BAXTER'S BUTTERFLIES

Donald Thomas

Author's Tranquility Press
MARIETTA, GEORGIA

Copyright © 2021 by Donald Thomas.

All rights reserved. No part of this publication may be reproduced, distributed or transmitted in any form or by any means, including photocopying, recording, or other electronic or mechanical methods, without the prior written permission of the publisher, except in the case of brief quotations embodied in critical reviews and certain other noncommercial uses permitted by copyright law. For permission requests, write to the publisher, addressed "Attention: Permissions Coordinator," at the address below.

Donald Thomas/Author's Tranquility Press
2706 Station Club Drive SW
Marietta, GA 30060
www.authorstranquilitypress.com

Publisher's Note: This is a work of fiction. Names, characters, places, and incidents are a product of the author's imagination. Locales and public names are sometimes used for atmospheric purposes. Any resemblance to actual people, living or dead, or to businesses, companies, events, institutions, or locales is completely coincidental.

Ordering Information:
Quantity sales. Special discounts are available on quantity purchases by corporations, associations, and others. For details, contact the "Special Sales Department" at the address above.

Baxter's Butterflies/ Donald Thomas
Paperback: ISBN: 978-1-957208-21-3
EBook: ISBN: 978-1-957208-22-0

This novel is dedicated to my two beloved sisters, who left this earth way too early. First, Joanne Kennedy of Windsor, Nova Scotia who loved golf. I miss you and may your golf shots in Heaven be long and straight. And my beautiful sister Barbara Yorke of Fall River, Nova Scotia. My quirky, funny humorous sister always made me laugh and when I said, "I am your older, wiser brother," she would respond by saying "Well you are older."

I miss you both. R.I.P.

If you want to go fast, go alone...If you want to go far, go with others...African Proverb

Contents

Girl Meets Boy 8
In the Library 19
The Neanderthals 26
Suspension - The Beginning 35
Superman 41
The Mind of a Ten-Year-Old 53
Mother 64
Professors Everywhere 78
Bud 88
Into the Unknown 95
Charity Cottage 103
Iron Tank 113
Cora 123
Gerald 135
Doug 142
Foot Soldiers 153
Clive 159
The Torture Room 169
Ray and Wendy 180
Dreams 191
Butterflies 215
Joanne 239
Billy Ray's 249
Baxter and Linda 265

CHAPTER ONE

Girl Meets Boy

Linda had tried. She gave it a shot but it just didn't work for her. She'd tried this online dating thing that her girlfriends had talked about and it left a bitter taste in her mouth. In fact she had never seen or experienced first-hand the worst of the male of the human species until she tried online dating - liars, cheaters, manipulators, game-players, degenerates - at least she'd found out where all the perverts and whackos hung out. They were all online. She even met a couple of them. What a disappointment that was.

They didn't look anything like their online photos.

How does a man go from having an athletic body to being overweight - fat - when I meet him? Or look ten years older than his online age?

They all want to drive motorcycles. Organ donors, I call them.

And where is that beach that they all want to walk on?

They can't spell and their vocabulary consists of four words. 'How ya doin' Honey?'

Don't they wear shirts?

And no, I don't want to see their manhood!

She had to laugh. At least she maintained her sense of humour and was glad she tried it.

Now she knew, because if she hadn't tried it she would always wonder.

But she was lonely and really wanted to meet a good man. In her opinion and from recent experience, they were not online. She figured she would have to meet a man the old fashioned way - falling down drunk in the bars, as her girlfriends joked about.

No. That wouldn't work for her. It would have to be just meeting someone in her daily activities. It had worked for the older generation. After all they didn't do online dating...*most didn't even have computers!*

At that moment Linda noticed the tall slender male walk into her third year Economics 303 class. It wasn't his height that caught her attention. She secretly scanned all the males in her classes for someone who qualified as her perfect *'physical male'* - she had a thing for short men. Normally she didn't give tall guys a second glance. Though this guy didn't qualify on the short end, he was good-looking and exuded a quiet confidence that he carried in every step. She was intrigued by him.

If only he were shorter.

I hope he's not online....

Full medium-length brown hair parted crookedly in the middle with his slightly rounded face, gave him a rugged Robert Redford-like appearance. He was not as handsome as some men she knew, but he was handsome.

If he were only shorter, he would be almost as appealing as John.

She thought of John, her former fiancé, often. John was shorter than most men and because of his smaller physical nature he made up for it with greater ambition and drive that taller men did not possess. It was an attractive feature of John. He was the only lover she ever had. She remembered that first time...the day she lost her virginity down at the lake.

Just awkward...humping, thumping, panting, sweating...it wasn't great.

Is that what it's all about?

No wonder she hadn't had sex with another man after John.

He had left her high and dry at the altar. In the last six months he came back into her life and promised that he had changed and that he loved her and couldn't live without her. He confessed that leaving her was the worst mistake he made in his life. She had been weak when she took him back and she didn't know why. Maybe it was the prestige she felt as the girlfriend of a med student. She had let her guard down and again he disappointed her when he left her for the second time.

She had finally given him the boot, but he was still in her thoughts. Whenever she let her mind wander, there he was and she couldn't shake his image. Her girlfriends said she had to sleep with another man to get John out of her mind and then move on.

She couldn't do it. Her strong morals and values stopped her.

I just can't sleep with a man for the sake of sex. It's not me.

Her girlfriends did it all the time, but she had to have strong feelings for the person in her life and the constant thought of John prevented any new deep connections with another man. She had to shake John out of her thoughts and out of her life, one way or another.

"I am weak and stupid," she said over-and-over to herself...she was not. She was exceptionally bright, with a superior IQ and was strong of character. Yelling at herself was her own way of kicking herself in the butt when she thought of John.

She just could not understand the paradox of being emotionally manipulated by a man who professed to love her, yet not commit to her. She wanted to meet someone new, to be able to put her trust in a man again, to fall in love. But it seemed like more of a pipe-dream to her with her guard wall up so high.

She noticed the quiet stranger look at a seat in the class near the football players. Obviously he was not aware of the trouble he could get himself into sitting in that particular area. Everyone else in the class knew better. They stayed clear of those Neanderthal football players. She had learned the hard way, why they did.

She had mistakenly sat in the first aisle on the left side during the first economics lecture of the semester. A huge linebacker, about two hundred and fifty pounds of muscle and bone, hoisted his legs in front of her across the aisle at the same time that another hulk of a football player blocked her exit from behind.

"Anyone coming into our aisle has to pay admission," blurted out the mountain of a man at her back. "And for a woman, the cost is to feel her tits." He laughed with the other animals in the front aisle when he reached from behind and grabbed her breasts.

Linda shuddered when she remembered that incident, his clumsy hands and then the feeling of exhilaration when she turned around and slugged the guy in the nose with a strong right cross. A bright red gush of blood spurted from his nose and he screeched in pain.

"You bitch, you broke my nose. You're dead bitch, you're dead. I'm gonna get you for that." Too late. Linda had raced up the steps to safety.

It was with that incident fresh in her mind that Linda became acutely aware of the imminent danger this new guy had placed himself in when he entered the domain of the football players - that same first aisle. Almost immediately his exit from the aisle was blocked from behind, when a three-hundred-pounder stood up at his back. The player in front of him raised his massive legs across the back of the seats and blocked any avenue of escape.

"Hey punk, anyone entering our area has to pay the price of admission, so fork over twenty dollars, asshole, or pay in pain," recited the massive hulk of a man who stood up directly in his face.

A hush came over the rest of the students in the lecture room as they became apprised of the trouble that brewed for the undersized prey caught in the football player lair. The silence in the room seemed to freeze time. No one moved until the silence was broken by the young man.

"You want me to hand over twenty dollars or you will beat me up. Am I correct?" He responded in a calm, clear voice. He stared directly into the football player's eyes.

"You got it asshole," replied the football player.

The tension seemed to expand along the aisle as the two stood toe to toe; a three hundred pound animal faced directly with someone half his size. The outcome of any altercation between the two was never in doubt in the minds of the spectators in the room.

Suddenly the football player stepped aside and said, "I'm sorry, sir, if I caused you any inconvenience. Please go ahead...and again accept my apologies."

The stranger walked down to the end of the aisle and took a seat in football player row. The other players dumfounded by his gall, stood and walked menacingly toward him.

"Leave him alone," said the three-hundred-pounder, "or you'll have to answer to me."

Linda couldn't believe her eyes. As far as she knew, no one but herself had challenged the animals in Neanderthal row. Except for her own experience of punching one of them in the nose, no one had escaped until they paid the price they demanded. Unaware that she spoke out loud, she exclaimed in a quick burst.

"God, I hate football players. They are Neanderthals with the brains of a flea. And I apologize to all fleas."

The girl beside her laughed. "I totally agree with you, but did you see how that cute guy stood up to that animal and how the animal backed down. How did he do it?"

Linda did not respond. Her eyes were focused on the back of the slight figure in Neanderthal row. He calmly leafed through a note book in preparation for the lecture. He was oblivious to the antics of the Neanderthals who still milled around in a state of confusion and anger - but held in check by the three-hundred-pounder who had initially challenged him.

She decided, at that moment, that neither hell nor high water was going to prevent her from meeting this man, but she didn't know how. As lectures passed, she pondered various methods of 'bumping into him' accidentally. She focused her attention on him and noted that with every lecture he continued to sit in Neanderthal row, not ten feet away, oblivious to the animals - perhaps to taunt them. But she didn't have the nerve to sit in that row near him.

Her amazement and interest grew as she observed his movements from afar. He didn't appear to have any friends, always came into the lecture hall alone and quietly took his seat. He spoke to no one.

During one class, she felt brave and attempted to get closer to him. She took a seat two rows back just over the stranger's shoulder. She noticed the icy stares of the animals leer at her for testing their boundaries. The animals had come to accept the presence of the stranger on their turf, but were determined not to allow anyone else to claim their territory.

"*Don't test us, honey,*" sneered one of the animals as he gestured toward her in a threatening manner.

Linda ignored him and she noticed that the stranger did not move - seemed uninterested in her safety. This disturbed her and she leaned forward to say something to him when she noticed that he skimmed through a book in his hand so fast that the pages appeared to fly by.

He's speed-reading.

He laid down the book and quickly replaced it with another one out of his backpack. Linda squinted and strained her eyes to see the title of the book he had laid down.

Applications of Advanced Quantum Physics.

This intrigued her even more.

What the hell is that guy reading? It has nothing to do with economics.

Her amazement multiplied when she noticed him flip through three more books during that one hour lecture. He did not appear to pay any attention to the economics professor or to the subject matter of the lecture, even as she scribbled notes as fast as she could in an effort to grasp the context of the lesson.

She had to get to know this mysterious man and when she fumbled with her notes at the end of the lecture, she dropped her books as she exited the aisle in back of him.

She cursed silently, 'Sacre Bleu' and bent down to pick up the books scattered in a disheveled pattern across the steps. A long tanned arm came into her line of sight, offering one of her books.

"Do you need some help?" said the stranger calmly. "I hope you don't intend to drop economics so early in the semester."

He laughed and handed her the economics textbook.

Linda looked up and swept away a tuft of her hair that was a constant irritant in her eyes every time she bent over. Very seldom did she find herself at a loss for words. If anything, her friends had labelled her Chatty Kathy, the babbling doll that speaks repeatedly whenever its string is pulled.

She looked straight into the stranger's clear blue eyes and sensed a quiet strength that ran deep as a calm pool of water. Up close, she looked at the broad smile on his face and melted like an ice cube on a hot summer day. Her knees felt weak and she stumbled forward.

He caught her arm, steadied her.

When she looked up their eyes met for a quick instant that seemed to last forever. A momentary silence was broken when Linda stuttered in quick, sharp words. *"I'm alright... I'm alright!!"*

He backed off at the abrupt tone. Linda noticed she'd given him the wrong impression.

Stupid, that was so stupid of me!

She had an unintended aloofness in her voice. At a time when she wanted to project her female charms, the exact opposite had come about. *I could kick myself!*

"Oh, I didn't mean to turn your offer of help away. I'm so sorry and very grateful. But those football animals in that row make all of us feel uneasy. And being so close to them...I'm sorry, you're not one of them, though you sit with them."

He smiled and nodded his head at the same time. *"No, I certainly am not one of them."*

Baxter looked deep into her hazel brown eyes.

He dropped his gaze from her eyes in a way a man does to appraise the physical features of a woman.

She was not a beautiful woman, but very attractive with full round breasts, slim waist and hips that perfectly augmented her five-foot-five-inch frame. Her closely cropped brown hair enhanced by her pouty lips and a slight pudgy nose made her a woman that would make any man's stare linger.

But it was her eyes that captivated him. Strength of character and passion burned within them.

They momentarily stood on the lecture room steps, unsure of what to do next. Side-by-side they started up the steps in complete silence. Linda broke the awkwardness when her quick mind snapped into action. She blurted out the first of many questions that were on her mind about him for some time.

"How'd you make that huge football player back down from you last week, when you were standing eye-to-eye with him?"

"Well...before I answer any questions, maybe you should tell me your name," he said laughing.

"Sorry, my name is Linda. My question may be a little bit improper, but everyone saw how you handled that football player"

He smiled, feeling a little bit more at ease. She was nervous and it showed but her interest was there.

"My name is Baxter, and I'm glad to meet you and to answer your question about that football player... I think he just saw the error of his ways."

Baxter was prepared to expand on that answer, since it may not have sounded believable, but to his surprise she never followed up. She just simply asked another pointed question.

"And I saw you flipping through those books, page-by-page so fast I couldn't believe it and I think they were on physics or something totally not economics. What were you doing?"

Baxter looked at her.

"I read fast and have interests outside economics and besides." He laughed out loud, recognizing she was genuinely interested. "I knew that you were watching me read those books and wanted to throw you a curve, so to speak."

"Well your curve ball really worked, because I completely missed it."

They continued from the lecture hall and their conversation, unabated, expanded into other unrelated topics.

Linda was attracted to this mysterious man, named Baxter. Her attraction grew stronger with each minute that passed and with each amazing insight that their conversations explored.

He is not smug, nor arrogant, just insightful and slightly guarded about his obvious intelligence.

Her female intuition at full force... there was something very special about this man. She did not believe for one minute that the Neanderthal football player had just come to his senses, as Baxter had suggested. She was determined to find out more about his run-in with the football players that day. But not now; her attraction for him grew stronger and she was not going to screw it up with a stupid question about something that might embarrass him.

Wait till I get to know him a little bit better and then I'll embarrass him.

She chuckled.

CHAPTER TWO

In the Library

Linda was in love. Being in a relationship with Baxter was all she had hoped for, and more. Her strong love for this man grew a little bit each day as she absorbed the little details about him that amazed her. He was not an ordinary man, no matter how hard he tried to prove otherwise.

She would often catch him speed-reading about subjects that had no connection to his studies. The hours that he spent in the vastness, the endless aisles and rows of the library were not only a reason to admire him, but also a source of jealousy because those books took him away from her. Made her feel less interesting. Thoughts milled over and over in her mind.

Is he really committed to me?

Is he thinking as much about me as I am about him?

It was early in her new relationship with Baxter and her experiences with her old boyfriend, John and his commitment issues gave her pause for some doubt. The crazy stories that her girlfriends conveyed to her about their experiences with men only added to her feelings of insecurity.

I am so much more mature than my girlfriends...aren't I?

Linda's self-doubt did get the better of her one day after Baxter had been late for a dinner engagement the night before. Although she accepted his apology for spending too much time at the library where he lost track of time, she decided to follow him to the library the next day.

Is there another reason why he lingered there instead of coming home to me?

In her mind, it was only to alleviate her suspicious feelings and not because of any distrust she had about him. It was with twin feelings of guilt and determination that she followed Baxter that morning. She took the added precaution to wear a dark wig and different clothing to hide her identity.

She thought she knew his schedule and interests, but to her amazement he went directly to the university medical library. She hadn't expected his interests to lie there and the layout of the medical building made it very difficult for her to remain undetected and still observe what he was up to. From a distance she observed him stop casually at the reception desk and exchange polite banter with the receptionist on duty. Linda stayed well back and then saw Baxter, through the large open-spaced windowed structure, stop at a computer. He proceeded to click through page after page in rapid fashion.

He can't be reading each page that fast. I know he speed reads but, it's impossible. He looked like he is reading about five book-pages at a time. No one could absorb that much information that quickly.

Whenever anyone came close to him, he slowed down to a normal pace. It was obvious to Linda that he did not want to be seen working the computer so fast.

She was fascinated by her observations, but after one hour was also fatigued and decided to cross the street and have a cup of coffee in the nearby coffee shop.

Refreshed with the quick caffeine fix, she returned to the medical building a half hour later. Baxter was nowhere to be seen. Perplexed, she went to the reception area and feeling embarrassed, asked the young receptionist if she had seen where the fellow at the nearby computer had gone.

"You mean that amazing guy who reads so fast that it looks like a blur," said the receptionist. She adjusted her posture to an erect, attentive position and smiled in a dreamy way.

"He's so cute. I've noticed him for a couple of weeks now, first at computers, the fiche machine and then he goes upstairs to one of the stack areas and reads. I think you'll find him on the second floor."

Linda found Baxter flipping through a book, and as she suspected, he was speed-reading page-by-page in a flash. She stayed well back out of his line of sight and marveled as he leafed through the pages, book after book. He went from aisle to aisle and the index subject in each aisle changed from concepts beyond her comprehension. They were medical in nature and from his satisfied expression; he must have absorbed the information like a sponge.

But Baxter was also being watched by another older, balding man and Linda didn't notice the older man approach her.

"**I couldn't help** notice that you are watching Baxter." The older man said as he walked down the aisle toward Linda.

Startled, Linda turned around and saw a tall, distinguished, elderly gentleman holding an armful of medical books.

"Are you as much intrigued by this remarkable young man as I am?" Asked the gentleman, while he shuffled an armload of books and stretched his hand out for a handshake.

"My name is Dr. Shultz and I teach here at the medical school."

He had a gentle handshake for such a large man and a very trustworthy manner. His sudden appearance was nonthreatening. Linda smiled at him.

"Hello, my name is Linda and yes the young man also intrigues me - he's my boyfriend."

"And you're following him?"

"It seems strange, I know," replied Linda.

"Not so strange," said Shultz. "I've noticed him for some time and perhaps I'm following him as well. He has captivated my attention both as an educator and as a student of the human condition. So I hope you don't mind my abruptness in approaching you."

"Not at all. I'm just trying to understand him a little bit better. He's very mysterious and doesn't completely open up to me, and being a woman I need to know my man."

Linda chuckled out loud and it brought a smile to the professor's face.

"I know what you mean," replied Dr. Shultz. "I noticed him flipping through complex medical journals, that even my most advanced medical students have difficulty understanding. When I approached him about his interest in medicine, he became evasive."

"Dr. Shultz, I don't know whether you know it or not, but he is enrolled here at the university in the third year commerce program and as far as I know, he doesn't have the slightest interest in medicine. But he reads everything under the sun. He is truly brilliant but he does everything he can to hide it."

"But why would he do that?" queried the professor.

"As far as I can tell he doesn't want people to recognize his special abilities or be singled out as being anything other than a normal average-type student. His course marks in commerce are just average and I think he deliberately keeps them low to not bring attention to himself."

"Well I originally noticed his speed-reading skills a couple of weeks ago and approached him about it," said Shultz. "It was odd since those books can't be easily assimilated by cursory examination, as he apparently was doing. So, I asked him about his interest in medicine and how he could possibly ingest so much information so quickly. He just said that he had a keen interest in medicine although he wasn't a med student."

"And quantum physics," said Linda. "I saw him speed reading on that, too."

"Remarkable," said Shultz. "He also said the oddest thing to me when I suggested that he talk to some renowned colleagues of mine if he had any specific questions about certain topics. He simply said: I doubt if they could teach me anything."

Shultz stifled his statement with a slight cough.

"That shocked me from someone so young. I readily admit it took me by surprise and when I talked more with him I realized that he was anything but ordinary. Out of curiosity, I tested him on his medical knowledge and asked him a few questions. He was quite forthright and correctly answered every one. It amazed me."

"That surprises me, Doctor. I would've thought that he wouldn't expose his medical knowledge, especially because you are a stranger to him."

"Well I can't account for that, but perhaps having caught him speed-reading through those medical journals might had something to do with it. He also made me promise that I wouldn't mention it to anyone. And as I continued to talk with him, I found out that he has a keen interest in parapsychology, specifically, mind-reading. He also asked me directly if it is possible to read another person's mind."

"He really opened up to me," continued Shultz. "So much for his evasiveness. I think it was on his mind and he just had to get it out."

"I wish he had opened up to me as he did with you," said Linda. "But tell me more about this mind-reading thing that he is fixated on. I have another theory about what he might be doing that involves you - and perhaps even me."

"I can't be truly certain about mind-reading," said Shultz who mumbled slightly. Shultz had a prestigious position as an educator and medical doctor and the subject was a touchy one. "I told Baxter outright that mind-reading is not a medical subject and very little is known about it outside the parapsychology field. But it does not mean that it doesn't exist, considering the enormous potential of the human mind."

"I think he has ulterior motives," said Linda. "I don't think for a minute that Baxter would let his guard down so easily and quickly to a stranger like you are to him."

"But why do you think he opened up to me like that?" said Shultz.

"I don't know, but, the more I think about it and knowing the extent that he has gone to hide his special abilities, the more I am convinced that he is planning something."

The professor continued. "If that is the case, then I postulate that perhaps he singled me out for some reason and thinking in the absurd, I can further postulate that perhaps in some manner, he read my mind."

He suddenly became noticeably uneasy with the slant in the conversation.

"Linda, I am a Doctor of Medicine and I have to keep up my professional image here. I think we are getting way ahead of ourselves with this mind-reading subject. There's no evidence that it has happened and it appears to be pure conjecture. I think

"I'm going to leave that topic alone but if you follow-up on mind-reading with Baxter, I will certainly entertain future discussions with you on the subject."

Linda looked disenchanted.

"I don't have to be a mind reader to see that you are disappointed with my stand on this Linda," said Shultz with a short chuckle.

"I understand Doctor. You're in a difficult position here. But I really think Baxter picked you to confide in, and in a way he has never done with me."

With a determined voice she said, "I intend to get to the bottom of this and have a revealing conversation with my man."

Dr. Shultz covered his mouth and laughed. "I don't think Baxter will stand a chance in a debate with you, my dear. If there is ever anything I can help you with, please call me."

He handed Linda his card shook her hand and then departed, saying.

"I will definitely keep Baxter on my radar,"

Linda watched as Dr. Shultz ambled down the aisle to the escalator, then turned her gaze toward Baxter and noticed that he still flipped through books, page by page.

Maybe I should walk over to Baxter and talk to him about meeting Dr. Shultz. But not at this time. I would be embarrassed.

She headed toward the escalator.

I have to pick the right time and place then have a talk.

She didn't notice Baxter turn his gaze from the book in his hand and watch her descend the escalator from the medical library.

CHAPTER THREE

The Neanderthals

In economics class the next day, Linda leaned over to Baxter and whispered softly in his ear. "A movie and dinner tonight? It's on me." Baxter smiled and looked into her eyes, "I like a woman who knows how to treat her man. You're on."

Linda packed up her notes and books and shoveled them haphazardly into her backpack as the class dispersed in its usual noisy, clattering manner. "I already picked the movie and it is playing at Parklane Theatre at 7 o'clock," she shouted above the din of the class as they departed the lecture hall.

Mike Cicerelli, the biggest of the animals in Neanderthal row overheard Linda mention the 7 o'clock movie at Parklane and mumbled. "It's payback time." He gestured to the other animals to stick around after they packed away their books.

"Huddle up guys. We've got some business to take care of tonight, and that means you too Meathead." He pointed to the animal who had previously balked at going after Baxter. "We have to restore our honour that the little shithead over there stole from us." He glared after Baxter who was climbing the steps that lead to the exit from the lecture hall.

Meathead spoke up. "I'm telling you guys that there is something about that little freak that we shouldn't mess with. I can just feel it."

Cicerelli countered Meathead's hesitation, sensing the conflict between the two. "If you're chicken, then go home to Mommy, but the rest of us have some payback to dish out."

Baxter picked Linda up for the fifteen minute walk to the theatre. They walked hand-in-hand down the street past the many small boutiques and coffee shops that lined the way. They didn't talk much. This wasn't normal. She always chatted away leading a conversation, but not now and she had an inquisitive, distant look in her eyes. There was something amiss. He sensed it.

Maybe I'll try to read her mind.

It was something that he had practiced since he found that when in close proximity to a person, he could actually pick up the electrical circuitry and impulses that came from the brain.

By reading the nuances of facial expressions and movement of wrinkles around the eyes and mouth, along with the position of the little hairs on the upper lip and on the eyebrows and different mouth contortions, he could interpret what the electric impulses told him about a person's thoughts. It was like reading a book. He did not actually hear or see thoughts. It was similar to braille, where blind people run their fingertips over the bumps on a page which represent letters that form words. The electrical impulses were the bumps that he interpreted into thoughts.

He was determined to improve this marvelous skill he had recently discovered about himself. It required a tremendous amount of concentration and brain energy on his part, but those were things that Baxter had in abundance. With practice the thoughts came faster and clearer.

Linda started to talk about her day. Baxter looked into her eyes and read her face and then her mind. She was going to bring up how she saw him at the medical library and how she talked to Dr. Shultz. It was clear in her thoughts although she had not talked about it yet.

He saw the flow of thoughts in her head. She was troubled by spying on him at the medical library. Her thoughts were like words written in plain English on a school blackboard directly in front of him.

It amazed him how clear the sensation was. Linda was about to say, 'I saw you at the medical library on Thursday and I am curious what you were doing there?'

He didn't want to get into a deep discussion about why he was at the library, although the conversation could not be put off. It was inevitable. Linda was determined and she would continue to bring up the topic until she fully satisfied her curiosity.

I better bring up the library first before it becomes a big issue with her.

"I met a very interesting person at the medical library some time ago," said Baxter in a quickly-fashioned statement that caught Linda by surprise.

"Funny you should say that, I was just going to mention to you that I saw you there yesterday," said Linda.

"I go there to read about medicine just to expand my knowledge. It interests me. Weeks ago I met a very distinguished person, Dr. Shultz, who noticed that I looked out of place and he befriended me."

He sensed she was seeking an opportunity to question him further.

"But Bax, I don't understand your interest in medicine. I know that you're brilliant. You can't hide that from me, like you hide it from others. But medicine and those physics books I see you flipping through in Economics class... what is it with you? You have to explain?"

The conversation was about to become awkward. It was not the time to give up the many secrets about his abilities he had pledged to keep to himself. He also had to ward off the thought that was forming in her mind. The 'I love you' was about to come out and he was not ready to hear it. He didn't know how he would respond.

The Neanderthals resolved Baxter's dilemma for him. They were carefully hidden in an alley offshoot from the street, which had to be passed on the way to the theatre. When Baxter and Linda approached the alley, the Neanderthals stepped out directly in front of them.

Baxter felt danger and fiery red anger that came from them. He called upon his special physical abilities. He tapped his left hand with his fingers in rapid succession. It was the technique his mother had taught him as a child to bring out his abilities. He could feel the small hairs on the back of his neck stand up. Trouble stood right in front of them. He halted his step as Linda looked back with a slight sense of bewilderment, not having noticed the Neanderthals.

The first thing that caught Baxter's attention was a wisp of hot breath that escaped from Linda's mouth, captured like mist in the coolness of the air. He looked beyond Linda as the first of the Neanderthals approached from the dark shadow of the alley. Instantly, Baxter's entire muscular structure loosened and became supple and coiled at the same time.

"Step behind me Linda," he whispered into her ear.

There were four of them and they approached together like a wall from the dark alley. They were a menacing sight, four huge, hulking men weighing over one thousand pounds, collectively, and each well over six feet tall. They took up the full width of the sidewalk as they strode forward almost shoulder to shoulder. An elderly couple who walked ahead of Baxter and Linda stopped in their tracks and looked at the huge wall of muscle and bone that blocked their path. They turned to step off the sidewalk with a look on their faces that resembled awe and fear.

Cicerelli hardly noticed the couple with his gaze firmly fixated on Baxter and Linda. He brushed the elderly couple aside with a huge sweep of his left arm. The couple, unhurt, looked back.

"What the hell is going on?" yelled the old man in a squeaky voice.

"Shut up you old fool or we'll squash you like a bug," replied one of the Neanderthals.

The old man, in a fit of defiance, raised his index finger and angrily shook it in the air before he grabbed the arm of his female companion and quickly proceeded on his way.

Time seemed to stand still as the Neanderthals and Baxter and Linda stood within twenty feet of each other. No one moved. But the burning eye contact from both sides could have blown a hole through solid steel. The Neanderthal's eyes were filled with hatred and anger and Baxter immediately sensed the depth of their feelings. His quick scan of their faces, posture, bodily movements and especially the electrical circuitry in their brains had opened their minds like a book. Physical harm was rampant in the minds of three of the four, but he sensed a deep respect and apprehension in Meathead's thought processes.

"Meathead, I know what you all intend to do and I know that you're not with them," said Baxter in a soft, calm voice.

Cicerelli responded, leaping forward and yelled for his comrades to follow him.

"Ok, shithead and your bitch woman, you're both gonna pay for your disrespect. You've got it coming. We're going to mash your faces into the sidewalk and rape the bitch right in front of you."

Three of them ran toward Baxter. Meathead stayed back. Cicerelli grabbed for Baxter but grasped nothing but air. He kissed the concrete sidewalk when Baxter in cat-like fashion gently pushed his shoulder and used his forward momentum to send him sprawled, face down. Baxter could see the ridiculous slow movements of the cumbersome football players who in turn saw nothing but a blur where Baxter had stood. They toppled in succession like giant trees felled by a lumberjack's chainsaw in the forest.

They were baffled and infuriated. Three of them came at Baxter again. He was not where they saw him. They tumbled again. This time two of them stayed down, in total bewilderment. They couldn't believe his speed or their own eyes. Their facial expressions said it all. They were finished. Cicerelli's resentment at being humiliated by an inferior person drove him into a blind rage.

He took a switchblade out of his back pocket, flipped it open and made a beeline toward Linda. Baxter read his thoughts. He had to do more to restrain him in his crazed state. He was on Cicerelli before he had taken two steps.

Cicerelli's whole body went limp. There was a distant look in Cicerelli's empty stare. He passed out as Baxter loosened his pinch-like grip on his neck muscle that controlled the blood flow through the body's main artery to the brain. He slumped to the sidewalk in a heap.

The silence of the moment was as loud as if a screaming siren blasted away. No one on the sidewalk moved. Dumbfounded looks of total awe were on everyone's face. How had a mere minute-of-a-man put down a towering giant like Cicerrelli with such ease?

Linda gasped to catch her breath. The whole incident took about thirty seconds, but left an impression on her that would last a lifetime. Many questions had to be answered. People began to approach them when the spectacle of the confrontation became evident to the other theatre goers.

Baxter broke the silence.

"Meathead, get your buddies and leave. Remember what happened here tonight and understand that all the power of your size and strength is misguided if used for the wrong reasons."

Meathead looked down at Cicerrelli, lying prone on the sidewalk, still groggy but recovering. He lifted him up and steadied him on his feet with the aid of the other Neanderthals.

"Don't worry, Baxter," muttered Meathead in a conciliatory tone. "I don't know how you beat us so easily but things are gonna change in our group. I'll make sure of that."

Meathead gave Cicerelli a quick jab in the midriff to indicate that leadership had just changed hands. They ambled down the street in an almost comical fashion, lugging the still unsteady Cicerelli with them.

Baxter turned to Linda and took her by the arm. "Let's get out of here. People are starting to look at us."

Rather stupidly, he blurted out, "do you still want to go to the show?"

Linda laughed. "No, I don't want to go to the show and besides those people aren't looking at me they're looking at you. How the hell did you do that back there?"

Baxter feared what was coming next from Linda. He didn't have to actually read her mind to figure that out. He feared the onslaught of questions to come more than an hour long fight with the Neanderthals.

"We're dropping into Starbucks. You're buying us a coffee and you're going to talk to me." There was firm resolve in her voice. She meant business.

The coffee had a bitter taste as Baxter gulped down the first few steaming mouthfuls. Perhaps it wasn't the coffee taste that was so bitter but the inevitable line of questions that were about to be fired at him. Linda looked him straight in the eye.

"Start talking buster. That was no ordinary thing you did back there on the street."

How am I going to handle this situation?

He didn't want to jeopardize his desire to lead a normal life. He had worked so hard for it, but at this moment a special degree of brinkmanship would be required to keep Linda's questions at bay.

Should I trust her and tell my secrets?

The thought swirled over and over in his mind.

"There is something that I have to tell you," he said in a low voice. He hesitated. He thought of his mother and how she drilled into him 'never tell anyone more than they have to know about your special powers.'

But Linda knew already that he was different and that there was something special about him. Denial wasn't going to work and Linda was different. Special.

"There are things about me that few people know. I have some abilities that not many people possess and you've seen some of them tonight and earlier."

He resigned to tell her the truth, but only as necessary and nothing beyond what she already knew.

"I can speed-read, I can move fast, I want to know as much as possible about everything." That's why you saw me in the medical library. But there is nothing special beyond that. Maybe I am smarter than most people. And beating up the Neanderthals was nothing. They are big, but slow, and no match for my speed. There's not much more that I can tell you about myself other than what you've seen and know already. Linda smiled. There was a puzzled look on her face.

He sensed she knew that there was more about him than he was telling, but he would explain in his own time

Baxter read her mind and trusted her even more.

Maybe someday.

All this talk about his special abilities made his mind wander back to his youth when his abilities first appeared. He streamed through the hallways of time to the period when he became aware of his special abilities. It was like a video that he clicked to play. He saw himself as a young boy. He played the video and reminisced.

CHAPTER FOUR

Suspension - The Beginning

He was six years old when it happened the first time, the feeling of suspension as he came to call it. He stepped on the ice for a hockey game at the old Ice Arena in Portland, Maine and the feeling just came over him. The twenty or so six-year-old-boys fell all over the ice. Their ankles bent as they floundered comically and chased the puck from one end of the rink to the other. The way he moved made the game look easy compared to how uncoordinated and slow the other boys skated. Like the rest of the players, most of whom were boyhood chums, he had difficulty at first to maintain balance to stand and move on skates. He fell numerous times but adjusted and picked up the coordination and rhythm required to effortlessly glide over the ice, while his friends continued to struggle with little in the way of anything that resembled skating skills. He felt the puck on his stick and moved it back and forth instead of just slapping at it like the rest of the boys. He was exhilarated and stick handled through the entire team. He mastered the skill of hockey in his very first game.

It wasn't that he scored ten goals in his very first hockey game that made him happy when he jumped over the boards for his next shift. It was that first feeling of suspension. As a six-year-old-boy he had no understanding of the significance of the feeling. He only experienced it - the sensation that the other players on the ice slowed their body movements while his remained the same and he could control how fast or slow the others moved like in a video replay. This was his first experience with suspension.

He was the golden one. He continued to shine and outclass all players in his age group. Even at such a youthful age he began to attract the attention of hockey scouts from the higher levels of hockey when they heard about a future superstar. They came out to his games, called his home and enticed his father with offers of fame, fortune, and stardom. His father understood the potential for his son and the fortune that he, as the father of a super-star could reap. He would rant about how Earl Woods had molded his son, Tiger, into the greatest golfer of his time.

"Earl Woods gave up everything for his son." It was a constant refrain that rang in Baxter's ears and he grimaced each time he heard his father's words.

"I plan to do for you what Earl Woods did for his son. When you are a star you will have your old man to thank. Don't ever forget that."

Baxter hated Earl Woods, even though he had no idea who he was. He only knew he was the reason he was forced to spend hours each day as a youngster on the home made hockey rink in his backyard and the reason he practiced boring skating, stick handling, and puck control drills - and the constant drudgery of shooting on the target goaltender made for practice. His father had named the goaltender "Jacques Plante" and in bold white paint hand painted his name on the front of his sweater. At night after a hard day's practice shooting at Jacques Plante, Baxter had dreams seeing the goaltender chase him around the rink, swinging his goalie stick like an axe to even the score for being hit with the puck so many times. The harder Baxter worked to score on Jacques Plante, the worse the nightmares became. But it didn't stop his father from pushing him harder in practices.

"Even Bobby Hull couldn't score on him," quipped his father. "So work like hell to score."

It wasn't that he hated hockey; it was that he hated practicing when he didn't want to play. It irritated him that his father didn't allow his friends over just for fun. He wanted so much to just play hockey with his friends but his father went into shouting tirades when they asked to come over.

"You are too good to play with those worthless kids. They aren't good enough to step on the same ice with you. You can't learn hockey playing with them. Now get out there and do those skating drills. You are going to thank me someday."

He would invite teenage boys over to play full contact hockey with instructions to 'lay on the body' against Baxter. Baxter hated those older boys but his father justified bringing them over.

"This will toughen you up and those bumps and bruises you get will remind you that life as a hockey star is tough."

Baxter would go to bed black and blue from hard hits and often would cry himself to sleep after he practiced with those older boys. The worst part was he could not invoke the power of suspension when he wanted it most - in those brutal practices. The power of suspension would not come out on cue. He had no control. He hated those practices more and more and suspension came out less and less.

He tried to talk to his father about his dislike for the practices and the toughness of hockey. He only responded by saying, "I know what you got in you, son. You've got to bring it out more."

"What do you mean, Dad? What've I got in me, a bug or something?"

"No son. You've got a special power. I can see it in you when you skate. You skate like the wind; no one else on the ice can touch you. You're special, Bax. But your mother would kill me if she knew I told you this. Don't mention it to her. Promise me, Bax."

Baxter was bewildered. He didn't understand. "Ok, Dad, I promise, but I don't understand what you're talking about. I don't feel special."

"Your mother will explain it to you someday son."

"But, Dad, I hate those older boys and those practices."

He flushed with resentment and anger.

It was around this time, as an eight-year-old hockey prodigy, that he started to lose suspension. By then he was the star player on the Starbucks "Stars" team in the elite bantam hockey league in Portland. The boys on his team were twelve to fourteen years old and he was the smallest, fastest, smartest and the scoring leader for the team. But being an eight-year-old, he had nothing in common with his older teammates who constantly seemed to talk about sex and screwing girls with big tits. It was always about sex and dirty jokes before, during and after the games. He didn't really understand what they were talking about but laughed along with them to fit in. He remained an outsider with nothing in common but hockey. They were, after all, five grades ahead of him in high school.

He could count on suspension kicking in when he was wrapped up in the adrenalin-rush of a game but his desire to succeed and win for his team started to wane. Once his desire faltered, suspension also faltered. It was like there was a correlation between his innermost desires and his ability to call up the powers of suspension. It was a control thing and he had none. It was at this point in his hockey career that a vicious cycle developed. His desire to play for the Stars abated; suspension left him, the team started to lose and his teammates resented him.

He recalled how sad he was at eight. His boyhood friends never came over to play. His teammates were jealous and hated him. His father pushed and pushed at something he didn't want. Suspension had caused nothing but pain, disappointment, and rancor in his life.

He wanted normalcy in his life; needed to play with his old friends again. To run, jump, and play like a normal happy eight-year-old. With his loathing toward hockey, he looked forward to summer. He was frustrated that suspension didn't just show up when he wanted and he really wanted it to show up when he played on the Orioles little league baseball team.

It was a near-perfect situation, that summer in his eighth year, when he was up at bat in the ninth inning of the league championship game. The bases were loaded and his team behind by one run. He wanted to bring out the power of suspension. The league champions, the Cardinals, were strong and their left-handed ace had struck out most Oriole batters. Baxter had already struck out twice by the overpowering fastball of the sleek, tall left-hander. He felt weak-kneed when he stepped up to the plate.

I want that fastball to slow down. I want the pitcher to move in slow motion. I want that ball to float to the plate and look as big as a beach ball.

"Strike three, you're out!" bellowed the umpire when the ball zipped through the strike zone.

Baxter had let his team down and he was frustrated.

"Why didn't it show up?" He muttered as he walked back to the bench.

His disappointment compounded.

It almost always comes out playing hockey when I enjoyed the game. So why not when I play baseball? I enjoy so much more than hockey? What is this mystery within me?

He didn't know when it would come out. It was random, like the time he'd been tackled hard and dirty in peewee football. The next play he took the ball and everybody shifted into slow motion. He moved through the line and spun away from the linesmen. They merely waved at him in desperation while he ducked under their outstretched, slow-moving arms. He danced around the linebackers as they lurched toward him while he evaded their grasp, and then raced toward the goal line. The exhilaration of that touchdown was sharp because suspension never occurred before when he played football. It was another part of the jigsaw puzzle that he grappled with while trying to understand the meaning of his special power.

Why did it come out without thinking about it?
It was his power alone, one he neither understood nor controlled. At that point in his life it shaped who he was and that vexed him.

CHAPTER FIVE

Superman

When he was nine, he learned a little bit more about suspension and how and when he could expect it to show up. He was walking with his close friend, Stevie, on a path which leads down to the railway tracks when four older and bigger boys came up the path from the opposite direction. He had a sinking feeling in the bottom of his stomach when he saw who they were. We were in big trouble because it was the Hardiman gang.

"Stevie, it's the Hardimans, let's get the hell out of here," Baxter said as they approached.

He wasn't a coward but he sensed real trouble straight ahead and an unfair fight was about to develop. Every kid knew that the Hardimans were evil. The neighbourhood kids said that if anyone stepped on their shadows the Hardimans would beat the shit out of them. They were the most feared gang in the neighbourhood, the neighbourhood bullies and they would not back down from anyone.

Baxter wanted to run but he knew Stevie wouldn't. Stevie was stubborn and wouldn't back away. He never had and never would, no matter the circumstances. It was one of the things that Baxter hated about his friend Stevie. He was tough and his toughness came from some secret place deep inside him. He wasn't big or strong but he simply believed that he was tougher than anyone else. He was one of those stubborn kids that had more pride than brains and whatever the odds, he would fight rather than flee.

"Stevie, let's get out of here. There are four of them and they'll kill us."

"You go if you want. We were here first and I'm not afraid of them," said Stevie. He marched forward.

We're in big trouble!

Stevie continued down the path straight at the Hardimans. He was fearless.

"You little squirts better get off our path if you don't want your skinny little asses kicked," bellowed one of them.

Stevie kept going.

"You little jerk, I warned you to keep off our path," yelled the biggest of the Hardimans. He kicked Stevie in the stomach.

Stevie dropped to his knees and gasped for breath, but he wasn't down for long. He rebounded to his feet and swung both arms wildly at the closest of them. He was only half the size of the smallest Hardiman and Stevie's viciousness temporarily surprised them. They were used to most kids running away in fear because of their reputation.

They froze for an instant. But only for an instant. Surprise may have been the reason why one of Stevie's wild swinging blows landed squarely on the jaw of one Hardiman, knocking the brute off his feet. It took a couple of seconds before the four Hardimans came at Stevie, but those seconds were like an hour to Baxter. He flew into action to help his close friend.

The Hardimans had Stevie surrounded but before they could strike, Baxter was beside him. It was the first time in his life that he was in a real fight. He felt exhilarated. A blood rush pumped through his arteries at super speed and his muscles flexed like a taut bow string ready to send something flying.

Everyone around that circle appeared to slow in motion. He could see the Hardiman's faces contort with rage and excitement at the beating that they thought they were going to inflict. They were going to teach a painful lesson about respect.

Fists and feet flew at Baxter from all four sides and that's when he realized he abhorred violence. If he struck back at them he would be just like them.

The fight didn't last long. In fact it wasn't even a fight. No return blows were exchanged. Baxter ducked under their slow leg kicks and swept them off their feet with his outstretched leg. Adrenalin pumped through his veins and their swinging arms and fists slowed. All he did was side-step their fists and shove them when they were off balance. All four of the Hardimans were down in an instant.

They were totally surprised but still sprang to their feet and flew at Baxter in a fit of rage. Again they landed flat on their backs.

"You're gonna regret that." One of them picked up baseball-sized rocks and hurled them at Baxter. It was easy to avoid the slow-moving rocks thrown from five feet away. He braced for another attack when they picked up thick four-foot-long sticks from the rubble strewn around the edges of the path. He ducked and moved under, around and over the swinging sticks and again deposited the Hardimans on their backsides.

They realized the futility of their efforts and rose to their feet. The leader yelled. "Holy shit, let's get the hell out of here." They ran down the path, looking over their shoulders as if they were pursued.

Stevie had a look of total awe on his face.

"That was incredible. You beat the Hardimans...all by yourself. No one has ever done that before. How did you move so fast? You were like a blur out there. Why didn't you hit them?

You coulda creamed them. All you did was push them down. You shoulda punished them, like they would've punished us. How did you do that?"

"Stevie, slow down. I don't know what happened. Something just came over me and I reacted."

"Just wait till I tell everyone," said Stevie.

The very next day the story of Baxter beating the Hardiman gang was all over the school. The story was passed from person to person and it seemed his exploits grew by leaps and bounds. His reputation was way overblown even as he denied and downplayed the encounter. It didn't help that Stevie was doing the exact opposite and bragged Baxter up while he exaggerated the event. Baxter was irritated by Stevie's persistent story and the close bond between him and Stevie changed.

It came to a boil in phys-ed class one morning when Baxter slipped in a rope-climbing relay which caused his team to lose. One of his teammates yelled. "What's the matter with you Superman, the rope got kryptonite on it?"

Stevie was one of the first to laugh followed by more raucous laughter from the rest of the class. Mr. Burchell, the phys-ed teacher was also caught up in the moment and laughed as well, though he tried to control the class. Embarrassed, Baxter sounded off.

"Stevie, it's your fault spreading those rumours about me being some kind of Superman. You've turned me into a laughing stock."

Shortly after that, Stevie stopped coming over after school.

Baxter wasn't comfortable with the hero, super kid reputation that Stevie had built up around him. He wanted to be like his schoolmates. It reminded him of being a member of the Stars hockey team where he was looked up to as the best, the fastest but didn't really fit in. He wasn't one of the team. He didn't want that happening again in his everyday life. It was the reason he hated hockey and he pained over the thought that it was happening again. Suspension, once again was setting him apart from a normal life and normalcy was something that he craved more and more.

He had become increasingly isolated in his school life during those early years. He never had many friends and they became fewer when his reputation as a super kid grew out of proportion. Other kids would avoid him or snicker and whisper behind his back calling him Superman. Who he was and would become were more clouded than ever before. He was also more aware he had to get suspension under control. He vowed never again to use the full power of the unknown force within him. It was destroying him as much as he felt isolated by it.

It was a strange twist of fate that the Hardiman gang came into his life again and actually helped him realize this new self-imposed control over suspension that he was determined to find. The Hardimans were school dropouts and had a habit of taunting and intimidating kids who used to be their schoolmates. They no longer fit in with the school crowd and they had no friends outside of school. They were bullies and bullying was one of the only activities that filled their empty lives. They showed up at their former school on a daily basis. It had become a ritual with them.

They lingered around the outskirts of the school yard, on that particular day.

"Hey Superman," yelled one of them when Baxter rounded the corner of the school yard. Baxter was alone, behind a crowd that had just streamed out of class.

"Hey hotshot, think you're man enough to take us on, you fucking asshole?" said the biggest of the Hardimans. They circled him in tandem before he had a chance to avoid them. Baxter could have ignored their taunts since they hesitated about directly confronting him - still respectful of their last encounter. But he recognized an opportunity to test his new resolve to change the way suspension had affected his life.

The situation was tense but Baxter had a slight grin on his face when he responded.

"What did you call me?"

"I called you a fucking asshole, you little freak," said the biggest of the Hardimans. "What you gonna do about it, piss your pants?"

His adrenaline began to pump and blood rushed through his veins. That was the first sign that suspension was about to kick in. The world around him moved in slow motion. His breathing became rapid and he took a moment to sense all the changes that were going on in his body as well as the changes in the environment around him.

The strength in his limbs increased as his muscles flexed ready to spring with a force he could not imagine. The hairs on the back of his neck stood up and his ears picked up the honk of a car horn that must have been more than a block away. Normally, he would never hear that.

His brain absorbed all information it encountered. Just for an instant he looked around and noticed that the flight of a bird in mid-air had slowed. It was in slow motion. He marvelled at this experience and knew that no one around him felt the sensations of this heightened sensory response that had overcome his body. It was critical - a moment of enlightenment for him and he thoroughly studied this amazing transformation. He realized that suspension was triggered by a combination of emotions such as anger, fear and anxiety. It was also at this moment he knew what he was going to do with the Hardimans.

They continued with their taunts but still seemed reluctant to initiate any action against Baxter. They remembered what happened on the path down by the railway tracks. For a brief instant there was a standoff. The Hardimans frozen with respect and Baxter, with wonderment at the changes he felt building up inside himself. School finished for the day and many of the kids began to gather around in the yard when they saw a fight was about to begin. Stevie was in the crowd and it was his remark that broke the ice in the brief standoff.

"Take a hike, scuzzballs, before Baxter and I kick your asses all over town like we did down by the railway tracks."

The Hardimans were bullies. They knew it and basked in it and they would never cower and lose face in front of those they considered to be inferior. Stevie's remarks set them off and the respect they had formed for Baxter was offset by their own pride. They came at him in full force.

Baxter saw them coming. They moved slowly, but this time he did not move out of their way. A fist hit him square in the jaw but he cushioned the blow by moving with it and absorbed most of the punch. The force was enough to knock him off his feet and the four Hardimans jumped him. They punched and kicked. Baxter used his arms to block most of the blows but allowed some of them to strike and those hits drew blood. He knew exactly what he was doing even as the Hardimans continued to pummel him.

He heard their taunts about Superman.

"Come on Superman, why don't you use your super powers and fly away."

They continued to kick and punch him while he lay on the ground in a defensive position. He fended off most of the serious blows that were aimed at his head though he allowed a few blows through to maintain the realism of the situation for the audience. He also punched back and struck a Hardiman in the nose. Blood gushed like water out of a spigot and he backed out of the fight for a moment and placed his hand and then a sleeve over his bleeding nose. When the blood flow stopped he jumped back into the fight and aimed a vicious kick at Baxter's head. He deflected that blow with his left arm but by all appearances it looked like he was helpless. The fury of the attack continued, unrelenting and the crowd of school kids increased as more gathered around at the spectacle of the fight. They all stood there and witnessed the unfairness of the situation. Four were beating on one.

No one moved to stop it - perhaps all waited for the next guy to respond, to help. It was the psychology of group mentality at its worst.

Stevie shouted, "Bax, use your speed and get out of there. They're killing ya!"

He jumped into the fight and tackled a Hardiman around the legs which brought the much bigger boy to the ground. The Hardiman's attention then turned to Stevie and just as they were about to vent their built-up rage on him, Mr Clancy, the school principal and Mr. Burchell rounded the corner and saw the fight in progress.

Clancy yelled. "Hey, you kids, what's going on over there?"

They were familiar with the reputation of the Hardimans and as soon as they recognized them in the fight, they started to run. The Hardimans saw them and bolted like frightened rabbits from the scene, but not without a parting barb at Baxter and Stevie.

"We'll finish this another day, assholes."

Stevie was shaking when Burchell and Clancy arrived.

"Are you okay?" Asked Clancy who looked distraught at the sight of Baxter on the cold, cracked asphalt of the schoolyard.

They didn't notice the wry little smile on his face, behind the mask of blood that formed from the red liquid that flowed from the deep gash over his right eye.

"Don't move Baxter, stay on the ground. You might be seriously hurt," said Mr. Burchell with a concerned tremble in his voice.

"There's nothing wrong with me. I probably look worse than I really am," Baxter jumped to his feet. "I got a couple of bruises and a cut over my eye, but that's all - other than a torn shirt."

By this time the crowd of bystanders came closer, attracted by the sight of blood. Baxter did look quite a mess with the torn shirt and blood dripping down the side of his face, and his usually clean, closely-cropped hair strewn about in a dishevelled manner.

There was concern in the crowd. Betty Johnson, one of the prettiest and most popular senior girls in school, stepped forward and wiped his face with a handkerchief she pulled from her pocket.

"You look terrible. Are you sure you're not hurt?"

"Only my pride."

"But I heard that you were some kind of Superman, or something."

"A slightly exaggerated rumour. You see, I can't fly and don't have x-ray vision."

He chuckled as more of the crowd circled around me.

He recognized the change in attitudes toward him as more and more of the school kids came closer and questioned him on the fight. But Stevie looked disappointed.

"What kind of freak are you?" he said. "I know what you did down by the railway tracks and you just did nothing today."

Baxter shot back. "Stevie, what happened by the railway tracks was a fluke. I just got lucky and threw them off me. I'm the same friend you've always known. I'm not Superman as much as you've spread around that story about me."

Stevie was taken aback by his angry retort.

"I'm sorry, Bax, maybe you're right. I got carried away. I hope you're not mad at me."

"Naa. Just stop calling me Superman."

Mr. Burchell ignored Baxter's protestations that he was alright and drove him to the hospital outpatient department. Baxter knew there was nothing wrong other than the cut over his eye and a few minor scrapes and bruises.

He had blocked the majority of the Hardiman's blows that would have inflicted serious damage. In spite of the pain that had just begun to creep into his muscles and bones from the conflict, he felt both relief and accomplishment. Relief from the fact that he now would no longer be Superman to his school chums. The Superman myth had been destroyed with his sorry performance in front of everybody. He was now sure that he could be more like everyone else.

Normal.

But he felt great gratification and a sense of accomplishment to be able to control suspension at least to a certain degree. He was cognizant that the fight had brought suspension out in full force. He could sense it. Everything about suspension was there: the power in his muscles, the quickness in my mind although without the strength of his willpower, he would've succumbed to the temptation to dominate the fight.

He learned a lot about himself that day in the schoolyard…about how he wanted to lead his life and especially how he wanted others to perceive him.

The short fifteen-minute drive to the hospital with Mr. Burchell was a time for reflection. He came to a conclusion that day, in his ninth year of life, that never again would he bring out the full power of suspension. He didn't understand its full power but he did know that he could control it with his willpower. The fight with the Hardimans had taught him that. If he let it out in full-force he would become abnormal, like Superman that Stevie described. He didn't want to be a Superman. He didn't want to be abnormal.

That was when he thought about how lonely the real comic-book character "Superman" must have been. He felt sorry for him because he was different from everyone else and had so much strength, power and special abilities that he had to hide his true identity in the character of the bungling Clarke Kent. He must've been the loniest man in the world and he never allowed himself to reveal his true identity to anyone. He could never have true friends considered his equal. He had no one who could relate to him on a one-to-one basis. Everyone looked up to him. His alter-ego, Clarke Kent, was the one with the friends. Not him.

Superman had a sorry life. He saves people, like from burning buildings and he just flies away. He doesn't stay around and chat with them or joke with them. He doesn't socialize with anyone, other than love-struck Lois Lane. He could never have a relationship with any human female. Clarke Kent was the socializer. He enjoyed his everyday life as an ordinary reporter, interacting with his fellow workers as an equal and leads a normal life.

Superman needs Clarke Kent. Without Clarke, Superman would have no life but for a lonely existence as a super-hero.

"I don't want to be Superman," Baxter said under his breath on the long ride to the hospital. "I don't have a Clarke Kent."

Mr. Burchell talked up a storm, but Baxter didn't hear a word about the championship school basketball team that he coached. His mind drifted to the mysterious power that he possessed and his resolve to come to grips with the power within himself was greater than ever. He knew one thing. He could not talk to his father about it. His dad had barely talked to him since he stopped playing hockey and denied him the chance of being the father of an NHL superstar.

He remembered something that his father had said to him once.

"You're special, Bax. But your mother would kill me if she knew I was talking to you about your special power."

"Mother." Baxter muttered and didn't realize he repeated the word, 'mother' over and over again.

"What did you say?" Asked Mr. Burchell.

"You want me to take you to your mother?"

"No," he responded. "It's just that soon I have to speak to my mother."

CHAPTER SIX

The Mind of a Ten-Year-Old

That morning the entire Grade Seven class was nervous. The girls chattered louder than normal, almost to the point of a low roar. The boys were the opposite. Quieter than normal, reserved and when they entered the classroom they simply took their seats. They generally joked around with each other and teased the girls. But on that day they didn't. They opened their notes and books and crammed up to the last minute for the final history exam of the term.

The girls dealt with the tension of the exam in their own way. They interacted with each other and exchanged possible questions and answers. The tension in the air could be cut with a knife and when Miss McKinnon walked into the room, the tension heightened.

"Good morning class." She smiled and strode to the pine desk at the front of the room and dropped a large pile of examination papers, with a loud thud, squarely in the center of the desk. She did it that way on purpose.

"I hope you studied long and hard for the exam," she said. "Because you're going to need it."

Miss McKinnon had a dry sense of humour and often sprinkled her daily lessons with sarcastic taunts at her students. The students didn't appreciate her humour. They thought she was warped when she laughed at their discomfort. She used sarcasm as a valuable teaching aid and often told the class, "with sarcastic humour comes a great amount of respect."

Al Almon looked up while he shuffled through his history notes and noticed that Baxter sat calmly with his arms crossed.

"Hey what's with you? Aren't you worried about the exam?"

"Not really," Baxter replied. "I think I pretty well got it cased."

"What do you mean you got it cased? This is the hardest exam of the year. Everyone is worried about it. What makes you so special?"

Maybe Baxter carried an air of superiority, but he didn't do it on purpose. He just told the truth. He wasn't worried about the exam. It was part of how he saw the world. It was black or white. There is no grey. There is the truth or there are lies. He simply stated how he perceived the history exam. But the other kids his age had to deal with emotions and perceptions about how they fit in with their peers. They would lie at the drop of a hat if they saw gain. He couldn't lie. It wasn't in him.

Al Almon didn't like Baxter because of the way he confidently carried himself and the way he looked - always so neatly dressed. He was different from the rest of the kids in school and being different was an instant mark for ridicule. Al leaned toward him and before he could speak Baxter replied in anticipation of a confrontational remark, not quite sure whether he was mad at him or frustrated at not being prepared for the exam.

"I'm not special," Baxter replied. "I just see the answers in my head."

That was the truth as far as he was concerned and it should've ended the conversation.

"You're weird," responded Al, determined to get the last word in. "Wait till I tell Miss McKinnon that you already know the answers."

Baxter didn't think much about the short conversation with Al Almon until two weeks later when Miss McKinnon stood in front of the class and proclaimed, "I have the results of the history exam and they are terrible. I am not happy."

She walked slowly from student to student, passing out exam papers and yelled each result, "fifty-two, sixty-five, sixty-six, seventy-one, and forty-five." She had that warped smile on her face, the one we all hated so much. She had just about finished the morose task when she stopped. There were three papers not yet distributed and she turned to face the class from the back of the room.

"I have three papers remaining to pass out," she said and waved them in the air high over her head. "Two are terrible like the rest of the class." She walked over to Patricia Purcell, placed her exam paper on her desk. "Fifty-seven!" She bellowed out to make sure that everyone heard. She was not concerned with the look of humiliation on Patricia's face.

She yelled again.

"And a mediocre sixty-one for Virginia. I have one paper left and I hold this paper up high as an example of exemplary effort."

Baxter knew that she was talking about him because he hadn't received his paper. He felt slightly embarrassed since he overheard whispers around him from some of the others..

"Who's Miss McKinnon talking about?"

"Who's the suckhole?"

"Whoever it is must've cheated."

"McKinnon's pet, I bet."

Miss McKinnon walked over to Baxter.

"Baxter McPherson had a perfect score of one hundred percent He answered every question on the exam correctly."

The whispers in the class became louder and above the whispers Al Almon yelled out.

"Cheater! He cheated. He told me he saw the answers."

Miss McKinnon looked surprised and turned directly toward Baxter.

"I am assuming that Al is wrong. But is there any truth to what he's saying?"

"I never cheated, Miss McKinnon. I don't know what Al's talking about. I think he mixed up what I said, a while back - about the exam."

Miss McKinnon doubted about how he could have possibly aced the exam. It was a hard exam and no one scores a perfect mark in her examinations.

"Baxter, come with me to see Mr. Clancy."

Mr. A.P. Clancy, the school principal, was a short man considered ancient by the school kids. He had a full head of white hair and wore very expensive three-piece suits which made him an easy target for jokes among the school staff. He smothered himself with Old Spice after shave lotion and it was common talk among students that you could smell "Apey" – as they called him - before you could see him.

The strong spicy, sweet smell of after shave was evident in the hallway air as they approached Clancy's office. It made Baxter sneeze in short rapid bursts when they got closer.

"Mr. Clancy must be in," laughed Miss McKinnon when she noticed his sneezes. "Are you okay, Baxter?"

"I'm alright. The smell of after shave lotion is strong, but I kinda like it."

"So Baxter is a wonder kid," said Mr. Clancy in a bad attempt to make a joke. Miss McKinnon had explained Baxter's exam results and the charge by Al Almon that he cheated.

Clancy opened a file in front of him and leafed through a series of papers.

"I am assured by Miss McKinnon that there is no way that you could have cheated on the exam."

He regained his composure after his bad joke.

"The questions were not released until the examination began and they were only known by Miss McKinnon. Baxter, I have your personal records in front of me and see that your marks are quite extraordinary. I have to admit that I am very impressed."

Baxter shuffled uncomfortably in his chair embarrassed by Clancy's remark.

"So how do you explain Al Almon's contention that you saw the exam results?" said Clancy.

Baxter recovered from his embarrassment and responded.

"I remember talking with Al about the history exam. He asked me why I was feeling so confident. I think he misunderstood what I meant about seeing the answers."

Clancy was curious.

"Exactly what do you mean?" he said.

"I don't actually see the answers, because I don't know the questions. But I see the page in the book where the questions come from?"

"Again, Baxter explain about the page?"

"Well...when I read the question on the exam I immediately see the page in the textbook where the answers are. I see every word on the page as if the book was open in front of me and it's as if I am reading the words right off the page. You see, I don't really need the textbook because I see the words in my mind."

Silence.

Clancy cleared his throat with an abbreviated cough. He looked over at Miss McKinnon who was at a loss for words.

The silence was broken by Clancy. "You mean to say, that you actually see a photograph in your mind of everything that you read."

"That's exactly what I see. The pages are like photographs. I didn't cheat."

"I know you're not a cheater. But the way you describe it, you have a photographic mind. But, how extensive is your memory? By that I mean, as an example, if you read a book two hundred pages long, can you remember every word on all two hundred pages?"

Baxter searched for an answer in terms of pages in a book. He had never really thought about his memory like this. The number of pages he could remember was far beyond the two hundred he had asked about. He answered with pride.

"I suppose I would remember all the words in the two hundred pages."

Clancy pressed him further.

"Do you mind if I give you a little test?"

He nodded.

"I have your history book in front of me and there are five hundred pages in the book."

Baxter interrupted, "I read the whole book, Sir, so you can test me on any page."

Clancy flipped through the book and stopped with his finger on a certain page. He counted down the lines and posed a question.

"What is on line twenty-five on page three hundred and ten?"

Without hesitation, Baxter quoted the correct words on the line, including punctuation. Clancy was astounded. He looked at McKinnon and in a soft voice said, "that is one hundred percent correct."

He flipped to another page and repeated the test with the same result. Another page. Another correct answer. Clancy closed the book and laid it down on his desk.

He wanted to learn more... the extent of Baxter's memory.

"Baxter, how many books can you memorize?"

"I don't think in terms of books, Mr. Clancy, I think in terms of libraries."

He had overwhelmed both McKinnon and Clancy. The cold silence in the room and the surprised expressions on their faces told him that.

His desire for normalcy became a little bit more distant than it did five minutes ago. But he had to continue. His mind was different from everyone else's and never before had he a chance to talk about it openly without holding back from fear of being ridiculed.

Miss McKinnon continued to question him after Clancy's momentary loss of words.

"I don't quite understand. How could you possibly see every word in every book in a library?"

"It's not that way. First of all I've never read every book in a library, not even in our own small school library. It's not the size of the library or the number of books or anything like that. It's how my mind works. It organizes things almost the same way a library does. You would go to an index card in a catalogue and pull out the name of the book you are seeking. I do the same thing in my mind. I draw out the name of the book from an index, flip through the Table of Contents in the book, and go to the page for the information."

He might have lost them so he tried to simplify.

"Once I read a book it is in my mind's library."

It was the best way he could explain what he saw in his mind, the best way he could explain how his mind worked.

"You must understand that I don't actually see every word, on every page, in every book in a library, all at once. I narrow it down to one page and then I see the words on that page. It's not as unbelievable as it sounds. My mind pulls up exactly what I am seeking - almost immediately."

"Okay," interrupted Clancy, "I think I understand how you think. It's absolutely incredible. Let me go a step further if you don't mind. How do you solve problems? For example, how would you think about solving a problem like say, world poverty? I hope I'm not pushing you too far. It's a complex issue, I know."

Clancy was testing Baxter. He didn't expect him to answer. But he did.

"Do you play chess, Mr. Clancy?" He asked.

"Yes. I'm quite fond of it. It's a great game of strategy and a wonderful mental exercise. But what does chess have to do with solving world poverty?"

"It's the way I think about a problem. But first of all, I have to say that I know I would not be able to solve world poverty. Gosh, I'm only a kid."

Clancy looked over at McKinnon. They laughed. It broke up the seriousness of the moment.

Baxter continued, "I know it is really important and it means that certain people are poor and other people are rich. But if I set my mind to solve it, I would first have to study it and all the issues involved in it and then I would go and play a game of chess with all the issues."

"You've lost me. I don't see what you are getting at," said Clancy. He was worried about being seen as inadequate in front of a ten-year-old kid.

Baxter added, "It's difficult to tie together the two concepts of playing chess and solving poverty, but chess as you said, is a game of strategy and world poverty is a problem that would involve using different strategies to solve it."

"I see where you are going," said Miss McKinnon. "Continue."

"As you know, in chess one has to think three or four moves ahead, anticipating moves that your opponent will make. A certain move sets in motion a chain of moves to defend and/or attack against that move. A whole series of combinations and permutations of moves becomes possible - each with a different outcome. It becomes more involved as the game progresses. I think of chess and all the combinations of moves that become part of its strategy - as a giant tree with many branches and twigs that all eventually lead to the trunk of the tree. Chess is a lot like that tree."

He broke off for a second.

I'm getting way over their heads

He enjoyed it.

"The idea behind my tree story is to get to the trunk from the top of the tree in the least amount of time, in the most efficient manner. Down one twig and up another twig may lead to a dead end, so I have to retrace my steps and take another route, another twig, until I come to a branch and I follow that branch through a series of branches, backing and retracing, until I come to a main branch, a limb, which leads to the main body of the tree, which takes me directly down to the trunk."

He stopped. *Did they follow me?*

He knew what he was talking about but he wasn't sure they did.

"I hope I haven't lost you. I'm throwing a lot of information in the pot and I hope I haven't spoiled the stew. But I have to explain this in the best way I am able...and don't forget, you asked the question."

"I follow you." said Clancy. "Please continue."

I don't think he did...there was the look of doubt in his eyes, but Baxter wanted to finish.

"To solve a problem I would use a strategy, like a chess match and the many routes to get to the bottom of a tree. If I see an obstacle, I will take a different route, until I encounter another problem, which opens up other routes. Like in chess, I see many different options that each move brings up and finally I travel the distance to the roots of the tree with the least amount of effort."

They didn't ask questions, so he either lost them or they understood. He thought he lost them, but he continued anyway.

"Problems of any nature can be sized up with any criteria to measure the various twigs and branches of the tree. You can use economic criteria, financial criteria, political criteria, social criteria, environmental criteria all of which would be parts of the tree. Of course, each criterion, to simplify matters would be a tree, for instance, an economic tree, a political tree, a financial tree and so on. And at the trunk of each tree, you would have the most efficient answer to that problem as measured by each of the criteria."

Was I overwhelming them?

He added one final remark.

"That's how I think my mind works to solve problems, both big and small, from world poverty as you had suggested, or to find the quickest route to the corner store. It happens instantaneously in my mind based on information available to me."

Clancy pulled himself together, cleared his throat and tried to maintain a professional image.

"Baxter," he stuttered. "I want to get you tested."

"What type of tests?"

"I want to set up a series of IQ tests for you, so we can make sure that you receive the attention that a child of your intelligence deserves. You understand about IQ tests, don't you?"

"I understand," he replied. "But it won't happen. My mother would never allow it."

CHAPTER SEVEN

Mother

There were so many things that Baxter had to talk about with his mother. More people became aware of his special abilities and he had become some kind of weirdo or a freak to them.

I just don't know what my special powers are; their extent or where they come from or when and how to bring them out. I just don't know whether to show them off or to hide them.

Thoughts swirled in his head.

If he showed them off it made him feel good, but gave him a superman complex which he didn't want. It meant that he would lose his friends. They didn't understand him and made fun of him; like the time he walked home after school by himself when some of his classmates yelled at him. *"Geek. There goes that little geek who thinks he's so special, so smart."*

"I don't know what a geek is," he tried to explain.

Someone in the group shouted, "It's someone who farts in a bottle and saves it to smell later."

"Geek, geek. Baxter's a geek."

They picked up rocks and hurled them at Baxter. He ran, they chased and he left them eating his dust.

He was sad. He wasn't a geek, but he wasn't like the rest of his classmates. He would burst at the seams, holding back so much of his capabilities and at the same time being the source of ridicule from his classmates and friends. But he still wanted to be accepted by them. It was a major dilemma for him.

I don't want to hide my abilities any longer.

His mother had to have answers about his abilities and to resolve the dilemmas his powers had caused. He had to speak to her in a way to skirt around his father, although he also had issues with his mother that had to be resolved.

Why had Mom totally ignored me when I needed her to speak out against Dad when he was driving me too hard in hockey?

Mothers were supposed to stand up for their children and she wasn't standing up for him.

She must've seen the bruises and lumps on my body when I was knocked around by those older boys in those brutal hockey practices.

She must've heard me cry myself to sleep every night when I had those nightmares about Jacques Plante coming after me swinging his goalie stick like an axe.

She said nothing on my behalf. Why? And why not stand up for me?

All the dilemmas in his mind were a jumbled mass of thoughts. That particular Saturday morning, he leaned across the breakfast table.

"Mom, I've got to talk to you," he said softly so that his father couldn't hear. It was one of his commandments that all meals had to be taken at set times for each meal of the day, with all the family together. No one was allowed to talk until he blessed the meal.

"Not now, Bax," said his mother. "Wait until we finish breakfast."

He wasn't sure if he had picked the right time to bring up the discussion about his abilities and the dilemmas in his life. He feared his father would find out. But after we'd eaten and his father left the room, his mother glanced back at him.

"Come with me, Bax. It's time we had a good talk."

She led him into the living room and sat down on the sofa, then gestured for him to sit beside her.

"It's okay, your father is outside packing his golf clubs in the car. He'll be away for most of the day, so we can talk as long as you want. What's on your mind?"

He stammered, not sure of exactly how to broach his dilemmas.

"I-I-I don't really know where to start, Mom, but there's something different about me that sets me apart from everybody else. I don't know what it is and I don't know what to do about it - and especially, I don't know how to control it."

Tears swelled in his eyes.

"I think I'm a freak and there is nowhere to turn. I can't talk to my friends. They laugh at me and call me names. Dad turned against me when I wouldn't use this special power - I call it suspension - in hockey, and it's making me miserable because I feel so alone."

He gasped for breath and barely finished his sentences. His shoulders heaved and he broke down from the pressure that had been on his mind, not just at that moment, but for all the time in his short life.

Everything came to a boil in the living room that day.

The floodgates opened and tears streamed down his cheeks. He was relieved and embarrassed; relieved from the release of pressure that had built up over the years and embarrassed because he cried in front of his mother.

Twelve-year old boys don't cry.

"**Baxter, it's okay,** it's okay. I know what you're going through. I really do." She slid across the sofa and consoled him in her warm, soft arms.

"I have a lot of explaining to do. I was going to wait until you were thirteen years old to tell you the family secret that is part of you, but I see that now is the right time."

She stood up and stared at him with a pensive expression on her face.

"You're special in a very good way, Baxter. You've nothing to be ashamed of. You're not a freak. You inherited the family secret that has been passed down from my side of the family, to the first born son generation after generation, from my mother and her mother before that for hundreds of years."

She chose her words carefully.

"I knew you had it, even when you were in my womb. I felt it in you. When I was pregnant with you, my mother - your grandmother beamed with excitement when she talked about a boy child being born. He will be very special. She repeated over and over. And it's true. You're very special. You began walking, almost running, when you were three months old. Most children don't start to walk until nine or ten months. When you were four years old it was apparent that you had the family power. I can still remember that day like it happened yesterday. We were in the park, myself, you and your father. Your grandmother was looking after David and Barbara and we were just walking on a beautiful summer day. You picked up a football that the older teenage boys were playing with and ran. They chased you and to their amazement, they couldn't catch you. It was then that I knew for certain that you possessed the special family power."

Baxter was puzzled, but remained silent. She paced in front of him.

"But you see, I had to wait - and it was the hardest thing I ever did - till you were older, a young man, to explain this power, this special family thing that you have. But it killed me to see you suffer and struggle with it and I couldn't come to your aid. I couldn't interfere with you."

Her voice cracked with emotion.

"You had to experience the power on your own, both the good and the bad of it. It's part of you and it's going to shape your life. You had to learn about it in your own way, while you were still young. You had to experience and cope with the strong emotions that are a side effect of its powerful physical and mental force. You must understand son that I had to let you deal with all of it by yourself."

Her eyes started to water but she held back the tears. Her voice cracked again.

"You have no idea how many times I wanted to take you and hold you and explain what is so special about you. But your grandmother talked me out of it. She kept warning me every time I was tempted to help you, that it would only harm you, if you didn't learn to grasp it and learn its power through your own experiences when you were young, like you are now. She saw it destroy your Uncle George who couldn't handle it and committed suicide. She told me many horror stories about long-dead relatives who couldn't handle how it affected them."

"Mom, I still don't know what it is, this family secret, this power in me."

She settled down and wiped the moisture from her eyes with a tissue she pulled from her hip pocket.

"Son, all I know is that it is nothing abnormal or supernatural or anything like that. It's completely natural. Other people may have it in certain degrees but not as strong as in our family. Just like some people can see better than others, hear better, throw farther, run faster, some are smarter than others, taller, heavier, stronger. The variation is part of the human condition. The differences between people makes those with greater abilities stand out. In our family, our gifted first sons have always stood out to the highest level of intelligence and physical prowess that is humanly possible."

She fumbled for the right words. It was a sensitive subject for her.

"I know this sounds hard to believe, but bear with me for a minute. This suspension, as you call it, is but only one manifestation of the power of your mind. You see most people can only use about eight to ten percent of their brain's power, but you are able to use up to ninety-nine percent of yours. This makes you unbelievably quicker, stronger, and smarter than most other people. You have been born with this power, this special condition that is part of our family's heritage."

She stopped for a moment and paced in front of him. His eyes riveted on her.

"Some families may have conditions that show up in their family history, passed down from generation to generation - medical problems such as diabetes, the breast cancer gene, male-pattern baldness. These are conditions that persist generation-to-generation. For example, look at your best friend, Stevie. His father is bald, his grandfather is bald and if you go back far in history, I bet you will probably find a pattern of baldness in most men in his family. Chances are that Stevie will also start to lose his hair when he turns into a young man. It's the same biological reasoning that red-haired parents have red-haired children. Look at the Budden's. It's genetics."

She questioned, "do you see where I'm coming from?"

He nodded.

"But our family is blessed with a genetic trait on my side of the family - the Thomas family - whereby the second female child passes the family trait to her first born son."

She was relieved...finally to tell the family secret to him.

"I am the second female child of my mother, who was the second female child of her mother. And Baxter, you are my first born male child and you possess the family trait. Another point, Baxter, is that it gets more powerful in each successive generation. This makes you the most powerful recipient of this gift in our family's history."

I had been right. There is something different...something special about me.

Baxter questioned and answered at the same time.

"That means then that Joanne, will pass our family trait on to her yet-to-be-born first son?"

"That's right," she replied. "Your children will not possess your special powers. I don't know why it happens this way, but this will be the way it will work for Joanne's first son. So, Baxter, always watch out for your sister, Joanne. She is the key to the continuation of this marvellous human condition that only exists in our family. I haven't told her about this yet, but I will at the right time. But now I want to make absolutely sure that you are aware of the special gift that you possess."

He wanted more information about himself - he wanted to understand the mysteries of his life that had perplexed and frustrated him for so long.

There is more...I know there is.

"Mom, I understand I have these special abilities. But there is something that always intrigued me that I can't figure out. Why can't I bring out this special power, suspension - on cue when I want? I can never be sure that it will come out."

Past events swirled in his mind. When he played hockey and baseball - sometimes it came out, sometimes it didn't.

Why did it come out in certain situations and not in others?

"You can control it. It's within your powers, son. You just don't know it yet," she responded. Her tear-stained face brightened with a broad smile.

"I can give you a very simple method to control it. Just tap your hand with two fingers five or six times and the power of your mind will bring it out on cue. You have to charge up your mind and this little trick can help you do that. It's like you would pull on a bowstring, building up tremendous power that will be released in an instant, propelling an arrow with tremendous speed toward the target. Your mind is the bowstring. You just have to train it to release your power and its full potential when you want it."

"Practice this technique," she said. "It will focus your mind on the immediate task at hand and transmit great power and speed directly to your body and expand your mind's capabilities."

Suspension had perplexed him for so long, his whole life that he had to try it right away. He tapped his hand.

She laughed when she noticed him tap his hand.

"You are wondering why it didn't come out in your baseball and hockey games when you wanted it to. It has to do with emotions, strong emotions that seem to block powers of concentration. Clear your mind of strong emotions and it will allow you to instantly pull back that bowstring and unleash its power. That's what the tapping will do for you. It will trigger the clearing of your emotions and allow complete control of your mind."

He didn't think about it and as he tapped his left hand his senses heightened, he emptied his mind of all emotion. The blank expression on his face startled his mother. She watched him with amazement. She witnessed first-hand, the workings of perhaps the most powerful mind in the world - her son's.

"How do you feel? What are your senses telling you? You have to learn to understand the changes that your body goes through to fully control your powers. Tell me everything you are experiencing."

"I feel fine, Mom. I can feel myself charge up. I experienced this feeling before, but I didn't understand it - on the hockey rink, in the fight I had with the Hardiman gang. It's like things slow down. I can feel my whole body charge up like a giant magnet. I feel strong and quick and light-headed."

I can control it...it's amazing!

"Let me try to explain it to you as I see it. My perceptions and all my senses feel like they are on alert. It's like I am pumped up on adrenalin, like I am plugged into an electrical socket. I feel so much potential. My mind is racing two hundred miles-per-hour down a speed track and it's starving for information like a sponge wanting to soak up water. Yet I am really just standing here talking to you. Not even moving and yet feeling all this awareness and strength surging through me. Thank you. Now I know I can control it and can turn it off with the blink of an eye."

He blinked his eyes in rapid succession and could feel the rush of heightened strength pour from his body like water flowing out of a tap.

"Though I'm down now, down from the peak of the mountain, I feel I can climb the mountain any time and descend it whenever I want."

He was exhilarated with this new-found knowledge about his powers, something that had eluded him all his life - the source of so much frustration.

His mother hated to bring him down from his high but there was more she had to tell him...not so pleasant things...things that may happen because of his powers - as if she knew he would not lead a so-called normal life.

"Remember the time when principal Clancy tried to give you an IQ test? Under no circumstances would I ever allow that to happen. I remember you being so proud about impressing Miss McKinnon and Mr. Clancy, especially after all the pain you were going through just being yourself. I know you wanted to be recognized for your special talents, but I couldn't let that happen. You didn't understand the enormous potential you possessed and the real danger to yourself if others became aware of it. That was neither the time nor the place to advertise your talents. But Bax, I knew how proud you felt about being admired for being yourself, for being smart and you wanted others to know it."

"Mom, what happened about that IQ test? For the longest time after that, Miss McKinnon and Mr. Clancy avoided me like the plague. I tried to talk to them about it, but they just ignored me. I don't understand what happened?"

His mother gritted her teeth and grimaced as if someone scraped their fingernails down a blackboard. It was an unpleasant memory and it showed on her face.

"That time was one of the most difficult times I had with your special abilities in your young life and it was important for me to protect you. Clancy knew you were special. He wanted to exploit you. He wouldn't let go. He constantly pressured me about getting you tested by professionals, medical doctors and other specialists. He said I owed it to the human race to develop your special mind properly and professionally. I had to get him to back off."

She hesitated and swallowed hard.

"You would've been a guinea pig, Bax, to all those so-called experts. I wouldn't allow that to happen. Your life would never be your own and this would have been before you even had a chance to start it."

"But I'm only twelve years old, what would all those people want with me?"

"You don't understand." She shifted forward in her seat to emphasize what she was about to say.

"Greed and power are big motivators in some people, some organizations, and they will do anything to retain power. They also determine threats to their power as dangerous. Power comes from independent thinking and brainpower that smart people like you possess and those people would want to control or eliminate any people that would affect their power base. That could be you."

She paused for a moment. This was difficult for her.

"It may seem hard for you to believe, son, while you're so young but you might be the smartest human being that ever lived. Powerful agencies and people would desperately want to learn our family secret - and your secret - for their own purposes."

He fidgeted as he digested what she said. She saw his apprehension.

"How would they use me? I'm only a little kid."

"To gain power and money. Like when you played for the Stars hockey team, they wanted to use you to win. Sports teams would want you to play for them for the great wealth that goes with winning. Powerful governments and agencies would want you for the same reasons. It's time for you to be fully aware of the world around you and to take your rightful place in it as you develop your marvelous potential. I will do everything I can to protect you as you turn into a young man, but you have to be prepared to face uncertain realities in your life."

He sighed...*What would my life be like?*

"Cheer up Baxter. I think things are not that bad. I've had a lot of time to think and the best advice I can give you is that you have to be very careful not to draw attention to yourself."

He nodded. "But how?"

"You can't go out and score ten goals in a hockey game every time you lace up a pair of skates. You have a special gift and I'm not completely sure what you're going to do with it - but I do know that it's for much more important things than scoring goals in hockey. Your destiny is to do greater things."

He laughed.

"You have to appear to be normal. I know that you are smarter than other kids in your classes - even smarter than your teachers but you can't get a mark of one hundred percent on every exam you write."

She paused for a moment, looked straight up in the air, and shook her head.

"I can't believe that I am saying this to you, telling my son not to excel. I almost feel like I am betraying you, but you know what I am talking about. Do not bring attention to yourself, under any circumstances."

Those words resonated in his ears.

"Do not bring attention to myself," he silently repeated, over and over.

"In sports, or school, or with your friends," she continued. "But what I want you to do is use every possible moment of your time, and use that marvelous mind of yours to expand your horizons, to learn everything you can about every possible bit of human knowledge, in every subject in the world."

There was worry in her voice.

"I have to also tell you that I do have fears that your special skills are already known by some powerful people and organizations. They might already be watching you. So it is even more important, now, that you don't tweak their interest further."

She stopped when she heard the sound of a car come up the driveway.

"Your father's back. We'd better stop talking now. We can talk further at a later time, but there is one more thing that I have to say to you about your special powers, Bax, and it is perhaps the most important thing that you can take away from our talk today. You know the difference between good and evil and you've been brought up to respect people, to have morals and values and I hope that whatever path you take in life, you will take these important Christian values with you. I certainly don't mean to preach. Where you go in life, you will have a profound effect on those around you and on society."

"Now go help your father take his equipment out of the car."

He walked away and pondered the conversation with his mother that changed his life.

He didn't sleep well that night. He was restless and his enormous mind was adrift in a sea of thought about the conversation he had with his mother. He thought about not drawing attention to himself - about maintaining morals and values in his life when dealing with others. This stuck in his mind.

How am I going to accomplish things in life without bringing attention to myself?

It was a question that spun over and over in his mind that night. He knew the importance of his mother's advice and he resolved to do just enough to be normal.

How to mimic normality? It was simple. No more ten-goal hockey games or moving at super-normal speed in sight of people. I have to keep suspension under wraps...and under control.

He thought hard that night about what type of person he wanted to become. He didn't know what he wanted to do and surmised that the answers would come to him later in life. He did know that he had a soft spot in his heart for the underdog, the misunderstood and for strength of character against adversity. After all, it was the story of his own short life.

He tossed and turned in bed. His mind raced. A burning desire overcame him to learn everything he could about everything under the sun. Tomorrow morning was the start of the rest of his life and it was to start at the library.

He was tired and wanted to sleep. But in his mind there jogged a question that unsettled him.

Who is watching me?

He tapped his hand and thought deep, comfortable sleep.

Lights out.

CHAPTER EIGHT

Professors Everywhere

Baxter and Dr. Shultz strode to the podium of the small amphitheatre where Baxter placed a bunch of papers down in front of him. He adjusted his glasses to hang below the bridge of his nose, similar to the way the six distinguished professors in the audience wore their eyeglasses.

At least I look like the intelligentsia.

With 20/20 vision, he didn't need to wear glasses, but it helped his persona by displaying some human frailty. He shuffled the papers around as if they actually had a purpose. He was comforted because they projected a normalcy, something he strived to achieve. Dr. Shultz also adjusted his glasses on the end of his nose to the preferred eyeglass position of the distinguished guests.

Dr. Shultz started. "Gentlemen, as you know, I have been telling you for some time now that an exceptional student has become a close personal friend of mine. He stands before you in the person of Baxter McPherson. He looks like a normal student; however I can assure you that is not the case. He is the most brilliant person I have ever met and that includes all of you."

There was a hint of laughter in the audience and one of the professors stood up. "And does that include you, too John?"

Dr. Shultz smiled. "Most of all me." He looked around at his colleagues. "We are fortunate because it took all of my persuasive powers to have Baxter appear before you. And you all know the condition that I asked you to abide by: to abstain from discussing this meeting with anyone. I gave my oath to Baxter that you would not speak of this meeting."

He looked around for any comments.

"I would like to start by introducing you, my esteemed colleagues, to Baxter. On my extreme left is Professor Ken Casey, renowned scientist and a specialist in astrophysics, professor emeritus at Harvard and presently on assignment to NASA. Next to him, Dr. Gary Brown. Again professor emeritus at Harvard and a practicing clinical psychologist. And Baxter, you no doubt recognize Professor Charlie Pye, Nobel Laureate in economics and your current professor in Economics 303."

Professor Pye stood up and looked at Baxter. "I hope Baxter that you plan to do better than the C+ mark I gave you for the first semester."

Baxter laughed. "And I thank you for that because I didn't think I even deserved that high a grade."

There was a bit of a buzz among the distinguished group in the room. They couldn't believe what they had just heard. C+ was a mediocre mark for a mediocre student.

Professor Pye spoke up. "Is this a charade? Is someone putting us on here? What type of joke is this?"

Dr. Shultz recognized a potential problem had developed and he raised both his arms to settle and reassure them. "If there is one thing I learned from Baxter, it's that he doesn't want to stand out. He could ace your course, Charles, with one hand behind his back, but that would put him in the spotlight and he'd stand out from his classmates. He strives to be accepted as normal. Am I correct, Baxter?"

Baxter, still behind the podium, was deep in thought.

Now I know how gay people must feel when they first decide to come out of the closet.

He had decided some time ago that he had to reveal his exceptional abilities to some people. It was now the time. But he was not certain who these people might be. Professor Shultz had persuaded him to speak to his esteemed colleagues about his abilities. They seemed like a good choice. But, it still felt awkward.

Stepping away from his defensive shield which had comforted him for years was his first step. The shield that had made him feel normal and had protected him.

Let the chips fall where they may.

Meeting with Dr. Shultz and his small group of academics was the first step away from his shield. He hadn't formulated a definite plan and despite his all-encompassing intelligence, he still possessed human frailties of doubt, anxiety and logistics about where his life was headed.

He decided to just go ahead and 'out' himself.

"You are correct, Dr. Shultz," said Baxter. "Gentlemen, I know who I am and I know that I have a special gift that few, if any people possess." Baxter took over the meeting and relieved Dr. Shultz of the responsibility. He continued with the introductions.

"Calvin McInnis, renowned medical doctor - and like the rest of you - professor emeritus at Harvard where he studies the human brain and its functions. I welcome you."

Baxter looked at the stout, middle-aged man seated directly in front of him.

"I have read all of your books Dr. McInnis, and appreciate that you have pioneered fantastic revelations on the mapping and delicate intricacies of the human brain. I admire your work and I can share some very relevant observations to clear up most of the problem areas of your research."

Professor McInnis frowned. He didn't relish the idea that someone of no apparent esteem, or distinguished letters after his name, suggested that he struggled with his research. Worst of all, for this young man to suggest that he had relevant insight into his research was unbelievable. Calvin McInnis was more than upset with this young upstart who stood in front of him.

"Who the hell do you think you are, son? What letters of distinguishment do you have? You're a third year student."

"I am sorry if you feel threatened Professor McInnis. You're right. I have no distinguished letters after my name. But I would suggest that the frontal lobe, left cortex is the area of the brain where you should concentrate your efforts to resolve the immediate problem with your research." Dr. McInnis was irritated. Baxter had known he would meet with suspicion once he revealed some of his special abilities to this group of Harvard professors. He saw this suspicion right now.

I am swimming but I feel like I have a lead weight tied to my ankle.

For a brief moment Baxter noticed that Dr. McInnis's train of thought shifted to his sick wife, Merideth. He read McInnis's thoughts.

Baxter continued. "But I see you have something important that is weighing heavily on your mind. Your thoughts are centered on your wife Meredith who recently found out she has a growth on her breast. You worry because of her family history of breast cancer."

Baxter had stepped beyond the boundaries of the meeting with these distinguished gentlemen, but he persisted. He indirectly revealed his mind-reading skills. Repeated practice had improved this special ability.

He observed their reactions.

The cat is out of the bag, now. Will they accept what I just revealed to them?

Baxter scanned the neural pathways of the scholars in front of him and read deep revulsion. The revulsion didn't surprise him. They would not be open to a new idea of this magnitude.

Dr. McInnis had been affected most by what Baxter had shared and now was the main source of the negative thoughts that Baxter picked up.

"How'd you find out about my wife's condition?" said McInnis. "No one here knows. I told no one. Have you been sneaking behind my wife's back, talking to her doctors?"

Feelings in the room grew negative, but Baxter had opened this door and would continue to walk through.

"Dr. McInnis, no one talked to me about your wife's condition. But I do know that you want to discuss this with your fellow colleagues so I tried to help. I brought it out in the open."

A pin could have dropped in the room. Then all hell seemed to break loose, with one professor after another directing questions at Baxter.

Both Baxter and Dr. Shultz raised their arms, simultaneously. Baxter raised his voice over the commotion. "Gentlemen, please bear with me, I am neither a carnival freak nor a physic pretending to foretell the future. I know about Meredith McInnis's condition because those thoughts were on Calvin's mind. I knew because I read his mind."

Chaos.

He sensed their thoughts.

Mind-reading....something out of a cheap sci-fi movie.

In unison, the group of Harvard's most distinguished stormed from the small amphitheatre, disgusted and indignant at the deception that one of their own, Dr. Shultz, had inflicted upon them - a young upstart charading as a mind-reader.

"Hear me out. Let me finish. Don't leave," shouted Shultz. But to no avail. They left the amphitheatre and slammed the door behind them. Baxter and Shultz stood there for a few seconds in the empty room and looked at each other.

"I am so sorry, Baxter", said Shultz. "Everything went out of control so quickly."

Baxter felt Shultz's disappointment. He tried to console his friend.

"They're all great men, John, but they aren't ready to accept a person like me. Please do not feel badly. I don't. It verified that it is the time for me to tell others who I am and share my abilities. It was a step forward for me. But this wasn't the place to do it."

The Harvard professors considered themselves to be privileged, elitist members of society and possessed super-sized egos to match. Baxter picked this up from their thoughts. They were not his type of people. He would have to 'out' himself in a different manner. He did not want to reveal this to his friend, Dr. Shultz.

Baxter looked straight into his friend's eyes.

"John, I now know that I have to find myself. No one can really help me do that, but I thank you for trying." He clasped John Shultz's hand in a firm handshake, hugged him and handed him a letter.

"Do me a big favour and please don't open this letter until tomorrow morning."

Baxter walked out of the amphitheatre. Alone.

***

Linda studied in her dorm room a lot instead of in the library where there were too many distractions. She would sometimes go to the library when she wasn't too serious about her studies. She would often end up gabbing with her girlfriends and watching the boys. It was like a display with the guys strutting their stuff like male peacocks in mating season. The girls acted similarly - in their own way. The library was more like a bar on campus. Another meeting place but without the booze.

It was close to the midterms and she had to do some serious studying. No library for her this week.

Baxter knocked on her door.

The talk he planned was the most difficult thing he was about to do in his life. He had to leave and he had to explain why... and why he had to leave her behind. He would have a lot of things to explain. Saying goodbye would be painful. It weighed heavily on his mind.

"Bax, I can always tell your knock. Come on in," said Linda through the closed door.

He walked in and she didn't even look up.

This is going to be soooo difficult...and my timing sucks...right before her midterms.

"Hunkering down with the books ...ehhh...good for you," he said.

Linda got up from behind the large oak study desk, pushed her books aside and wrapped her arms around his neck.

"Now this is the type of study break I need," she kissed him. "You surprised me. You normally let me know in advance when you're coming over. So what's up?"

Baxter had thought about how he was going to tell her. There was only one way to do it. The band aid approach - just rip it off as quickly as possible and get the pain over with, all at once.

Easier said than done...

He looked into her eyes.

"There is something very important I have to tell you."

She noticed the serious expression on his face and backed away a couple of steps.

"Linda, you know I love you. I may not have said it before. But I do."

"Baxter...ohhh," her eyes puffed up. "And I loved you from the first day we met."

She wrapped her arms around his neck again. He took hold of them to momentarily restrain her.

"I have to leave Harvard. It's time. It's what I have to do...and I have to leave by myself."

The joy he saw on her face disappeared. A forlorn look took its place.

"But...but what are you talking about? And why? Has it something to do with me?"

"God...no Linda. It hurts me like hell to tear myself away from you. You know there is something different about me. You told me so many times yourself...and it's true...and I have to find out who I am and what I will do with my life and my abilities. It's not you, my love. I have to leave everything in my life to discover myself...and that means leaving Harvard and my friends and you, too...but only until I find out who I really am...I hope you understand."

"No I don't understand. Take me with you." Tears flowed down her cheeks.

"I can't...but I'm not leaving you for good. You have to trust me...I love you and I will be back and I will be in touch while I'm away.

He took her in his arms and smothered her with kisses.
He then backed out the door turned and walked away.
It hurt like hell!

***

The next day Professor Shultz picked up the letter and opened it before he prepared his ritualistic morning coffee. He had waited, as Baxter had instructed, till the morning after the disastrous group meeting in the amphitheatre. The short letter was in Baxter's handwriting and was succinct.

John:

I have left Boston and am totally on my own now because it was time for me to leave. I will miss you greatly, as I will Linda, my family and my friends. I have talked to Linda and it was very difficult for me to leave her. I have not told the others of my departure and I will leave it you, my dear friend, if you would be so kind.

You know why I had to go and I leave it to your best judgement when they ask for an explanation. But for the most part, they will know and understand.

I left a cell phone in my apartment. Find my apartment key taped inside this envelope. Please protect the cell phone so I can get in touch with you. It is a special cell phone that I altered so that it cannot be traced. I will call when I am able. Keep the cell phone close to you and safe at all times.

Rest assured you are on my mind and I will see you again, God willing. Please destroy this letter.

Your life-long friend.
Baxter

Professor Shultz read the letter over and over and felt a great loss. He swept away a small tear in his eye and tore up the letter in fine pieces. He would pick up the cell phone from Baxter's apartment that afternoon.

CHAPTER NINE

Bud

Bud Brown rolled out of bed on a cold blustery January morning, shivered a bit from the lack of warmth outside the bed covers and looked at his naked body in the full length mirror of the hotel room. As much as he sucked in his stomach and posed in a body-builder stance, he couldn't hide that old age was wearing down his once slim, athletic body. He didn't wear pyjamas - slept 'au natural' - as he called it, and he loved the sensation of being unencumbered in his nakedness. But this morning he thought he should wear at least a tee-shirt to bed because January in Boston was damn cold.

His job made the coldness of the morning and the shivers it brought, even harder to bear. He picked up the file on one 'Baxter McPherson' while he dressed, then flipped it open to the last memo CIA headquarters had sent him the day before. He read it again and slapped the file shut. It didn't feel any better when he read it now than it had when he received it yesterday.

He reflected upon his past cases for a moment and how badly they had made him feel about himself and how he earned his living. He hated his job as a CIA domestic operative even more as he mellowed with age. At the ripe old age of sixty-two and as a grandfather, he valued the development of the human spirit and soul, even more each time he looked into the questioning eyes of his beautiful little granddaughter and grandson.

He had softened with age...*that is natural even with the harshness that is required in my profession. I'm human after all.*

His cases involved young, brilliant people with exceptional talent...some with physic abilities, the highest IQ's to be searched out and used for CIA purposes.

His profession disturbed him.

Freedom of youth is what it's all about...and I take it away from them.

He was never privy to what the CIA wanted with these people, nor how they used them. He just had to find them and convince them to use their talents for the good of the country. But he had his own sources of information after being in the organization for twenty years. After twenty years, you learn things and suspicions often come true.

They are discarded like a piece of garbage when their usefulness runs out...*they are good people and their country abandons them.*

He didn't want this to happen to Baxter. The CIA heard claims that he possessed special abilities. Bud had to learn as much as possible about him from as far back in time as he could.

Bud tracked down A.P Clancy, the former principal of St. Agnes School where Baxter had received his early education. He was in an upscale nursing home....u*pscale it was but it was still a place where old people go to die.*

Bud hated nursing homes.

I'm gonna be in one of these places soon enough.

He smelled ammonia when he walked into that brightly lit senior's nursing home and was chilled by the pervasive sad feeling that permeated the air. Old men ravaged by age; some slept in their wheelchairs, some shuffled aimlessly in any direction, slowly with support of their walkers. The nursing staff talked to each other, oblivious to the concerns of the inmates.

Bud picked out A.P Clancy in the corner of the living area looking out the window as if there were actually a reason for doing so. He was wheelchair bound and looked like the rest of the inmates - lonely and depressed. The unmistakable smell of Old Spice after shave was difficult not to notice. A helpful nurse said that Clancy suffered from second stage Alzheimer's disease and Bud had doubts whether the elderly man would be rational enough to remember one student among the thousands that he had been in charge of during his years at St. Agnes.

As soon as Bud mentioned the name Baxter McPherson, Clancy perked up and his dull, grey, empty eyes lit up with intelligence.

"He was an amazing young student and one that I'll never forget," said Clancy. He straightened himself from his slumped position in his wheelchair.

"And as far as I'm concerned he was a freak of nature. He has a remarkable photographic memory." The old man paused, shook his head and coughed. "Absolutely out of this world...I tried like hell to get him tested and I can tell you that his mother ruled the roost. She completely stymied every attempt I made to get him tested. The kid wanted to, but it was a losing battle fighting his mother."

He squirmed in his wheelchair.

"The only information that she admitted to was that Baxter was an exceptionally smart boy - but no more than many other smart children. But that didn't stop me. You see, I didn't believe her. So I followed him as secretly as I could. Do you believe that? Me, the school principal following a student."

"He was exceptional?" said Bud. "So what did you find out about him?"

"I saw marvellous examples of his scholastic and athletic prowess in his years at my school. But apparently this prowess dried up when he became a teenager. In his teens Baxter appeared to be just a normal kid and that change baffled me. I figure that there was a very effective cover-up by his family and extraordinary restraint on young Baxter's part - to hide his God-given, super-human talents.

Clancy had spent long, meaningless days waiting to die in the nursing home but at this moment his voice filled with purpose.

"I was like a detective. I followed him and watched him. But he held back in just about everything he did at around the age of thirteen. It was like he just stopped in his tracks and I know that his mother was behind it, controlling him and guiding him to act normal."

Bud had learned all he could from Clancy and was about to leave - perhaps a little bit earlier than he had planned, due to the unpleasantness of the nursing home environment. As he rose to his feet, Clancy spoke up again.

"Watch his sister, Joanne," he coughed. "She is also special in a certain way. I found out that she has inherited the McPherson family special gifts and when she gets older, she will pass it down to her own first born son."

This revelation startled Bud. He hadn't known this. Earlier he had checked the family history but had not realized the significance of Baxter's sister in the scheme of things.

He questioned the old man. "Why do you believe this?"

"I talked to the grandmother in their family, who quite openly said Baxter's sister is special. She is the second daughter of the second daughter in the McPherson lineage and her son, when she has one, will be special - inheriting the family's special traits. Baxter is the best of the McPherson family right now, and his sister Joanne will pass these special gifts on to future generations."

Clancy started to cough again. A nursing attendant noticed his discomfort and motioned to Bud.

"I am sorry Mr. Brown, but you'll have to leave now. It is time for his medication." Bud thanked Clancy and walked away with a sense of relief. He hated those homes but he was glad he'd talked with the old man. He was now more convinced than ever that he had to confront Baxter and help him escape the clutches of the CIA.

The CIA knows things and had tracked down Baxter's presence at a special amphitheatre gathering at Harvard University with a group of professors. Bud was informed of this meeting. He had to act quickly. It was now the time to meet Baxter.

The cold wind swirled around Bud's feet and he instinctively fastened the top button of his coat. He could have picked a warmer place to confront Baxter but he sensed urgency. He had waited outside the locked door of the amphitheatre at Harvard University and he now saw his chance. He stepped in front of Baxter as he exited the amphitheatre. He lightly grabbed him by the arm.

"May I have a word with you Mr. McPherson?" He spoke in a firm voice.

"I've been expecting you," responded Baxter as he stood face-to-face on the snow-cleared steps. "I know you have been watching me and we should have a long-overdue chat - but not here. Let's duck across the street to the coffee shop."

Bud hadn't expected such a congenial first meeting when he made his abrupt approach. But right now he needed that hot coffee and was thankful that a coffee shop was close by.

Bud had the first sip of hot coffee, then blurted out, "I work for the CIA and the CIA wants you because of your special abilities. I told them how special you are. They will eventually get you. You cannot hide from them. They will find you no matter where you go. They are the eyes of the devil, itself...email, telephone, cell phones, credit cards, debit cards...they relentlessly track them all; they will find you if you use any of them."

Baxter knew all this and said, "I know the CIA is watching me, but I will hide in the best place possible, a location so safe I will be untouchable."

"I doubt very much that there is such a place. I speak from experience. But go ahead, prove me wrong. Where is it?"

"In plain sight."

"It won't work. You don't understand the CIA's broad-reaching power. They can swoop down and take you tomorrow, right off the street, and you will be gone, lost forever - forced to do whatever they want. I've seen this done before."

Bud swallowed hard and gulped down the hot coffee. He burnt the inside of his mouth. It hurt but it warmed him up.

"You have to leave immediately. Go anywhere, but get out of sight quickly and don't leave a trail or they will find you."

The urgency in Bud's voice was not lost on Baxter.

"You have a couple of day's grace - then they will start looking for you," said Bud. "My report on you is due tomorrow and I can delay it a couple of days before they see through the stalling and come after you."

The information confirmed the thought patterns that Baxter picked up from Bud's mind. But one thought he picked up startled him.

"You know about my sister, Joanne, don't you?"

"Yes, I found out. But don't worry. Your sister's secret is safe with me. I'll never reveal it."

Baxter knew that was the truth.

CHAPTER TEN

Into the Unknown

Baxter was alone. Never in his life had he experienced the feeling of utter isolation. He had his family to support him in the worst of times during his childhood, but now there was no one for him. He had no support, no friends, just complete strangers who passed by and ignored others - including him - in the pursuit of their own petty lives. He was not only completely alone, he was overwhelmed with feelings of sadness, nervousness and even fear about the trek he had put himself on - to discover his life mission and what lay ahead.

All those feelings overcame him when he slumped deep into the coach seat of the Amtrak train headed to Chicago. He had paid his bills and bought the train ticket. He had severed all ties to his former life, disposed of his physical assets and emptied his bank account. That left a grand total of two-hundred-and-fifty dollars in his pocket as he headed into the unknown.

How far will two hundred and fifty dollars take me?

He was at the beginning of the next stage in the theatre production of his life. He was both excited and afraid.

He read the minds of the people around him on the train.

God, I hate my job. If I had enough balls, I would stand up to that bastard of a boss.

If I have to argue again tonight with my wife, I think I will shoot her.

Where am I going to get the money to pay my bills? I'm broke. Maybe my luck will turn at the blackjack table tonight.

I am getting so old and frail.

I hate my husband. He's a conniving prick.

I think I fell in love with the wrong man.

God... would I love to screw that new secretary.

I am ugly and fat.

What is the purpose of me living?

The empty faces of the people on the train showed their lot in life. Their thoughts were a jumbled mixture of worry, anguish, sadness, hopelessness and anger over all issues in their daily lives.

Baxter was about to shut off his mind to prevent himself from being overwhelmed with their depressing thoughts when one solitary man in an aisle seat a row over caught his attention. He seemed at peace among the throngs of people around him. He was the only one and he exuded a sense of tranquility and happiness. Baxter read deeper into his mind and found that his happiness came from 'giving' not 'taking.' The man had built up a small fortune in his work life and given it to a hospital for sick children. He stamped this man's identity into his brain...*this good man would someday, somehow, be rewarded for his unselfish deeds.*

That moment, seated on a train to Chicago, Baxter had a revelation. It was the proverbial light bulb going off in his head. The light bulb turned on after he read the mind of the good person seated one row over.

There are a lot of good people in this world...I will seek them out...it will be part of my new mission in life - to reward good people.

He thought more and more about this revelation. He set it as a personal and strategic policy - to promote human welfare. It was to become a main tenet of his journey.

How can I ever accomplish such a noble task with but two hundred-and-fifty dollars in my pocket?

He set his great mind for a task to work out the details of his life mission.

The train screeched to a halt in central Chicago and when the kind stranger was about to disembark, Baxter approached him, touched his shoulder and stated, "I know what you have done and you will be rewarded. Remember the name, Baxter."

Baxter left the train and stepped into the cool air of a clear Chicago morning. He smiled as he read the man's reaction to his outburst.

There are a lot of crazy people in Chicago.

Baxter had no idea where he was going. He just walked and trained his thoughts to read the minds of people he passed on the street. He sensed more evil than good and that worried him. He walked and walked that first day in Chicago and he grew tired.

He sat on a park bench and despite all his observation skills; it had escaped his notice that he was in a very run-down area of the city. When he looked around, he observed the dilapidated condition of houses that had not received a coat of paint in decades, the broken windows on buildings no one cared enough to fix, garbage lined the street - and most obvious of all, the people. They looked as run-down and forgotten as the buildings that surrounded them. Most were African American with very few white faces among them.

So this is an example of American blight.

His mind raced over economic theories of decay in the urban core of cities. It seemed obvious to him how these rundown neighbourhoods could be re-claimed, one neighbourhood block at a time, through the regenerative effects of small business activity.

Why hasn't it happened here?

A scream from across the street startled him away from economic revitalization theory. Four large men kicked and punched a frail-looking old man who attempted to defend himself by swinging a cane at the younger, stronger men. But his was a fruitless effort. It was a robbery in progress. They shouted at their victim, "Give up ya money, old man, or you're dead meat."

Baxter recognized the seriousness of the situation and the danger that the old man faced. He raced across the street in an instant and grabbed the thug nearest to the helpless old man who was being pummeled by vicious kicks and punches. Baxter threw the thug ten feet in the air.

For a brief moment there was calm. No one moved. The four attackers couldn't believe what had just happened. They looked at one another, looked at Baxter, then looked stupidly at the old man. Baxter read their thoughts.

No one comes to the aid of anyone in this neighbourhood and certainly not a honky helping a black man.

"Who da fuck you, Honky?" shouted the downed thug in dismay. He scrambled to his feet.

"You're gonna pay for laying hands on Leroy, Honky!"

Leroy came at Baxter and was sent flying face first to eat concrete as Baxter tripped him up. The others, in a coordinated fashion - from years of experience in urban battles - rushed Baxter.

Baxter read the rage and violence in them. In that split second he grasped how sheltered his life had been. He couldn't imagine the violence that these young men faced in their lives. He felt sympathy for them but they had murder on their minds and Baxter's sympathy could mean his life.

He had to subdue them or they would kill him. No fancy moves in this situation but aggressive tactics would be needed to stop their attacks.

The first thug was downed by a straight, open-palmed thrust of the forearm to the chest. The second man was tripped up by a leg sweep and a quick pinch to the main artery in his neck that rendered him unconscious and harmless. The third thug was sent flying in the air and landed heavily into litter and foul-smelling trash cans. He didn't move.

Baxter looked around and his attention turned to the old man, who lay on the sidewalk. The old man had watched the battle between the four street hooligans and this miraculous white man who had saved his life. He was dumfounded. Baxter approached him and helped him to his feet.

"Are you all right, mister?" asked Baxter.

The old man had never seen a person move as quickly as the white stranger who stood in front of him. He was in shock, and so awed that he could not feel the pain in his beaten body.

"Who dis white man?" he said under his breath, "and in ma hood?"

"I am fine, mista...but watch out!" the old man screeched.

The warning came too late. A heavy wooden pole crashed down solidly on Baxter's head.

A foul smell of rotting, musty clothing was the first thing Baxter noticed when he awoke out of a complete daze. He looked around and saw that he was covered in filthy mats that provided a certain degree of protection from the coldness of the late evening.

He was in a large, abandoned, underground railway station. His body ached. He felt his ribs and grimaced in pain at the light touch. He felt dried blood on his forehead and he had a tremendous headache when he swiveled his head around to observe his surroundings. He had been severely beaten.

Baxter felt himself all over and was thankful that no bones were broken. His individual pride had suffered a blow because the four thugs he had encountered had gotten the better of him. He had read their minds and had seen murderous hatred and knew they wanted to kill him.

How did I survive?

"You lucky man, Mista." The old man, silhouetted against the fading daylight, approached Baxter. "Leroy and his gang of thugs woulda killed ya dead if my buddies hadn't come lookin' for me at dat time. Dey drove dem off."

"Dey got your wallet, though," continued the old man. "And dey sure did kick and beat you up after Leroy hit you over ya head with dat pole." The old man paused for a second then offered Baxter his hand in a vigorous grip. "What's ya name, Mista? Ya saved my life. I'm Jefferson."

The old man reached his hand out and shook Baxter's hand. Baxter grimaced, and felt the pain in his head with even the slightest movement of his facial muscles as he smiled, ear to ear.

"My name is Baxter and I also owe you my life, Jefferson."

He moved his arms. His shoulders throbbed. He winced when he bent over to shake hands. His gut hurt from the many kicks and punches that Leroy and his gang had given him. He commanded that pools of life-giving blood pour to the injured parts of his body to heal his wounds. Jefferson handed Baxter a cup of bitter tasting tea that he had just brewed in his rail track home...*it was pungent to taste but nothing tasted so good.*

"Youse gonna need a few days' rest," said Jefferson. "Ma humble home is yers fer as long as ya needs."

Baxter thanked Jefferson, but he felt the healing properties of pools of blood already flow to the injured parts of his body to mend his wounded flesh.

"Thanks, I will be recovered in the morning." Baxter was injured and tired and he pulled the foul smelling mats over his body and fell into deep slumber as easily as if he had been lying in his own bed covered with freshly washed cotton sheets.

The rats that crawled over his matted bed covers woke Baxter early the next morning. He looked around and whisked away the cat-sized rats that seemed unafraid of humans.

Jefferson was nearby.

"Never mind dose rats. Dey will only eat ya if ya is dead," he said as he handed Baxter a piece of orange. "Whatever I got is yers, Baxter. I don't got much, but it's all I got."

Baxter and Jefferson sat there in the filthy train station and talked for about two hours. It's what Baxter wanted to do, to get to know this good man, a good man in the bottom trough of society. He had a family, had lost them and his whole life's work through the ravages of alcohol. But he had given up the bottle in an effort to recover his life. It had been a tough go for Jefferson on his road to recovery. He had little in the way of education, a menial work history and was no longer young.

Their friendship was instantaneous.

Jefferson, a gentle, big-hearted man had received very few breaks in life. Baxter was proud to call him a friend. A friend, who within that two hours of engaging conversation, would do anything he could to help another human being.

Jefferson was also a judge of people and this young man in front of him was unlike any other person, black or white, that he had met before. He liked Baxter.

"Come on down to Charity Cottage and meet Miss Marie soon as ya wounds heal."

"I can go anywhere you lead Jefferson," replied Baxter. "I am perfectly fine now."

CHAPTER ELEVEN

Charity Cottage

Jefferson led Baxter through street after street. They all looked the same. Streets that suffered the pain of its inhabitants. Unemployment, poverty and crime existed side-by-side with uncollected garbage, scurrying rats and buildings as neglected as the people. Urban blight was everywhere.

One street was different. A house at street's end struck Baxter as truly singular. An exterior veneer of fresh white paint highlighted the house as something special. It seemed to attract the rays of sunshine that peaked through the clouds and shone on it like a beacon of light on a dark night. Charity Cottage was the house and it stood out in the middle of Chicago's urban jungle.

Baxter took in every minute detail when he and Jefferson walked through the door. It was freshly painted on the inside as well and had the sharp ammonia smell of a recent cleaning. Comfort and ease showed in the eyes of outcast men and women.

"Dees people are all homeless," said Jefferson. "But look at da pride in da faces."

The homeless filled the place, but they busied themselves with a variety of tasks: they cleaned, cooked and served food - helped out in whatever manner they could. Baxter was amazed at the coordinated effort in the busy, functioning operation of the homeless society that existed within the confines of that house.

"Come meet Miss Marie." Jefferson grabbed Baxter by the arm and pointed to a slight woman who barked instructions to the homeless men and women about chores to be done. "She's an amazin' woman, like none you'll ever meet. She did give up a life of wealth and privilege to come here and open up Charity Cottage. She just wants to help us type people."

Baxter was surprised. Marie was a white woman with premature greying hair, about thirty years of age and though she was attractive her face seemed older. One was taken by the strength of character that appeared chiseled in her features.

She noticed Baxter when Jefferson dragged him toward her.

"And who is this handsome, young stranger?" asked Marie as she walked away from the group of men who waited for instructions on tasks to be done.

"Dis ma new friend, Baxter, a stranger, but a good person. He did save me from Leroy's gang."

Baxter and Marie shook hands and there was an immediate connection between them. Baxter probed her mind and saw a person of the highest character.

"So Baxter, what brings you into this area of Chicago? You must know you look out of place." She did not mince words. Her direct approach impressed Baxter.

"Is it that obvious? I guess I don't look like most of the people here. But like Jefferson said about you, I also want to help people. Unfortunately, I have no money and don't have a place to stay.

They sat down and talked.

"You have no money?" Marie laughed. "Let me tell you about money. I had it once and could've had it again. I've seen the lifestyle that extreme wealth bestows upon the fortunate families with power and influence. They waste away without purpose in the lap of luxury. My family was lucky in that way and they cast me out, because I wanted to help people that were not like them."

Marie hesitated, then said nothing, from which Baxter could sense that she didn't make a habit of disclosing her family history.

"This is now my life in the slums of Chicago and I've never been happier," said Marie.

"So Baxter you're welcome to stay here at Charity Cottage - our home is your home," said Marie after about an hour of talk with Baxter. "But you have to help out around here. What can you do?"

That was a loaded question for Baxter. He laughed to himself. He was capable of doing anything in the world, better than the best expert in that field. But he didn't brag.

"I can fix things," he said. "And since I can't pay, I will trade my sweat and labour for food and shelter."

"Well then Baxter McPherson," continued Marie. "The TV doesn't work, the radio is broken, our only computer doesn't compute, the fridge and stove are on their last legs, and the washing machine doesn't wash. Can you handle any of those problems?"

Baxter smiled.

He was humbled. He was helpless and dependent upon the generosity of others. He had always appreciated people who were willing to help those in need...he was now in need. Charity Cottage was imprinted into the deep recesses of his mind.

"They'll be fixed immediately and will be better than ever."

It was not more than a week later that Marie, grinned as she approached Baxter. She put both her arms around him in a grizzly bear hug.

"Baxter, I don't know how you did it, but it's a miracle I never expected. Everything that I gave to you to fix has been fixed and they are all working better than they ever have. And it didn't cost Charity Cottage one red cent of our very small budget. How on earth did you do it all?"

Baxter was proud. He had accomplished something very meaningful for Charity Cottage. He'd helped them and it felt good.

He couldn't help but think back to the frustration he felt when he tried to talk and reason with those college professors in the university Amphitheatre, not that long ago. How meaningless it had been to try to impress those super egomaniacs at the university - they, who thought the world revolved around them - compared to the simple tasks of replacing a worn out part in the Cottage refrigerator, or the repair of a faulty valve in a vacuum cleaner... *Small things can mean big things in the proper circumstances.*

It was a lesson learned well by Baxter.

"I hope you don't mind," he said. "But I took it upon myself to make sure that all repairs were done without cost to Charity Cottage. I got the cable company to pay for something that I did to the TV. I tinkered with the TV set and opened up access to all TV signals from the cable company that they normally block and require payment to receive. It's a simple technical thing that the cable company imposes on all its non-technical customers."

"But isn't that illegal in some way?" said Marie.

"Not at all. It's your TV, not theirs and I simply re-arranged its circuitry to access signals. I also arranged to have them pay you $1,000 per month for five years by selling them the knowledge that bypasses their cable signals. Unfortunately for all others, the cable company will bury that information and never share it."

Marie looked worried. She stared directly at the computer that Baxter had also worked on for a few hours.

"I'm afraid to ask what change our little computer has undergone since you worked on it. It's a bit scary. Have you done anything to it?"

"I fixed it to its original specifications, cleaned up the hard drive, got rid of the malware and viruses but haven't really fooled with it. I could increase its capacity if you want, but I thought I had better ask your permission. It might bring notoriety to your organization if the computer companies hear of it. But it could mean a lot of money for Charity Cottage."

"Well Baxter. It may draw attention to Charity Cottage, but eventually that will bring notoriety to you. Is that what you want?"

Marie was right, though he wished she was wrong. He did not want to bring attention to himself. It would lead to unwanted scrutiny. He could improve computers at any time. He wanted to help Charity Cottage, but would have to find another way.

The loud crack of gunshots resonated loudly outside Charity Cottage. The crackling ricochet of bullets from automatic gunfire was very close. Residents in the house scrambled and ducked for shelter in all directions. Confusion reigned. Screams and cries were heard in the street above the rat-a-tat-tat of gunfire, and the sounds of men running, falling and knocking over things added to the confused state. The tension and fright in the air seemed endless but lasted for only a few seconds.

Then silence.

The silence was punctured by moans from the street. No one moved and the moans continued. Baxter was the first one out the door, while the many residents in Charity Cottage stayed down prone on the floor. Gunfire was part of life in this neighbourhood. The neighbourhood thugs were busy killing each other in gang warfare or over bad drug deals.

The man who'd been shot lay in the middle of the street. Baxter recognized him as the thug, Leroy, the one who had assaulted him a week and a half earlier. Leroy coughed up bright red blood while Baxter assessed his medical condition in expert triage fashion. He did not hesitate. The man needed medical attention to save his life and he had the medical skills. He would provide it regardless of the beating that Leroy and his gang had inflicted on him.

Leroy's wounds were not severe, but he was in immediate danger of losing too much blood.

Baxter ripped off Leroy's shirt and tore it into strips and applied a tourniquet to Leroy's wounded leg, the most serious of his wounds. The pressure stopped the flow of blood. Baxter lifted and carried Leroy to the safety of Charity Cottage. It was in a state of chaos when Baxter laid the unconscious thug on the living room sofa. Blood dripped and stained the upholstery. Many homeless residents of the Cottage were past victims of Leroy's gang activities and shouted, "Get that criminal out of here and throw him back in the street."

Jefferson stood beside Baxter.

"Whatever, I can do ta help, Bax. Let me know. You won't abandon him like everyone else has done. Da police on der way, but don't expect them to arrive too quickly in da hood."

"He lost too much blood and he won't survive much longer, the bullet just nicked the main artery in his leg and I've got my fingers on it now, trying to stop the bleeding"

Jefferson looked down and saw Baxter's hand inside the gaping wound on Leroy's leg.

"Jefferson, I need you to get me the medical kit in the bathroom, some duct tape, the glue in the hardware shop cabinet, a needle, strong thread, a razor blade, some rubber tubing and two syringes from any of the junkies here. Try for clean ones...immediately!"

Jefferson came back with the assorted paraphernalia. Baxter hands were a blur, he worked so quickly. He placed his hand on Leroy's head and transferred a thought to near-dead Leroy... *Don't wake up.*

Baxter taped up the artery with the medical tape in the kit, sewed up the wound and performed a blood transfusion from himself to Leroy. He placed both hands on Leroy's head for about a minute before a shroud of a heavy fog overcame his consciousness from his own loss of blood.

Baxter passed out.

Confusion was still rampant when he woke up, but it was focused on him this time.

Police questioned Marie, Jefferson and many of the homeless at the shelter. Medical personnel attended to Baxter. Baxter sensed he had transferred too much of his blood to Leroy and had lost consciousness. He was fine, but still weak as he felt his body regenerate from the IV solution that the paramedics dripped into his body.

"I've never seen anything like that in my life," said one of the paramedics who arrived on the scene. "This man saved the life of that common thug by a medical procedure that I've never seen before. He performed a blood transfusion on himself with absolutely no proper medical equipment. It is a medical marvel."

The paramedic approached Baxter.

"Mister what's your name, and how did you perform that transfusion procedure? Are you a doctor?"

"How is Leroy?" replied Baxter. "Is he okay?"

"He's just fine, thanks to you. He will have a full recovery, although he'll limp for quite a while yet. But what's your medical experience? Where did you learn that transfusion procedure?"

Baxter interrupted his endless questions.

"Jefferson, come here and talk to me," shouted Baxter over the confusion. He could see press reporters and camera men arrive to confirm a story that had spread fast. Baxter had to protect his anonymity.

"Get those people out of here - by any means," he whispered to Jefferson. "And don't let them take me to the hospital."

Another wave of nausea overcame Baxter, and he passed out.

The surroundings were unfamiliar and quiet when Baxter regained consciousness. He was alone in a darkened room, not in Charity Cottage. He tried to stand up. Marie and Jefferson entered the room when they heard him.

"Lay still, Baxter. You're weak," Marie said in a soothing tone.

"I'm one hundred percent fine, now…but where am I?"

"You're at my place," said Marie. "But I don't think you can stay long because the press are looking for you. You created quite a stir when you performed that medical procedure on Leroy - at great personal sacrifice, I might add."

"But how did you get me out of that media circus at the Cottage?" said Baxter.

"Well, twasn't easy," interjected Jefferson. "But it's amazin' how quickly a bunch of seemingly crazy, drug-addicted, homeless men can clear everyone from a room when they start acting nuts." Jefferson laughed.

Baxter laughed with him and then turned to Marie. "It seems being identified as crazy, dangerous and homeless has its advantages. But you're right, Marie. My stay here is over. I have to leave immediately."

The press knows something out of the ordinary happened here.

They are just like hound dogs...smelling out a story and following up on it.

The medical transfusion mystery talked about by the medical people...the cable company transmission-feed story. They will find out about that.

He thought about the CIA.

They also will be moving in.

Jefferson and Marie were sad when they heard Baxter state the obvious. He had to leave.

Jefferson spoke up. "Baxter, I know ya leaving, but I have ta ask: what were ya doin' when you placed both yer hands on Leroy's head? It looked like yose was praying."

Baxter didn't want to divulge much about his special talents, even to Jefferson and Marie. It would be dangerous - to them and also to him - if too many people knew his abilities. He was torn between telling them what he actually had done, or telling them very little. He had to tell them something. They deserved that.

"Leroy will now be a great help to Charity Cottage, Marie, and to the revitalization of the whole community. You'll be able to count on him to work for you and to use his street smarts for the benefit of the community - not for gang-related activities."

Marie and Jefferson were bewildered. They didn't understand what Baxter told them. They had only experienced the treachery of Leroy's gang life for years.

"But how do you know that?" questioned Marie.

"Let me just say that I now have a good feeling about Leroy."

He had imprinted good thoughts into Leroy's brain. It was something he knew he could do and it was a good time. He wanted to help Charity Cottage expand its message of hope and goodness further into the community and he chose Leroy to be that vehicle of revitalization.

Baxter embraced both of them in a huge, warm hug and looked into their eyes. He might not see them again for a long time.

"Good bye, my dear friends."

They will need money.

He walked out the door.

CHAPTER TWELVE

Iron Tank

Larry **Murphy** was excited. He expected great results from his 'Tough Guy' sporting competition. This venture promised to be a major success for him after so many failed business attempts. It had been a tough year since his social club for men had been shut down by the so called 'politically correct' town council of Oklahoma City.

He had high hopes for the now defunct social club, where women danced naked around a pole on stage in front of wildly cheering men - it was just a strip club. He knew that, but Murph was never afraid of a challenge and had tried to convince the town council that the so-called social club would greatly increase the town's tax base.

The social club did not fly in conservative Oklahoma City.

But it was part of his two-pronged business plan...*They will not turn me down twice...the Tough Guy events are less objectionable...and they need the tax revenue.*

So, the Tough Guy competitions just fit under the wire of the city bylaws on competitive sports events and had received approval...the tax issue was the deciding factor.

Murph was a slick marketer and the Tough Guy competitions were marketed to the many macho men between the ages of eighteen and forty who considered themselves to be tough guys. He had no problem to get contestants - the ones long on muscles and short on brains - and the majority of the population enjoyed the sight of two overly-muscled men who beat the living hell out of each other. So he also marketed it successfully to the masses.

It was the quarter final event of the first Tough Guy competition and Murph had opened up the spectacle to all takers who had the hundred-dollar entry fee to challenge the toughest guys in the competition. The 'winner take all' lure of five thousand dollars had attracted additional macho men who thought that they were tough enough to take on the seasoned quarter finalists. He was pleased by the number of applicants who had put up the entrance fee. This was another chance to prolong the event and wring as much money as possible out of it.

He had arranged that the winner of the newcomers would go directly into the semi-finals for a long shot to win the main prize. It was the underdog syndrome - the Rocky Balboa contest as he called it - that he had brought into his business enterprise. Another slick marketing ploy.

Everybody loved an underdog.

His slick advertising campaign had guaranteed full capacity for all the quarter-final events. There would be a packed audience of blood-thirsty fans to scream at every punch and kick to the groin. But none of the Rocky Balboa contestants would stand a chance against his own man he had planted in the competition. No one could beat 'Iron Tank,' the moniker for the professional wrestler and tough guy who had partnered with Murph to keep the prize money from falling from his hands.

'Anything goes' was the only rule in the competition. A match lasted as long as the referee ruled that a competitor could no longer continue. It was brutal - to overcome an opponent by any means possible - punching, kicking, wrestling, the martial arts and by the use of any part of the body except teeth.

Murph walked into the Oklahoma Arena early that morning and picked up a steaming cup of coffee for his breakfast meal that he'd have with a steady stream of cigarettes to feed his nicotine addiction. His love for cigarettes would lead to an early death. He ignored the little voice in his head as he sputtered and coughed up mucus - much to his own disgust. He headed straight for the office and bypassed the frenzied fans mesmerized by the match that took place in the wired cage in the middle of the arena.

"How are the gate receipts?" He called out to a busty middle-aged woman who stared intently at a computer screen in front of her.

She tapped a few keys and yelled out, "Another sell-out Murph and another big payday."

He walked over to the glass window of the office. It looked directly down on the wired cage where the matches took place. The busty woman sidled up to him, rubbed his back in a familiar motion. "Watch that young skinny kid in the ring now," she muttered as she lit cigarettes for the two of them. "He calls himself 'Hope' and he is unbeatable, defeating every opponent he meets and most of them were twice his size."

Murph looked down to the cage, unable to believe that the skinny kid could stand up against the mass of muscles that his opponent possessed. If he could wager on the outcome of the match, he would have taken one-hundred-to-one odds that the kid would be crushed like a bug on a windshield. There was no way he could stand against the three-hundred-pound opponent he faced. But Murph couldn't take a chance and make a wager because this was his business event and the gambling authorities might be watching him.

"There is no hope for Hope," he laughed to his busty assistant.

The mass of muscles in the ring snarled at Baxter, who was no thicker than one of his legs.

"Hey kid, you better get out while you still got a chance." He advanced and laughed out loud. Baxter back-pedaled out of his range.

Monster Mash was determined to end the match quickly. He could smell the five-thousand-dollar first prize and no skinny kid was going to keep him from it. He ran straight at Baxter and threw a wild haymaker with his right fist that would have felled a tree - if it had connected.

Monster's haymaker hit air. It was as if his opponent had vaporized - disappeared. One second the kid was in front of him, the next second he was not. Then Monster Mash felt strong arms around his head and a peculiar pressing sensation to the side of his neck. Everything went blank.

Murph couldn't believe his eyes as the skinny kid dispatched Monster Mash in the first ten seconds of the match.

It must be a fluke. Nobody can move that fast.

He reckoned that the hit of cocaine he had the night before played tricks with his head. He came back to reality when he heard the magnificent roar of the crowd overwhelmingly approve of the victory by the undersized underdog, Hope.

"This is fantastic," burst out Murph.

His business mind saw nothing but dollar signs for the final match against Iron Tank... *I can charge triple gate prices.*

He couldn't have asked for a better script; the skinny little kid as the crowd favourite up against the evil Iron Tank. Dollar signs flashed in front of his eyes. He had to talk with Hope and make sure that he could last long enough in the ring with the Tank, to not disappoint the crowd.

Baxter helped Monster Mash to his feet, steadied him as he regained his balance.

"Are you okay?" asked Baxter. "I'm sorry I had to do that, but I gave you a gift that will change your life."

Monster Mash still felt light-headed but he had no idea what this skinny little kid, who moved faster than a speeding bullet, talked about.

"I seeded thoughts in your mind tonight that will turn you into a very good man."

Such a simple message, I gave him.

Baxter left the centre of the ring stage. He had read Monster Mash's mind when he had him in a choke hold. There was nothing but evil and maliciousness in his thought patterns. Monster Mash was moving along a one way street to self-destruction. Baxter planted a message that would turn his life around.

'Do good unto others and good will be done unto you.'

Murph stopped Baxter on his way back to the dressing room.

"Son, you were fantastic. I have never seen a person move so fast. We have to talk."

He led Baxter up to his office and motioned for his assistant to leave them alone.

"Son," he began. "You're going to make me a fortune tonight and I want to thank you."

Baxter read a lot of suspicion in Murph's mind. He was suspicious of everything - of all the people who surrounded him

- from the many people who had double-crossed him in his business dealings.

He doesn't trust anyone.

Everything is about how much money he can make.

I have to be wary of anything he promises.

"I really don't think that you'll last long in the ring with Iron Tank, but I assure you that he'll not kill you. And you'll be paid well," said Murph.

He laughed and then stuffed another cigarette in his mouth.

Baxter read his thoughts again.

The Tank will eat him up and spit him out. Who cares if he gets killed? He did sign the waiver. What a schmuck this kid is.

Murph was out for himself. He couldn't be trusted to deliver the prize money and Baxter wanted the money. Badly. His plan depended on it.

There were other things that Baxter picked up from Murph's mind. He had great ambition to succeed in his business ventures by any means. This Tough Guy competition was his greatest success after years of failed ventures.

Baxter played on this knowledge.

"Mr. Murphy," Baxter replied. "I have a few things to tell you. First of all, Iron Tank will not kill me. I'll beat him. Secondly, don't expect to renege on the prize money, when I do win. If you try that, your business will be ruined - but worse than that, so will your reputation. I know that Iron Tank is in cahoots with you and if that information was ever revealed, you would have a hard time getting out of town in one piece."

Baxter paused.

"Do we understand one another? If I win, the money is rightfully mine."

Murph was bested. He could not afford to lose the most successful business venture he had in years. He nodded agreement. Baxter read his thoughts again.

There's no way that Iron Tank would lose against this runt.

Before the match, Murph pulled Iron Tank aside.

"My reputation and my business are at stake here. You can't lose. That skinny runt says he will beat you."

Tank didn't care about Murph's reputation or the loss of his business venture. He focused only on what this skinny nobody, 'Hope', had said about the match.

"He thinks he'll beat me, the Tank? I'll snap him in two, like a twig."

"I know you will," said Murph, "But he worries me. He's as fast as greased lightning and he beat Monster Mash in ten seconds. I couldn't believe it. I got a lotta money on you."

"Don't worry. Your money is safe. I didn't rise to the top of the Wrestling Federation for nothing. I won't lose."

"Ya sure," said Murph. "You just remember...you owe me big time. No one else gave you a chance...I did... you wrecked your career and reputation...the steroid use and cocaine abuse. You were once at the top of the world and you lost it all."

"You don't have to remind me. I know what I lost..and you're right. I owe you. This is my first chance to regain my lost career. I won't lose."

For a moment Tank's mind slipped back to all the glory he had experienced as one of the top wrestlers in America. He longed for those days again. Then being stripped of his belt by the Wrestling Federation. His sordid reputation made the Federation look bad, especially because young kids emulated him...and then his slow painstaking slide into obscurity.

Now, here I am in Oklahoma City...Shitsville...rebuilding my shattered life.

"I guarantee it, I won't lose," he said and walked away from Murph.

Iron Tank felt nasty when he stepped into the ring.

He was a magnificent example of the professional wrestler with bulging muscles everywhere, broad at the shoulder and narrow at the hip - a body builder's physique. He still had the magnificent skills obtained from endless, pain-filled hours of practice that had once shaped his rise to the top of the wrestling profession. His mind was molded in only one direction. To win.

Iron Tank looked across the ring at Hope who he saw as an immediate obstacle to regain his lost glory. But Tank wasn't only one of the world's best wrestlers; he was also an extremely intelligent man. His former rise to the top of the wrestling world was not only through pain-staking training, workouts and a strict dietary regiment but also through the overlooked practice of studying the game plan of all opponents.

He measured their strengths, their weaknesses, their favourite moves and also studied how other wrestlers had defeated them. But no one had beat Hope...yet. Overconfidence was a wrestler's worst enemy and had led to the downfall of many a champion in the past. He would not be overconfident.

He glanced at Hope across the ring. It was extremely hard for him not to be overconfident when he eyed his opponent's scrawny physique. Hope didn't have a wrestler's muscle definition. It was difficult to recognize any muscles whatsoever in his slim frame.

But Hope had not advanced this far - to the finals in the Tough Guy competition - by simply physically overpowering his competitors. He had relied on speed of movement in his path to victory. He liked to use the neck pinch to subdue his opponents. It was effective and was a formidable winning technique.

Iron Tank had watched some of Hope's matches and had never seen anyone move as fast. It was beyond anything he had witnessed in his many years of wrestling. Just the thought of Hope's skill set had an effect on his confidence. He couldn't allow Hope to get near his neck or he would lose. It was simply a matter to stay out of Hope's clutches and use his superior strength to grab him and finish him off.

The referee waved Iron Tank and Hope to the centre of the ring. He barked out last minute instructions. "You both know the rules. Everything goes but biting. If I see that one of you can't continue, I will stop the match. If one of you motions that you give up, the match is finished. Good luck to both of you. Shake hands, go to your corner and wait for the bell."

Hands were extended.

Baxter grabbed Iron Tank's hand in a firm handshake. Tank held on and squeezed tightly.

Baxter felt the strength of character in this man. He was not only powerful physically but also emotionally and mentally. He read his mind and knew Iron Tank's strategy. But more than that, to Baxter this was a man with a dream and ambition to achieve his lost spot in the athletic world of professional wrestling.

Someone at the top of the professional wrestling world could be a great influence on youth. Baxter saw an opportunity in Iron Tank to implant a positive seed, a strong message into his mind. A simple, but powerful thought.

Become the best man you can be and a role model for youth.

Both men went to their corners.

Iron Tank felt a funny feeling overcome him. He had no idea what it was except he recognized the intrusion of a thought about how he was going to change his life.

Baxter knew that Iron Tank would eventually achieve his professional wrestling objective, but it would not be at his expense. Even so, this was not going to be an easy match.

Iron Tank is a powerful man and one of the world's best-trained professional wrestlers.

He tapped his left hand three times. He could feel the power of suspension come over him and his life blood pool to his body's muscles. He felt enormous physical strength.

The bell clanged.

CHAPTER THIRTEEN

Cora

It was the rhythmical and musical chimes of the slot machines that caught Baxter's attention when he walked into the casino. The constant clang of the one-armed bandits was a lure that casinos programmed into the machines. He entered slowly and took in all the sights, sounds and smells that permeated the casino environment. The number of elderly women who sat on the uncomfortable stools and played the slots surprised him. Most had cigarettes hanging out of their mouths. He had heard stories that the true gambling addicts would wear Depend undergarments rather than give up a lucky seat.

Not only are these old women addicted to gambling but also to tobacco. Casinos are definitely in the sin business. They allow smoking. Maybe they should also pass out free Depends.

He soaked up information like a sponge on his walkabout. The pit bosses were handsomely dressed in suits and ties. *They look like funeral directors. All they do is take notes and walk from table to table.* The gambling public were dressed in casual wear that clearly distinguished them from the smartly dressed staff.

Baxter looked upward and saw the vast network of security cameras that overlooked the entire floor of the casino. More security cameras were located directly over all the gambling tables to record entire hands played, transactions, money changing as well as the faces of the people who played every game and hand. The security office in the casino constantly ran matches and checks on the identity of every person that entered their premises.

They are recording me now and checking my identity. I've never been in a casino before so they won't know who I am. The CIA has a file on me, but the casinos would not be privy to that information. But does the CIA have access to the casino files?

He walked by all the gambling venues and noticed that the blackjack tables were the most popular choice of the public. All types of people from all walks of life were trying their luck. *Doctors and lawyers...and Indian chiefs.*

He opened up his mind to get a general idea of the mindset of those around him while he continued his stroll. There were few surprises. It was what he expected. All the worst of human emotions: greed, fear, anxiety, stress, depression, evil and hatred. These emotions ran rampant in the people whose minds he read - more prevalent than the thoughts of happiness and goodness he read in the minds of a few people. He did not want unpleasant thoughts to crowd his own so he shut them out.

The gambling industry intrigued him. He had studied their business model and understood the statistical probabilities it relied on. He would play the odds to his advantage.

Blackjack is my game of choice.

He had four thousand dollars in his pocket. He sat down at one of the many blackjack tables frequented by the gambling public. The game was already underway. He waited and waited until the dealer started with new decks. Other games, such as roulette, craps and baccarat are games of pure luck and are so structured that the house never relinquishes its edge over the player. These games have no memory prior to the present spin of the wheel, play of the cards or roll of the dice and there are no influences over what will happen next. Pure luck. And the house had the odds in its favour in these games.

But the game of blackjack stands apart from all the other games the casino offered. A player may have an edge over the casino and may take advantage of that edge by raising his bets when the odds are in his favour.

He had waited for this moment. He wanted to get a correct count of the cards that were being dispensed and those that remained in play. The new decks allowed him to count cards. Three decks of cards were in play. Less than the maximum of seven decks that was allowed by the state gambling statutes and more than the one deck that gave card-counting gamblers good odds to beat the house. Baxter was patient even as the dealer prompted him for his play.

"Pass." He counted all the cards in play as well as those cast aside. He waited for the best opportunity. His chance came and he played his hand. The odds were in his favour when he drew an eighteen on his two cards. The probability that the house could match or beat his hand was slanted in Baxter's favour.

He quickly turned his one-hundred-dollar bet into two hundred. The player can win more money when he is favoured to win - if he's skilled or very lucky. The casinos made most of their money off poor and unskilled players. And there were plenty of them at the tables. Baxter was not one of them.

He waited again and he realized that if he read the minds of the five people at his table it would bring him a greater success rate when he placed his bets. He counted their cards and again the odds increased - in his favour. He felt sympathy for his fellow gamblers but his mind-reading skills did not affect the cards they held and how they played them.

I have to justify my actions somehow. He gave a silent laugh.

He kept on winning. Baxter's wins were noticed by the lady to his immediate right.

"You are doing great, sir," she blurted out. "So what's your secret? Are you counting cards or something?" She laughed.

"I'm reading everybody's mind," he replied with a chuckle.

"Nice trick if you can do it."

Baxter scanned her thoughts. She was an interesting woman. She was a hooker, but beyond her profession she was an innocent, pleasant and friendly young girl, down on her luck and determined to shake off the lifestyle that had dragged her into prostitution. Her trusting nature and her circumstances had landed her into the hands of evil men who had forced her into the trade.

Baxter felt a lot of sympathy for this young woman as he continued to scan her thoughts. Circumstances in her life had dealt her a very bad hand, not unlike the random nature of an unlucky card draw.

"Hi, my name is Cora." She stretched out her hand and shook Baxter's in a friendly manner.

There were no evil intentions in her mind. She had just run away and she knew that her pimp would find her unless she got out of town in a hurry. She'd taken a chance with the small amount of money she had saved and hoped to make enough in the casino to escape town...and her lot in life.

The goodness in Baxter's heart did not allow him to abandon this woman in her time of need. He also felt attracted to her. He gazed at her physical features as any normal male with a healthy libido would when facing an engaging female. She was pleasant of face and underneath her rather drab, full-length dress she possessed physical attributes of a healthy, sexy young woman. His mind strayed for a moment while he allowed himself to appreciate an attractive female.

"My name is Baxter, and it's nice to meet you. How's your luck going?"

"Not so good," she replied. "I'm down quite a bit and can't seem to catch a break. If it wasn't for bad luck I'd have no luck at all."

It was a dilemma for him to help this woman. He could not help everybody he ran into, but he also could not ignore helping a good person who wanted to escape a terrible situation at this early stage in her life.

He would help her.

"I might be able to help you with your luck, if you would allow me," said Baxter. "But it requires you to trust me."

Cora was surprised at the offer of assistance by this handsome young stranger. She could read people. It was the only good thing she had learned from the prostitution trade. The young stranger was totally unlike the many men that she had encountered in her disreputable profession. She didn't know why, but she felt complete trust in this man.

Baxter reached over and laid his hand on top of hers. His touch generated a tingling sensation throughout her body. She didn't understand the peculiar feeling, but at that moment any doubts about trust disappeared.

"I expect to be in Las Vegas for about three days before I move on, Cora. I can help you improve your financial fortunes which will help you get out of town."

All of a sudden her mind filled with information about Baxter - his brilliance, his trusting nature, the goodness in his heart.

"I don't understand how," she said. "But it seems, I know a lot about you and yet, we just met. It's almost like thoughts and memories about you were planted in my mind. I have never said this to a stranger before, but you have my complete trust."

Baxter had planted just enough information in her head so she would believe in him. Her trust was essential to his plan to help her in the short time he would be in Las Vegas.

"In that case then, your gambling lessons begin right away."

Baxter took her aside. "We have to set up a system, so I know what cards you're holding. I already know the card count and all the probabilities. You just have to hold or fold as I instruct you."

I don't want her to know about my mind-reading.

He set up a simple system with Cora, whereby she would touch her face with her fingers to simulate the value of her cards...*I will read her mind to corroborate the value of her hand...*He would respond with a tap on the table with his fingers once or twice to instruct her to stay or fold.

The system was amazingly simple and worked to perfection for Cora...and without her knowledge that he was reading her mind. Her luck immediately turned around and she and Baxter walked away on that first day with sizeable gains.

The casino now had a record of both of them on their computer system. That worried Baxter.

Would the casinos figure out what they were up to and share files with one another? How fast would they transmit them?

He was uncertain if all the casinos would be aware of his and Cora's success at the same time and ban them from their establishments. He had a small window of time before the casinos on the strip shared and collated computer information about client wins. He had to randomize their play as much as possible among the large number of casinos. Play different casinos at different times in order to avoid notice as a consistently winning couple.

His four thousand dollars had quickly turned into over seventy-five thousand and he reckoned that he was still probably just under their radar. He wanted to just stay long enough in Vegas to amass a one hundred thousand dollar stake for himself before his success was noticed.

It was the same for Cora. She accumulated just over one hundred thousand dollars and felt quite upbeat and confident about her changed fortune and having the means to escape town and her ill-fated lot in life.

But there was only so much time left.

"Cora if we linger much longer you will lose your opportunity to escape. I estimate that we only have one more day as a team before the casinos catch on to us."

They walked into the Mirage Casino and took their seats at the blackjack table. They had not played this casino before and Baxter hoped that their last day would pass without them being detected.

Rob Black was the head of the Mirage Casino's computer security system and he was very greedy. He never passed up the opportunity to make a buck. He had just received files on the previous day's activities from all the casinos on the Vegas strip. They shared surveillance computer files with one another. It made sense for the benefit of all casinos. He recognized Cora as a hooker from the computer security system of the Continental Casino.

She was identified as a prostitution trade worker who was missing in action. He dug around a bit, called contacts in the Continental and found out that the prostitution ring wanted her back and would pay for information on her whereabouts. She was a favourite of a very rich client who paid big bucks to have her satisfy his carnal desires.

Hookers are a special attractive feature of the gambling industry that helps retain a unique clientele and because of that hookers are given free reign of casino premises. It is a symbiotic relationship that profited both industries. They are usually left alone and Rob saw an opportunity to get paid for spotting Cora. He informed his contact, Bates Cattaglio, at the Continental of Cora's presence.

Bates was known to keep a junk yard dog chained in his back yard just to give it a kick every morning before he headed to work with the mob. No one messed with him…and he hated whores. He hated his mother. She would screw her clients in her one bedroom apartment right in front of him when he was a boy. They were worse than his junk yard dog.

He was dispatched to pick up Cora at the Mirage Casino.

The CIA was closing in on Baxter. They pursued all leads they uncovered about his activities. He had left Harvard and disappeared, but they tracked him to the Chicago area after news about an amazing medical procedure had been performed at a shelter called Charity Cottage. There was also an intriguing telecommunications trick reported at the Cottage that had avoided the billing of cable fees from the local cable company. Someone special had been there.

Bud Brown was dispatched to Charity Cottage to follow up on these leads. He interviewed Marie. She was dismissive and would not acknowledge Baxter's presence.

"So many people pass through here," she said. "I can't remember everyone."

Bud didn't believe her. She was hiding the truth to protect someone. He looked around the Cottage and was impressed.

Marie helped the down and out homeless in the area...and it was needed. His soft side got the better of him and he would not bring harm or disrespect to Marie and her work. But he had a job to do. Find Baxter and then help him.

An old homeless man sat in the back room of Charity Cottage. Bud walked in on him... *this is very strange*...the old guy was seated in front of a computer and tapped away on the keyboard. Bud walked over to him.

"Hey, you're pretty good on that computer. What's ya doin'?"

"I'm playing on the internet. It's fun. Never did it in my life before."

"I can see how good you are. Where'd you learn to do that?"

"Some guy named Baxter taught a bunch of us old wino's how ta play games."

Bud followed the trail of breadcrumbs left by Baxter from Charity Cottage to Oklahoma City and the Tough Guy competition and then to Las Vegas. He quickly tracked his presence to the Mirage Casino.

Bud was unsettled. He saw how Baxter had helped out Charity Cottage.

God...I know Baxter is a good man...helping wherever he can.
I can't let the CIA ruin him when they catch up to him.

He appreciated what Baxter was doing; helping people. The CIA had put their trust in him to find Baxter and bring him in. It was a major dilemma for him.

My career will be finished if I let him get away. But I have to help him.

Baxter had been spotted at the Mirage Casino.

Bud had a team of four agents with him at the Mirage. He was the head agent on Baxter's case and they were at his disposal and direction.

Baxter saw trouble when four burly, heavy-set, greasy-looking men in black suits rapidly approached their table. He grabbed Cora by the arm.

"We have to move...and fast."

The four mobsters started towards Baxter and Cora at a trot and surrounded them at the edge of the blackjack table.

"O-o-okay hon-ney, you're coming with us and we don't want no trouble," stammered Bates in his heavy Italian accent. The three other goons had their hands inside their jacket pockets as if they had weapons. Baxter stepped in front of Cora. He'd read their thoughts and knew their intentions. They would not back down.

"Back away sir, or you won't live to regret it," threatened Bates. "We got no quarrel with you. We just want the ho."

Seconds seemed like minutes and the six adversaries glared at each other in suspended animation. No one made a move since the wrong move could have deadly consequences. Baxter's mind raced as he considered the alternatives. He could not abandon Cora. People in the vicinity of the blackjack table began to scatter like frightened mice, when they sensed a fight. The situation was tense. The four mobsters moved closer to Cora.

Baxter tapped his hand. Suspension came over him. Out of the corner of his eye he recognized a familiar face. Bud Brown and his agents quickly approached at a determined but unhurried pace.

Baxter looked directly at Bates and his fellow mobsters. "Gentlemen, you lose."

Bud Brown and his team arrived with drawn handguns.

The situation was defused when the CIA agents patted down the mobsters, removed their weapons and handcuffed them.

An agent approached Baxter and patted him down as well. A female agent also checked Cora for weapons. One of the agents was about to handcuff Baxter but Bud Brown intervened.

"That won't be necessary. I'll take responsibility for these two. They're not dangerous," he spoke in an authoritative voice. "Get those mobsters outa here."

Bud led Cora and Baxter out of the casino to an awaiting car. The car tires squealed, burning rubber as Bud accelerated away from the casino.

Cora was the first one to speak.

"Who are you and what are you going to do with us?"

"You don't have to worry Cora," said Baxter. "They're the CIA and they are after me. If I read Mr. Brown correctly, it is very fortunate that he found me first."

A slight smile crept over Bud's face.

"You're right, I won't let the CIA get you. The agents who took the mobsters away know nothing about you. They're on a need-to-know basis about this mission and I told them nothing. But I can tell you that the CIA is determined to capture you and they were very close this time. Unfortunate for them, I was in charge of your file. But after you get away I will be removed from your case."

"More determined agents will pursue you from now on, Baxter," continued Bud. "You must get away, leave no clues about your whereabouts and change your appearance."

Bud pulled up in front of a bus station and turned to Baxter.

"Here is a bus ticket for one to Los Angeles. Take it and get lost. I will not see you again."

Baxter peered into Bud's mind. Bud was content with what he had done. Baxter touched his hand and implanted a message.

Bud sped away.

Baxter and Cora stood on the sidewalk outside the bus terminal. Baxter turned to Cora. She was silent but heavy tears streamed down her cheeks. He hadn't known her for long but he knew she loved him and that he had to leave. Her heart jumped when Baxter placed his hand on hers.

"Go back to the casino, Cora. It will be safe for a couple more hours. Cash in your chips, grab your belongings and leave this town. You are now a free woman, a strong woman, a woman destined to help others escape the prostitution trade."

Baxter placed both his hands on Cora's face and imparted strong, silent messages deep into her brain.

The Los Angeles bus pulled into the station.

CHAPTER FOURTEEN

Gerald

It was the sixtieth season of pari-mutuel racing at Los Alamitos Race Course in Los Angeles and the quarter horses assembled for the races were the best in the nation. Huge crowds had gathered for the race day and gambling fever was in the air. A small group of horse fans were allowed in the stalls before the race to see the horses. Baxter was one of them. He guided a hand over the head of 'Forever-in-Love,' a rugged three-year old quarter horse as it stood in its stall watching him cautiously.

Baxter never read the mind of an animal. Would it work? He had advanced his ability to read human thoughts by sensing bio-electrical pulses in the brain when he placed his hands on a subject. He considered it like hooking up a telephone to the electrical pulses between two brains that allowed him to read and send messages from another person's brain to and from his own powerful brain's electrical circuit.

He could not read horse thoughts. Horses didn't think; they sensed, but Baxter received a feeling about the physical state of the animal. Forever-in-Love was traumatized by physical pain in his hind quarter. He was the favourite to win the next race and the horse would not perform up to expectations.

He could not get near enough to all the horses to touch them. Security around the horses was tight. The horses streamed past the viewing stall and Baxter was as close as he could get to them. But close enough to sense their physical shape. The way they pranced...their calmness...were they restless...did they favour a leg? He studied them all. He relied on as much information as he could pick up.

If I could only touch them...I can only get a general sense of how they feel.

'Susan's Gift' stood out from the rest. The mare was a thirty-to-one long shot and was in great physical shape. She exuded confidence and Baxter sensed it. He looked at her record on the race sheet. The three year old mare hadn't won in her five most recent races, but in each race she had shown marked improvement in time. The mare was in peak physical shape and chomped at its bit for the race to begin.

He used a small portion from his casino winnings and placed ten thousand dollars on Susan's Gift to win.

The horses stampeded out of the starting gate. The intensity of noise from the crowd accelerated to a fever pitch of screams and shouts. For a brief moment Baxter opened up his mind and experienced the heightened excitement of people in frenzy. It was not something he would enjoy, but the temptation to understand such an excited state of the human mind was something he could not pass up.

Powerful emotions cascaded like an avalanche down a mountain. They didn't surprise him, yet the aggregate of strong emotions gave him a headache and he was about to shut down his mind when he noticed a single aberration in the crowd. It was an elderly gentle-looking man about seventy years old.

The horses thundered past the quarter mile mark. Susan's Gift ran behind Forever-in-Love within a tight crush of five horses. The jockeys bent their whips over the backsides of the animals at the three quarter mark - creating a mud-splattered, churning fury. Susan's Gift was ideally placed to explode from the pack. Seconds later, Susan's Gift made her move and broke ahead, overtook Forever-in-Love and crossed the finish line in a burst of speed - a three length victory.

Baxter sat down beside the elderly gentleman.

"I hope you had some money on Susan's Gift," he said.

The attention from a complete stranger startled him. Gerald Turner returned the comment.

"I was fortunate enough to place a couple of dollars on the long shot. I like the underdog and at thirty-to-one, it was a good gamble."

"I guess we think alike," returned Baxter. "I also placed a bet on the filly."

Gerald Turner had an eye for good people. Reading people was part of a necessary skill set that had made him a successful businessman for close to half a century. His first impression of the young stranger who sat beside him was favourable. He liked him.

"Good for you," said Turner. "So what are you gonna do with your winnings? Put it on the next race?"

"No, I'm really not a gambler," said Baxter. "This was a one shot deal and I got lucky. Besides I know some good people that could really use this money." He thought of Charity Cottage.

"If you got time, let me buy you a beer," said Turner. "I like the way you think about helping other people. It's something I've strived to do most of my life."

"I'll take you up on that beer. By the way my name is Baxter."

"Gerald Turner here."

He held out his hand for a handshake. Their hands clasped. In that moment, minds merged and Turner felt a strange tingling sensation over his whole body similar to a mild electrical shock. It shook him, but it was not unpleasant and made him aware of the strength of character of this young stranger beside him. An overall feeling of trust pervaded his mind. Gerald Turner knew that Baxter was a special person.

They walked toward the bar. Gerald had a noticeable slowness to his gait. Baxter saw it but didn't bring it up.

"Where do you work Gerald? And if you don't mind me asking - you like helping people - so how do you do it?"

"For some reason, my son, I feel I can trust you. I don't normally talk to strangers about what I do. But I can tell you. I am the CEO of Johnson & Johnson...you heard of the company...you know...the Band-Aid people."

"You mean this company." Baxter laughed and pointed to a band-aid on his little finger.

"Yaa, that's the one," returned Turner with a chuckle.

"Last year we had a profit of over fifteen billion dollars and I fought with our Board of Directors to put all corporate profits greater than fifteen per cent back into communities where we live and work...not only that, but the company supports medical facilities, poverty groups, recreation activities and social housing in areas of the country where we have offices. I started employees' profit sharing plans as well as activities related to health and wellness of company employees...and that's not all...but I won't bore you with more good deeds we've done. And that...to answer your question...that's how I help people...through my company."

"Wow...I'm impressed," said Baxter.

At Harvard, Baxter had been turned off by the arrogance of the Harvard professors. They had considered themselves to be elitist, at the top echelon of society. They paled in comparison to this man. Baxter thought of an old biblical parable.

It is harder for a rich man to get into heaven than for a camel to pass through the eye of a needle. Gerald Turner was a perfect contradiction to that theorem.

"A humanitarian businessman. That's hard to find in America today," said Baxter.

"And our company's social policy is spreading. Supporting the health of communities, where our employees and customers reside, helps maintain and enhance company goodwill, customer loyalty and profitability. It's a win-win situation for our company and for our communities. Other companies have noticed...and are following our lead"

"Gerald, you're a treasure for America...a trendsetter in corporate social responsibility." Baxter was overwhelmed. He had just met and talked with one of America's true heroes.

But Baxter was saddened.

A probe of Turner's mind had determined that cancerous tumours sucked his body's strength and vitality. The life force of an American hero was ebbing away.

"But you're deathly sick," said Baxter out of the blue. "Aren't you?"

"You can tell? It doesn't surprise me. There's something about you, that's special...and that's what I can tell about you, young sir. But you're right, though. Cancer's got a hold of me. Doctors have given me a year to live.

"Give me your hand," said Baxter. "You trust me, right?"

Baxter used the contact to probe deep into Turner's bodily activities. He felt the cancerous growth deep within his lymphatic system and sensed that he would be terminal if the cancer remained unchecked. The normal chemo and radiation treatments had run their course and could no longer arrest the growth of the cancer...his doctors were right.

"Gerald, I will be direct with you because I know that you are a man of conviction. You see yourself dying within a year and I am telling you that you are wrong, dead wrong if you excuse the pun."

Turner was shocked. He had all but accepted his fate. This revelation shook him.

"I don't understand," he stammered. "How do you know? I felt something when you grasped my hand. I have so many questions that need to be answered. How can you help me? And why would you?"

"You can't be allowed to die before your time. You are a too good a man with much more to accomplish in life. You felt something special about me...right...well it's true. You can be cured of your cancer if you put your faith in me and what I am about to tell you."

Baxter had Turner's complete attention.

"You have to put your trust and your financial resources into ongoing stem cell research. It's not as controversial as people in the U.S. believe. Stem cells can be created artificially in the lab without the destruction of life and it's no longer about taking them from umbilical cords or destroying a fertilized cell by robbing it of its life giving properties. All the controversies that presently surround research in this field are way off base."

"But my doctors told me that there was nothing more that could be done for my cancer and I have talked with some of the best medical people in America."

"Gerald," continued Baxter in a firm tone. "I know that you believe me and you know you can trust me when I tell you that your doctors are wrong. There is research going on right now in a little university in Canada, called St. Mary's University in

Halifax, Nova Scotia. Canadians are not so prone to political interference in biological stem cell research as we are here in America. There will be a major medical breakthrough on stem cells that will save countless lives. And you sir, are a prime candidate for a new life-saving procedure coming out of that research. You have so much more to give to humanity through your business acumen, your high profile and I want you to put your name behind this particular research and champion its cause as a living example."

"Who do I contact about this new stem cell procedure?" said Turner. "You perked my interest...I would welcome the opportunity to champion its cause...definitely... not only to save my life but for many other cancer victims as well."

"Contact Dr. Shultz at Harvard University. He will be expecting your call."

Turner was dumbfounded. He had accepted his pending death. For reasons he could not articulate, he trusted this magnificent young stranger who had just come into his life.

Baxter had implanted just enough information about himself in Turner`s mind to have him believe.

"I'll never forget you," said Turner. "You've tossed me a lifesaver."

Baxter shook Gerald Turner`s hand and said, "You'll be hearing from me again. I will be calling upon you sometime in the future when I need you to help me or someone else."

He left Turner at the race track. He had two thoughts on his mind; he had to collect his winnings and he had to call Dr. Shultz about Gerald Turner to have him contact the stem cell research team at St. Mary's University.

CHAPTER FIFTEEN

Doug

Baxter had a lot on his mind. He thought about family. He missed them all and he had not seen them in a long time. They were probably worried. He missed Linda - she was often in his thoughts...*but a man's gotta do what a man's gotta do*. And he was on a mission.

Thoughts floated in and out of his head when he thought of the different people he had met on his personal journey. He couldn't help have the floaters (in his mind) when he thought of Cora.

What did she charge for her services? Higher prices for certain acts? Or a standard price on a time unit basis? How many men did she lie with? Did she like any of her clients?

She was his friend and he cared for her...but...he still had those floaters.

He didn't have bad floaters when he thought about Charity Cottage, Marie and Jefferson...curiosity maybe.

How are they getting along? Are they progressing and developing and helping the homeless and the community? Is Leroy a help?

One overriding thought did occupy his mind.

I need money. Lots of it and in as short a time as possible to help my friends.

He had to get the money by himself. Thoughts about how he could do it swirled around in his head.

The casino industry must be aware of Cora and I after the fracas at the Mirage Casino. I can't go back to the casinos.

The CIA has probably traced me to the race track already.

I don't want to rely on Gerald Turner...I know he would help...but he has enough on his mind now...with his cancer and all.

He read copies of the Wall Street Journal with its stories of exorbitant wealth that the investment houses, like Merrill Lynch, pulled from the markets.

That's the place for me...and if they can do it!

He studied every aspect of financial markets and all of the market models that were used by the large investment houses. He could easily duplicate the obscene fortunes that padded their bulged pockets - with one big difference. He would use his fortunes to help Main Street, not Wall Street, to help the little guy not the big investment bankers.

Baxter walked unnoticed into a Merrill Lynch branch office in San Jose. He had changed his appearance to hide from the CIA whom he feared had ramped up their efforts to capture him. But a change of hair color and more facial hair would not fool the CIA for any length of time. He had to hasten his plans before any confrontation with them. He reckoned that he had a six-month lead before the long arm of the CIA caught up with him.

The young secretary at the front desk noticed Baxter as he skimmed through investment journals in the waiting room of the office.

"Do you need some help, sir?" she said in her best corporate and friendly manner.

"I am looking for a broker in the futures market to open an account and help me begin trading."

"Absolutely," responded the youthful secretary. "First I have to determine the amount of capital that you are planning to invest just so I can match you up with an appropriate broker."

Her response accentuated the corporate philosophy that permeated the investment industry - greed. The larger the dollars in an account, the more commissions that could be generated. He suspected that with close to six hundred thousand dollars available, he would attract one of their top account managers. He went along with the secretary's question and gave her that figure.

"Ms. Donna Spire, one of our top managers can answer your queries about setting up an account, sir."

"**Mr. Johnstone,** it's nice to meet you," said Donna Spire after a short introduction from the secretary.

Donna Spire was a smartly attired, stylish and attractive woman of about thirty-five years of age. The first impression Baxter had of her when she walked across the room with her hand outstretched for a handshake was that she totally looked the modern businesswoman - bright with a business school demeanour. A firm handshake allowed Baxter to probe her mind. Her thought patterns were consumed with her own best interests. She was the proverbial alpha female and only saw dollar signs when she looked at Baxter.

"Come into my office, Mr. Johnstone and we can quickly get you up and running with an account. You are coming into the market at the best of times in the commodity sector, especially in the oil market, where we are in an amazing bull market run."

Baxter had taken great strides to set himself up electronically with an alter alias, Alex Johnstone. It was necessary to sabotage any means the CIA had to track him down. With the use of a computer he put together fictitious data in support of his new identity. He did, however, feel uncomfortable being called by another name, but it was a necessary step.

He no sooner sat in her spacious office, which overlooked the San Jose waterfront, when Donna Spire began to talk about her track record and the impressive gains that her clients had achieved.

"If you work closely with me and under my tutelage, Mr. Johnstone, you can expect to achieve impressive profits." She glowed with an arrogant air when she pulled out a series of charts that depicted the path of price gains in a series of commodity markets over the past two years.

"I advised my clients to get in here and exit here." With self-assured pride she pointed to the exact bottom of the graph where they would have entered the market and then to the exact top where they exited the market. Baxter saw through her charade of false claims. She'd just pointed to a price pattern that had already occurred and then used it as proof of profitable returns. It was a ploy on her part to gain his acceptance as an investment advisor.

But what does that same chart say about future prices? I wonder if she tries to pull the wool over the eyes of every new investor.

"Those are remarkable results, Ms. Spire. I hope they can be repeated in my case - if I open an account with you." Baxter went along with the charade just to see how far she would go and to see how stupid she considered him.

"Let me bring in some forms for you to sign, Mr. Johnstone, and we can get you on the path to greater financial freedom." She pushed the intercom button and shouted into it. "Douglas, bring in form A210 right away."

The door opened and a young man of about twenty-one entered carrying a handful of forms.

"Mr. Johnstone, this is my young intern, Douglas Bannister."

No sooner had Donna finished her introduction when the young trainee tripped over an outcropping of carpet in front of the table beside Baxter. Papers flew everywhere and Douglas lost his balance and crashed into the table, spilling a jug of water over Baxter's pants.

"You stupid, stupid oaf," shouted Donna in a degrading tirade. "Clean up that mess immediately and apologize to Mr. Johnstone for being a complete imbecile."

Anger overcame Donna. She changed from the gracious business lady to a domineering woman who could not tolerate mistakes by subordinates in her presence, especially if it meant she was about to lose a prospective good stream of commission sales.

Baxter did not like what he saw in this woman.

Doug Bannister apologized and took out a cloth and attempted to wipe the moisture from Baxter's pant leg. Baxter took a moment to read Doug Bannister's mind while he continued to brush his leg. In contrast to Donna Spire, he liked what he saw in this young man. Doug Bannister possessed all the qualities Baxter had come to admire in a person. The trainee's sense of goodwill towards others was one of the dominant features that Baxter noticed.

Baxter read his thoughts again after the water incident.

I need this job at Merrill Lynch, but I have to suffer indignities from Donna. I feel I have to grovel at her feet. It's not in my job description: get me water, bring my coffee, get those forms and then to be called an imbecile in front of another person in a work environment. I could never demean another person in front of an audience like that. It's just not in me...and she does it all the time.

Baxter sympathized with Doug Bannister who took abuse from his manager and still maintained a positive upbeat attitude. It portrayed a strong character that Baxter didn't see in many people. He decided that Doug Bannister would be his account representative at Merrill Lynch.

"Ms. Spire," interjected Baxter in the awkwardness of the situation while Doug still sopped up water on the floor. "An immediate question I have for you is with regard to Douglas here. Is he eligible, as an intern, to offer to clients the services of Merrill Lynch that all of Merrill's account representatives can offer, including you?"

With a surprised look on her face, Donna replied. "Yes, he can offer Merrill's full services to clients, but he is just a minor intern in our office. Why would you consider such an inexperienced person over the credentials and experience that I can bring to your portfolio?"

Baxter gave a mischievous grin. "I like this young man and besides, he just anointed me with water."

Baxter and Doug laughed. Donna Spire did not.

Baxter had tuned himself into the study of the financial and futures markets. He digested massive amounts of information, catalogued, indexed, organized it all and applied it to his investment decisions. Counter to what Donna Spire had suggested about the oil market, Baxter concluded that the peak in the price of oil had approached, after he weighed all fundamental and technical factors at play on a worldwide basis. He reasoned that by just following the crowd, which was Ms. Spire's strategy - *lemmings off a cliff* - he would take a large counter position in favour of a dramatic drop in the price of oil.

Doug Bannister had entered Johnstone's trade in the oil futures market, even as he had concern that Johnstone's position was opposite that of all the smart professional traders at Merrill Lynch.

"All the smart money is buying," said Doug. "They can't be wrong. Everyone is on the buy side. The oil market is in a huge bull run. Do you really want to put on this trade?"

"The price run up in oil is over," said Baxter. "There is one thing that you can be sure of; trees don't grow to the sky. Oil is overextended on the upside. Everyone who is going to buy has bought. There are few buyers left, and without buyers, oil's price rise is over. I trust my judgement."

Two days after Doug had entered Johnstone's position in the oil futures market, the price of oil broke sharply to the downside. Johnstone's four hundred thousand dollar position immediately turned into four million through the leveraged position in his futures account. Baxter had also set aside fifty thousand dollars for Doug Bannister in a separate account without Doug's knowledge. It had quickly turned into five hundred thousand dollars. It was part of Baxter's plan to educate and partner with a person of good character. Doug was that person.

It wasn't easy for Doug to accept this magnificent gift. He was proud and possessed the moral upbringing to feel he needed to work for everything he received in life. It was only when Mr. Johnstone explained his plan for a partnership with him that he understood and accepted the financial reward. Through daily interactions with Johnstone, he realized the great privilege of being an associate of this man.

Donna Spire was not in a good mood when she stormed into her office the day the price of oil dropped another five dollars in price.

"The market must be wrong." She screeched in the morning meeting of all the high-powered executives in the firm.

"Everyone is getting killed. We're in an oil bull market and the price has to go up."

She swept a full file of folders and papers from the table in front of her, to the floor. Papers were still floating, butterfly-like in the air, as she continued her rant.

"Have any clients made money in oil lately?"

"I heard that a client of your intern, Doug Bannister, made a huge profit when oil dropped," said a subdued voice from the back of the room. The account executive had seen the fury of Donna Spire's rage in the past when markets turned against her, and he did not want to upset her further.

"Get Bannister in my office right away," responded Donna. "I have to straighten him out about how to play the oil market."

Doug was at his computer terminal when word came to drop everything he was doing and immediately report to Ms. Spire's office. But Doug had become emboldened with his recent success in the market and was considerably less threatened by Donna's overbearing attitude and treatment. He was staring at the computer screen, waiting for the price of oil to trade below one hundred and fifteen dollars. As per Mr. Johnstone's instructions, he was to add to both his and Johnstone's positions to profit from a further decrease in the price of oil.

Moments later, Donna burst into his office without so much as a knock.

"When I call, you come," she snapped.

The price of oil had just dropped below one hundred and fifteen when Donna entered. Doug's entire attention was focused on the computer screen. He entered trades for the two accounts. His attention to the computer screen and not to her only heightened her anger. "What the hell are you doing? When I speak, you listen!"

Doug used to jump to attention whenever Ms. Spire barked out orders. Today he didn't.

"I apologize, but I had been instructed to execute more trades for Mr. Johnstone as the price of oil drops."

Doug had not taken his eye off the screen while he talked. Her power over the intern eroded even while she continued her superior tone to demean anything that Doug had to say.

"Are you crazy? We're in a bull market in oil and I want you to cancel those trades immediately and execute new ones. The price of oil will rise."

This was all the abuse that Doug could take. He stood up and looked directly into Donna's furious eyes.

"I am under orders from my client, and Donna, his orders take precedence over yours." This was the first time he had talked back to her and the first time he had ever addressed her by her first name. It felt good.

"I w-w-will not t-t-tolerate your attitude, young man," stammered Donna. "You are about to be fired. Get Mr. Johnstone in my office so I can explain to him your impertinent attitude and the error of his ways."

They all met the next day in her office. Baxter had decided long ago, not to antagonize difficult people...and Donna Spire was difficult. She was the type of person who couldn't admit being wrong. Before Donna had a chance to degrade Doug in front of him, he defused the situation.

"Ms. Spire," began Baxter. "I want to wholeheartedly thank you for the great training and mentorship you afforded Doug here. With his help, I have amassed great profit that I otherwise would not have obtained. Thank you so much for your wise counsel to Doug. I have benefited greatly."

Donna was momentarily speechless - one of the few times in her career.

"Well, Mr. Johnstone, it's the policy of Merrill Lynch that our highly trained staff offer our clients the best service in the industry."

A slight blush came over her face. She was not a stupid woman and realized the profits that Mr. Johnstone had earned would endear him more to Doug Bannister than to her. She had been thrown a lifesaver which had saved face for her. She changed her attitude.

"Doug is our finest intern and I took personal pride in overseeing his training here at Merrill Lynch," said Donna. "I fully intend to offer him a junior account representative position with our office."

She wanted to grill Doug...*I have to find out what trading strategies Johnstone used to make such massive profits.*

"Thank you for offering me that position, Ms. Spire," responded Doug. "But I have accepted a position as Mr. Johnstone's personal associate and will be leaving Merrill Lynch immediately and partnering with him in our own trading business. We will be closing our accounts here by end of day and transferring all proceeds to our personal accounts."

Donna Spire stood in the middle of the office...disappointed. She'd lost an opportunity to learn trading secrets from the most successful client she'd ever met. For one of the few moments in her business life, she realized that she had treated a subordinate unfavourably and now it came back to bite her.

"I wish you all the best, Douglas," she responded. "I'll miss you. Keep in touch and I'll have your accounts transferred over by the end of business today."

Donna opened the Alex Johnstone account and she couldn't help but notice that he had gained a huge profit from his starting position of six hundred thousand dollars to over fifty million dollars. It had come from trades on more commodities than just oil and he had been correct in all his trades. She also noticed that Doug Bannister's own personal account approached ten million dollars.

She checked Alex Johnstone's largest position which was in the oil market. He would profit from a drop in price and oil had just dropped another ten dollars. She closed and transferred Alex Johnstone and Douglas Bannister's accounts.

She sighed heavily.

CHAPTER SIXTEEN

Foot Soldiers

Ads placed in major newspapers throughout North America read as follows:

Douglas A. Bannister

of

Bannister Commodities Inc.

is accepting applications

for Commodity Futures Traders

to expand his group of established traders

Mr. Bannister and associate plan to train a small group of applicants in their proprietary trading concepts. Successful candidates will be given $1 million to trade solely for Bannister Commodities Inc. Traders will keep 75 percent of their trading profits and will not be responsible for losses while using Bannister Commodities Inc. proprietary trading methodologies. Prior experience in trading is not necessary. Applicants should send a brief resume to:

Bannister Commodities Inc.
1881 Lawrence St., Suite 615
Chicago, IL
Atten: Douglas Bannister
All applicants must answer the following question in one page or less: What will you do with your trading profits?

Bannister Commodities Inc. was successful with assets in the many millions of dollars. It had become a very successful commodity trading firm in the United States. The proprietary trading techniques tested and employed by Baxter himself and applied to all commodity and financial markets were behind the success of the firm.

The ad they ran throughout the United States and Canada had a huge response. It was similar to the New York Yankees baseball team advertising open positions on the team regardless of age, sex, and talent or baseball experience. A chance to play for the New York Yankees - what a dream! People who responded to the ad saw it as an exceptional chance for instant wealth. The caveat, of course, was in the question about what a candidate would do with massive profits.

Baxter had hired human resource teams and psychologists to screen the thousands of applications received in response to the ad and to weed out the undesirable applicants. Under Baxter's instructions all successful applicants had to be of good moral character and exhibit the human values that Baxter himself possessed. To find the exceptional among the masses took months. Applicants came from different positions and walks in life with strong family values, concern for their fellow humans and possessed selfless personal attributes. These people were to become the foot soldiers in Baxter's army, dedicated to his personal quest: improvement of the human condition.

The large crowd of people milled about in the stately meeting room at the Congress Plaza Hotel's convention center in downtown Chicago. Those who attended had been notified by Bannister Commodities Inc. that they had successfully passed the first step to become traders with the firm and had been invited - all expenses paid - to meet for the final decision on their application. The crowd was diverse: short, tall, young, old, fat, thin, female, male, ugly, beautiful, educated, uneducated, all races, all occupations, all creeds - they were just people. But they all had something in common with each other; and it was what was inside them.

The group of three hundred strangers in the room chattered incessantly until Doug Bannister stepped up to the podium and tapped on the microphone a couple of times. He looked over the crowd, grunted a few times to clear his throat and said:

"Welcome to Chicago."

He lowered his voice as the high-pitched squeal of the microphone resonated throughout the room.

"You have all successfully passed the first step to a career that will change your lives. You don't know this at the present but I'm telling you a career with Bannister Commodities is not about making you rich. It is about goodwill to all and doing what is best for all people around us. That's the reason you've been selected among the many thousands of people who applied to our ad."

The crowd shuffled about silently and then settled. You could hear a pin drop.

"You are from all areas of Canada and the United States and the aim of Bannister Commodities is to benefit all people in your areas: all your family, friends, contacts and other people that you will identify as good people and good causes. You will be financed by Bannister Commodities Inc. and you will learn successful trading skills to help with financial support.

Doug felt no rush to hurry even when there was a slight applause from the crowd. He paused for a couple more seconds - beyond an acceptable time period expected for the occasion.

"I will tell you now that you have all been screened by professional people that we hired for that purpose and before we accept you in our program, you have one final task to undertake."

A definite buzz came over the crowd as people questioned one another about what that task might be.

Doug raised his hands to quiet the crowd.

Baxter roamed, incognito, among the crowd. He scanned individual thoughts and was impressed with the quality of the people. He wanted to gauge the mindset of those picked by the psychologists and resource people. He liked what he read in people.

But he became worried because he encountered an agent for Homeland Security in the crowd - an unassuming middle-aged woman who seemed out of place. Baxter probed her mind for detail. Everything appeared normal. She was there in the normal course of her daily duties to check out any large gatherings of people in her Chicago jurisdiction. Homeland Security would have a watchful eye on any such large gatherings as was the case here. The federal agency's presence was not out of the ordinary...but

If Homeland Security was around, the CIA could not be far behind.

"It's not a difficult task," said Doug. He sensed the inquisitive attitude in the crowd.

"My associate has been circulating among you. You will now meet him individually for a brief moment while he welcomes you to our organization. Before you meet him I want to inform you that, after the final selection, you will start training right away. In fact, tomorrow morning after tonight's welcoming dinner and reception. The reception will give all of you a chance to interact and get to know your fellow comrades.

Please proceed with me to Room A where my associate, Mr. McPherson, will personally welcome you to Bannister Commodities."

The crowd proceeded into the room in an orderly fashion for such a large gathering of people. Baxter stood beside Doug in a receiving line. Doug introduced him as his associate and founding member. The members of this diverse group of people from all over North America shook his hand that momentous day in Chicago.

It was Baxter's long-time dream to meet some of the best people in the land. They were not necessarily the smartest or most gifted individuals but were people of good, unselfish character who only wanted the best for family, friends, neighbours and their fellow man. They all possessed the basic human qualities that a society needed to thrive as a good and righteous nation. He sensed these attributes in the people whose hands he shook.

Each person in turn felt a slight jolt, similar to an electric shock when Baxter reached into their mind. In all, he implanted a general knowledge about himself and the purpose, goals and objectives of the organization he was setting up.

Baxter also shook the hand of Wendy Hunt. She was the middle-aged woman who worked for the Chicago office of Homeland Security. There was no CIA involvement when he probed deeper into her mind. He implanted a strong message into her subconscious about the nature of his organization. She would write a favourable report about them when she completed her investigation. His intuition told him that somehow he might need solid support from Homeland Security in the future.

Introducing myself with all the people in this room will be noticed. It is a matter of time before the CIA catches up with me.

Doug stepped up to the microphone as the last of the crowd was introduced to Baxter.

"There are a few more things I should mention to you before we all retire for the day and re-convene later for tonight's reception and dinner. First of all, the heart and soul of Bannister Commodities is Mr. Baxter McPherson who you just met. He is special beyond words, as all of you will understand in quick order and you may have felt something while you were being introduced to him. Take a moment to talk to people close to you and you'll know what I mean."

Doug paused for a moment and let what he had just said about Baxter sink in. Almost in complete unison, heads turned and a staccato of rapid-fire questions streamed from person to person. They had all felt the same jolt with the handshake. They understood - they collectively possessed similar human qualities and knew the intent of Baxter's plan. They felt complete trust in this person.

Doug tapped the microphone.

"Order, order," he said. "You now have a general feeling of our group's intentions and you will know more as we proceed with the training. One final thought before we re-convene tonight...." He continued to tap on the microphone to get complete attention.

"Take the form at the back of the room and make up your idea for a name and symbol for our group. It should be reflective of what you individually perceive about our group and its nature and goals. It's just a contest. Have fun with it and Baxter and myself will decide on a winning name. See you all tonight."

CHAPTER SEVENTEEN

Clive

Wally Campbell, the head of CIA's western division, slammed his clenched fist on the huge mahogany table top in disgust after he read Bud Brown's report on how Baxter McPherson had escaped the clutches of the CIA. It had been months since Baxter went off their radar screen and reading Bud's report hadn't made him feel much better. Wally didn't believe that Bud had done his best to capture Baxter. He couldn't prove it, but a man with Bud's experience should never have allowed a principal target like Baxter to elude capture. Bud had grown too soft in his old age.

He threw the report in the trash can and muttered an inaudible, derogatory remark about Bud.

"Obviously, you didn't like Bud's report," said a colleague who saw him throw the report.

"Bud's finished as far as I'm concerned," said Wally. "He's a fuckin' sympathizer. I will relegate him to a paper-pushing administrative position deep in a musty basement cubicle somewhere in the most far away office in the country. Don't mention Bud's name in my presence again."

"I want Clive Dunlop on the case," said Wally. "Baxter McPherson needs to be caught and he has just been sighted in the Chicago area"

Clive Dunlop was in the same building as Wally Campbell but another CIA division. It would take too many administrative steps to directly assign the Baxter McPherson file to him. But Wally was a specialist in avoiding administrative obstacles.

The Goddam paperwork that has to be undertaken to get things done these days in the CIA is ridiculous. It is blight on efficiency.

Though things were supposed to have improved since 9/11, Wally knew differently. There was only one way to get things done. Do it yourself and enlist people of action.

Clive Dunlop was at the skating rink this time of day.

The ice splintered into a thousand pieces as the knife-sharp edges of Clive Dunlop's figure skates cut into the smooth surface in a pivot turn that finished into a tight spin. It was a finely executed double sow cow routine that Clive was most proud of as he raced down the ice. Arms outstretched to generate greater speed and the jump, double spin in mid-air and a graceful landing that brought applause from the handful of figure skaters who had stopped their own routines to admire Clive's form.

Born and raised in a town close to the Canadian border had introduced him to winter sports. Snow and ice sports were the only activities undertaken in Minnesota during the cold and dead days of the dreary winter season. He had taken up figure skating and it was his passion as a child growing up in one of the coldest parts of the country.

He had a love for the sport. It was the only love in his life. He loved nothing else. He had no siblings, no friends and no girlfriends. He was a complete loner. His childhood was without nurture and it was loveless. As an orphan he went from foster home to foster home. He was smart and fought and scraped for everything he achieved in life. He was not weak. He had no pity, no sympathy, no tolerance, no empathy for the underprivileged, the poor, the weak, the disabled, and the uneducated. He lived and breathed the motto...*only the strong survive.*

He survived...educated himself and received a PhD in psychology from Yale which guided his understanding of the many weaknesses inherent in people. He had distinguished himself as a trustworthy, dependable and ruthless CIA agent who specialized in extracting information out of people of interest.

He relied on human faults and once discovered, used them to his advantage to collect necessary information from a specified subject. He was a master of his trade and the prominent go-to-agent when people had to be found and important information had to be obtained. He resorted to any means at his disposal to extract information. This included torture...one of the tools in his bag of tricks.

He had never failed in extracting information from subjects. Most of them were from normal, stable people. Maybe it was because he was mentally unstable himself. He knew that and it didn't bother him. It made him who he was...unstable but very efficient.

Clive laced up his figure skates and performed a series of pirouettes and double sow cows. He had perfected the techniques of many of the great figure skaters of the day and had formed a large following at the rink. He didn't mind. He appreciated an audience. It was the closest thing to love in his life. Something he never had in his childhood.

He sweated profusely. Great gobs of moisture ran down his face. In his final spin, Clive noticed Wally Campbell at the edge of the boards. Clive wiped the perspiration from his brow and glided across the ice to Wally, who had beckoned him. He approached and side saddled over the boards with an athletic jump.

The two men, though polite, didn't like each other and had a history of tolerating one another when their paths crossed in the past. They were too similar in many ways - both with strong personalities that clashed - especially when it came to control over others. However, they were both consummate professionals and didn't allow their personal feelings about each other to interfere with their responsibilities.

Wally held out his hand for a handshake when Clive approached. Just then an effeminate-looking figure skater came up behind Clive and smacked him on his butt.

"Great jumps out there Clive," said the effeminate figure skater in his high-pitched, girly voice. "Hope we can meet up later." He continued on by.

"If I didn't know any better I would think you were gay," started Wally.

"Who says I'm not?"

They exchanged awkward smiles.

"I'll get right to the point," said Wally. "We need your expertise to undertake a capture-and-extract case that is a number one priority. The man, Baxter McPherson, has eluded our grasp for some time now. I want you on this case because you're the best and we want this individual."

Clive admired Wally's direct approach. He didn't mince words and was flattered by Wally's admiration of his specialized abilities. Besides, it had been awhile since he had been on such a high priority case. He welcomed the challenge.

"At this point I won't tell you very much about Baxter McPherson," continued Wally. "This is not the place. But this man has extraordinary abilities that even you, with your many experiences, have never encountered. It'll take all your specialized abilities to succeed in this mission."

Clive was intrigued. The more Wally glorified this person of interest, the more he wanted to meet, capture and beat this man. It aroused his fiercely competitive spirit. *This Baxter character will be a worthy adversary to test my abilities.* His blood boiled at the thought that there might be someone that could better him...*impossible.* He grinned when Wally handed him a file.

"Study it intently," he said. "You will admire this Baxter character as much as I do, once you get to understand the depth of his talents and abilities. Then you'll understand why it is imperative that we capture him and bring him to our way of thinking. You have three days to study up on him and devise a method of capture. Your flight has been booked to Chicago and a team has been assembled and will be at your disposal."

Clive took the file as beads of perspiration dropped from his forehead onto its leather casing.

He accepted the task and the new challenge. He would begin immediately to study this new adversary. But first he had some unfinished physical activities at the arena. He noticed the figure skater who had just patted him on the behind, beckon to him as he entered one of the dressing rooms.

Clive poured over the McPherson file. His admiration for Baxter grew with each turn of the page. He was especially impressed with his ability to implant messages into people's minds with a single touch of his hand. Clive had never heard of this before.

That's impossible. But if correct, his mental abilities must be astronomical. I must capture this man.

He didn't understand how a person could implant messages. Clive was determined to see that ability for himself.

He reasoned that Baxter's secret abilities must have something to do with electrical impulses and circuitry that emanate from the core of the brain. His admiration for this special person continued to grow. *His brain's electrical circuitry must be beyond comprehension.*

Clive contacted the CIA's science branch and they confirmed that the only possible way to counteract Baxter's mind-messaging ability had to be done through specialized clothing made of rubber and lead. These materials had the properties to block the transmission of electrical currents. Clive reasoned that any physical contact with Baxter had to make use of these two materials. Rubber and lead had to be built into protective clothing.

***

Baxter and Doug, in their Chicago base, were going over the progress of the group's training sessions. They were pleased. The vast majority of the group had successfully passed the rigors of system training and testing and received a group average of 20 per cent return on invested capital in three months of simulated trading exercises. Baxter estimated that it would take another two months of simulated futures market trading before they would be capably trained to set out on their own with a million dollars of trading capital. It was an exciting period in Baxter's life seeing his personalized dreams become reality.

It was a brisk autumn day in Chicago when Baxter, Doug and two of his students put on their coats and left their training centre to cross the street for a cup of coffee at one of the many

Starbucks within walking distance. The opportunity to get away from the crowded centre presented a welcome break for them.

It was the time of the year in the windy city that the weather became unpredictable. The seasonal drop in temperature saw the sprinkles of rain become mixed with light snow flurries.

Sidewalk people scurried like frightened mice, at a faster than normal pace. They were apprehensive about the weather pattern that approached. It was one of those Chicago squalls that blew off Lake Michigan for which the city was famous. Snow was in the air and many of the sidewalk people glanced skyward as they hurried on.

Baxter's awareness of his immediate surroundings and his own personal safety had become somewhat diminished since he had allowed his great mind to relish and concentrate on the purpose and success of his group mission. The slow flow of traffic on the normally congested street shocked him back to reality in a hurry. He stopped and gestured to his companions to hold up.

"Something's not right." He noticed the trickle of traffic in the street. "There is either an accident further up or someone is purposely blocking traffic."

He sensed danger and that awareness was even more evident when he opened up his mind and read thoughts of people rushing past them on the sidewalk. He would normally be able to peek into the thought patterns of everyone in the immediate vicinity. But this was not happening, not totally. He couldn't read the minds of certain men on the sidewalk. They were wearing a similar type of toque headgear. Baxter couldn't read their thoughts, no matter how hard he tried. This was abnormal and a red flag flashed in his head.

Those toques must be laced with lead.

Electrical impulses couldn't penetrate the metal. The toques were oddly shaped. They looked like stiff metal cups disguised with a cloth cover.

Doug and the two students were oblivious to the danger that Baxter noticed along the street. They didn't see any unusual danger in the diminished traffic flow or in the number of men who wore strange toques on their heads. Baxter tapped his left hand with his right fingers.

Blood rushed to his big body muscles and to his brain. The world stalled. Snow had begun to fall quite heavily and to Baxter, millions of flakes appeared suspended in mid-air. It had been a while since Baxter had invoked his special powers of suspension. It hadn't been necessary while he set up his group activities. He appreciated suspension's special powers, but he did not relish using it - except in extreme emergencies. It still amazed him, the feeling of superior strength, power and speed that took hold of his body. Now, an extreme emergency was at hand.

Two black hummers raced down the street toward Baxter, Doug and his companions. Tires screeched on the wet, lightly dusted, snow-covered street and eight lumbering men in thick, black rubberized suits jumped out of the hummers. They brandished rifle-like apparatus in their hands. Two of the men immediately slipped on the ice that had formed on the street. They went down in a heap and triggered the weapons they carried. A net fired from one of the weapons and a tranquillizer dart from the other.

Baxter, now in a full state of suspension, noticed every little nuance of the ominous situation. He knew who they were. The CIA found him and planned his capture. He couldn't read their minds, which put him at a disadvantage to anticipate what they would do. He saw the weapons that had fired prematurely. They planned to use them on himself and his companions. He leapt with the grace of an African gazelle in front of his companions... sheltered them from the hummer agents and the frontal assault to come.

Six toque-wearing agents sprang into action and cut in front of Baxter and his companions. All exits from the street and the sidewalk were blocked. The toque-wearing CIA agents drew tasers and aimed at their targets. Zapping sounds filled the air. The tasers discharged.

No warnings were given.

Confusion and screams of pain were everywhere. Tasers, tranquillizer darts and nets were fired at Baxter's group - all at the same instant. Baxter summoned all his power and with the speed of light deflected as many of the darts and taser shots that he could. There were too many of them. He moved at incredible speed. To normal vision he moved at a blurred pace to protect his friends. But they were hit and dropped screaming to their knees. Baxter was also hit but he felt nothing. His superhuman power over his own body, his ability to direct his body's energy and blood supply to where it was most needed and to shut down the tranquillizing effect of the darts that struck his body, prevented the tasers and darts from overpowering him.

But the nets....

He could not combat them.

His friends were down and he was covered by nets. Taser strings and darts stuck out of his body. He was immobilized. All his life he had despised violence, but at this moment there was anger in his soul.

One of the toque-wearing agents came over to the paralyzed, defenseless, net-covered lump of a human being that he had helped subdue. He took off his rubberized glove and reached to feel for a pulse. His toque headgear slipped halfway off his head. Baxter grabbed his arm, held it for a second, implanted a message and then gave him a push. It sent him flying backwards, off his feet.

More darts hit his body and he slowed and was unable to move in the nets. The drugs started to overwhelm him.

Clive walked over and looked at his prized adversary - completely vanquished, wrapped in the nets and helpless. He kicked him.

"That's for throwing one of my men, asshole," he yelled in a rage. "So you are the famous Baxter McPherson. You don't look so tough."

CHAPTER EIGHTEEN

The Torture Room

Baxter woke up in a small, dimly lit, dingy cell. He was shackled in leg irons which only allowed him to move in half-step strides. He was drowsy and sluggish and still felt the effect of the drugs from the darts. He called upon the power of his mind to push a pure oxidized stream of blood to the parts of his body that were drug impaired. The healing process was underway but it would still take some time to completely flush the drugs from his body.

He looked around the cell. Not much in it: a bed, a toilet and a chair - a prison cell. He knew he was captive and alone. He rose up and moved to the bars at the front of the cell. He tested their strength, tugged at two of them with each hand. He couldn't move them even if he called upon the full power of his strength. They were specially constructed of heavy reinforced steel. This was not a normal prison cell.

The CIA has gone to great lengths to capture and contain me.

A voice boomed into the cell from somewhere in the ceiling.

"Even you can't break through those bars, Baxter. They were made special - just for you."

Baxter studied the ceiling. He was being monitored.

He felt a huge sense of responsibility for the people who were with him during the attack. "How are my companions? Are they hurt? Where are they?" He looked toward the ceiling, waited for a reply. None came.

Two men in bulky, rubberized body suits appeared in front of Baxter's cell. They wore metal cups on their heads. They looked silently at Baxter and Baxter looked at them. Baxter laughed harder than he had ever laughed in his life. His sides hurt.

He gasped for air between short bursts of laughter.

"I've never seen anything so stupid-looking in my life. What planet do you come from, anyway? Or are you clowns and come here to entertain me?"

Clive was not amused.

"Yes Mr. McPherson, I admit that we are funny looking, but we totally respect your special powers to read minds and implant messages - thus the need for these clown suits. Try to read our minds if you will."

The humour of the moment dissipated and realizing how serious the situation was, Baxter did attempt to read their minds.

Blank.

As stupid-looking as they are, their clown get-ups are effective.

"I can't read anyone's mind," returned Baxter. "Doesn't matter - I'm sure there is very little in your minds at the best of times."

It was not like Baxter to degrade anyone, but these people were to do him harm.

"Where are my companions? Are they hurt? What have you done with them?" repeated Baxter in a serious tone.

"I don't answer your questions, Mr. McPherson. You answer mine. Comprendez-vous?" replied Clive.

They had intelligence information about his abilities and Baxter knew what they wanted from him. They wanted to manipulate or control his powers. They would go to any lengths for that purpose.

These people scared him. He couldn't read the minds of the two clowns in front of him, but he knew that the head clown he faced was the dominant one and was in charge.

I'm in a battle with this agent. A battle of wits and strength of character.

The head agent spoke. "For further reference, Mr. McPherson, I will share a bit of information with you. I look forward to working with you and you are to address me as 'Sir.' One more thing, your quick recovery from the tranquilizer darts was totally astounding. Our medical people can hardly wait to get their hands on you. Rest now, our co-operative venture begins in the morning with a preliminary and extensive medical examination."

Baxter shot back. "There will be no co-operation until I find out that my companions are safe and unharmed."

Baxter waited for a response. There was none. The two agents in the rubberized monkey suits turned and walked away.

Two clowns approached Baxter's cell the next morning with a breakfast tray. It was obvious by their hesitation that they had heard about the special abilities of the subject held in the reinforced cell, in the mysterious wing of the premises where only top secret cases were housed. They carried the same net rifles and tranquilizer-dart guns that were originally used to subdue Baxter and his companions on the street of Chicago.

One of the clowns spoke. "We have your breakfast Mr. McPherson, and after you finish it, you are coming with us. You can do it hard or you can do it easy, but either way you are coming."

Baxter looked at the two clowns and waited a moment, then responded in a way that he gauged would raise their apprehension.

"You don't have to worry about me. How do you expect me to run wearing these leg irons? But maybe I will just get inside your heads and make you shoot each other with those dart guns."

They backed up a few respectful steps. They heard about his mind control. They persisted and escorted Baxter to a specially designed medical facility that housed a room that looked like something out of a science fiction movie. It was a chamber where the subject is enclosed in a small transparent room, separate from his handlers, where robotic arms, guided by men in white lab coats used computerized controls to perform the functions of a human doctor.

Baxter was impressed even as he was aggravated by the total invasion of his privacy. It would be pointless to resist the medical examination. They would force it upon him, if necessary. They were in control for the moment. He cooperated and laid on the examination table.

But he had some tricks of his own. They were looking for something superhuman from him and hoped that the medical examination would provide part of the puzzle of Baxter McPherson. Something they could use.

He would give them nothing. His strength came from his brain and he instructed his body to provide just normal human biologically measured results. The robotic arms poked and prodded and measured him in an assortment of medical ways. It included strength and stress tests. Baxter kept his cool and allowed the tests to proceed without incident. Clive looked on from the other side of the reinforced glass chamber. His medical advisory team read off the results of each completed test.

"Within normal parameters."

Clive became incensed.

"Baxter, you are holding back on us. I know that. You won't be able to totally resist our examinations," his voice reflected his irritation. "It's to your advantage to co-operate with us. The tests are only going to get harder. The medical tests show that you are normal and we all know that's not true."

Baxter noticed the team of medical personnel leave the chamber and a new group of three agents enter. They wore metal cups on their heads. They didn't need the rubber suits since Baxter was unable to touch them.

Clive grabbed the microphone.

"We want you to relax, Baxter. I will ask you questions, as will my new colleagues here, Dr. A, Dr. B and Dr. C. These will be questions about yourself and your special abilities. We are all trained psychologists so we will know if you are lying or holding back from answering correctly. You must be a little uncomfortable in there, all strapped down. Unfortunately, we will not be able to loosen the straps during this session. It's not that we don't trust you....well, actually it is because we don't trust you."

A quick burst of laughter from the group followed. They relished the power they had in this situation.

"You are also connected to a special lie detector apparatus that we control here. So if we determine that you are lying or not cooperating with us, you will receive a rather unpleasant shock. Just to let you know what we mean, here's just a small sample."

A sudden jolt of electricity poured through Baxter's body. He shrieked in agony.

"That was the lowest level on a scale from one to ten, and that jolt was only one second long. I can make the pain last as long as I hold my finger on the button."

Clive smiled to his colleagues.

"It's to your benefit to cooperate with us, Baxter," said Clive. "Because as much as I personally enjoy seeing you suffer, we need you. At your best."

Baxter called upon the strength of his mind to counteract the electrical charges that would soon race through his body. He braced for what was to come. They wanted information and he would not answer.

Let's begin with a simple question," said Clive. "Your name is Baxter McPherson. Is this correct?"

"Can't fool you," answered Baxter.

Clive hit the button and held it for three seconds. Baxter had readied his body to counter the charge. The pain was tolerable but he shrieked in pain to appease them.

"Please take me seriously," replied Clive. "Respect my position here and you will come through this without getting seriously hurt. Let's try this again and with a more pertinent question. Before you say anything, you should know the charge will set to level five if I press the button this time... if we don't like your answer...question: can you read minds?"

Baxter hesitated for a moment. "I can read your mind now and I know that you are a psychotic, evil person who likes to inflict pain and suffering on others."

He braced. The current would soon come.

"It hurts me to do this to you Baxter," replied Clive. "See how your non-responsiveness hurts us both? But perhaps you more than me."

He hit the button.

Baxter instantly jerked as far as his restraints allowed. His back arched in an unnatural, contorted bodily position. His eyes bulged, hair uncurled and his face contorted in a picture of agonized pain, he shrieked a blood-curdling scream that reached and filled the hallways to the torture chamber. One of the three agents with Clive backed away and vomited.

Clive stopped for a second and screeched into the microphone in a maniacal rage. "I want your total cooperation. I want nothing less - and I demand it now."

He slammed his fist hard on the button again and held it down.

Baxter jerked uncontrollably. His arm and leg restraints prevented him from flying off the metal table slab. Clive held the button down for a full ten seconds and Baxter's arched body position did not resemble anything that the human body could engineer. His great mind had reached its upper limits and had not been able to overcome the strength of the electrical current that surged through his body.

He blacked out, unconscious and his heart fluttered even as his body continued to dance. He was close to death. Clive eyed the monitors and recognized the seriousness of the situation. What had he done? He took his hand off the button. The current stopped.

One of the attendants screamed when he viewed the electrocardiogram machine results. "He's going into cardiac arrest. We have to get him out of there."

A team of medical doctors raced into the torture chamber. Turmoil prevailed as they worked on Baxter's now-limp body. Clive stood by, unmoved. He watched the medical team work their magic on his prime subject. The electrocardiogram attached to Baxter's body flickered in a life-affirming, oscillating pattern.

Baxter came back from the dead. He was still unconscious. Clive barked out orders.

"When he stabilizes take him back to his cell. We haven't finished with him yet."

While Baxter was flickering between life and death, where he lay prone on the torture chamber table, he had a dream…

I was ten years old.

I swerved left and shifted right and avoided the body check from the huge hockey player who wore a rubberized red uniform and a metal cup for a helmet. I deftly picked up the puck on my stick and darted between two slow-moving, rubberized opponents.

"Go Baxter go," shrieked the fans in the stands.

I looked over to the stands in full flight. I recognized them all, dressed in white, shining robes. They had an aura around them and glowed. My mother, father, brothers and sisters, Marie, Jefferson, Leroy, all the homeless I recognized from Charity Cottage, Gerald Turner, Cora, the stranger on the Amtrak train, the sick children from the Children's Hospital he helped, Doug Bannister and the people from the Chicago conference. Linda and Dr. Shultz stood in another row by themselves.

Linda pointed to an area of the stands to people I did not recognize. All sorts of people, hundreds of them. They all cheered in unison.

"We need your help. Win the game."

I moved into full stride and put a move on the lone rubberized defenseman in my path that left him flat on the ice, out of position…a breakaway…a clear path to the goaltender.

Clive was the goaltender. His mask was similar to the face of the devil...fiery red with smoke painted coming out of his ears. He stood erect and huge...entirely covered in rubberized goalie gear. He covered all angles of the net. There were few openings.

I ripped a slapshot from the top of the faceoff circle. The puck sailed over Clive's shoulder into the top corner. The twine bulged from impact. The red light flashed and shone throughout the arena. Beautiful monarch butterflies streamed toward the unknown people in the crowd.

Loud cheers.

A few minutes later, Clive stood at the foot of Baxter's bed watching him. Baxter was still restrained by straps attached to his arms and legs. He was groggy and had not fully recovered from the events in the torture chamber. He opened his eyes and saw Clive in front of him.

Clive almost seemed apologetic and walked back and forth in front of his bed. He spoke. "You gave us a bit of a scare, Baxter. We almost lost you in there and we don't want any permanent harm to come to you. You are too valuable to us. But you must cooperate. We need you on our side."

Baxter gurgled and attempted to speak. Phlegm had built up in his mouth. He coughed, spit the phlegm into a spittoon on his right, and then cleared his throat.

"You almost murdered me. The great CIA, a United States organization nearly murdered one of its own citizens," he spoke defiantly. "Under no circumstances will you receive any cooperation from me. Next time you will have to murder me."

Clive stopped in front of the bed and looked straight at Baxter.

"Mr. McPherson, if we can't have you, no one will have you. That's your only option."

Silence filled the tiny bedroom cell. The two antagonists leered at each other. Hatred and loathing clear on both faces.

Clive spoke first. "Baxter, you have not yet answered the question that I put to you before you so disrespectfully passed out on us in the examination room. Can you read minds?"

Silence shrouded the cell again.

Neither one would back down and the head games, so much a part of physical torture, had begun. Baxter cleared his throat and responded. "I want to personally thank you. Because of you, I experienced hatred for the first time in my life. Everyone should experience it because it shows the absolute beauty of its opposite - love. And hatred is something that I never want to experience again. Thank you for making me understand that."

Clive didn't expect such a response. It shook him - a 'thank you' from a torture victim. He nodded at Baxter and acknowledged the strategic attack that his worthy opponent had just delivered.

"I will never underestimate you again. You almost had me doubting myself. Congratulations. But the fact remains that you haven't yet answered my question. Can you read minds?"

"I can't read minds," said Baxter.

He didn't lie. The metal cups prevented him from reading the bio-electrical circuitry of the brain. Even in this moment of his life's greatest challenge, Baxter was truthful as a pious priest. The thought made him chuckle.

The chuckle infuriated Clive. Recovering from his momentary feeling of doubt, he snapped back to his old, evil persona.

"Since I believe that you won't respond favourably to the electrical stimulus that we introduced you to, we will begin the next step in our examination process. Some people have termed it waterboarding, but we like to call it the persuasive power of water."

He had a cup of water in his hand and poured it on the floor. He watched it bounce and bead.

"Soothing, gentle water cannot possibly hurt you, Baxter, but its hidden strength has an advantage if used in the proper way. I'm sure that you are aware of the waterboarding technique and I'm also sure that you can't resist it. We will give you time to think about cooperating with us and also let your body heal from our last examination procedure."

He departed the cell but turned back, "We will start in the morning. Pleasant dreams."

Baxter was in trouble. The waterboarding technique could not be resisted. It had the overwhelming infliction of a sense of drowning and no person could fight the feeling of losing the breath of life. Baxter understood that he would lose the next round to Clive and for the first time in his life, he didn't know what to do next or how he should attempt to respond.

He recalled his hockey dream.

I have so much more to do.

CHAPTER NINETEEN

Ray and Wendy

Things in life were not going well for Ray Jessome. He was fluent in Arabic and also a specialist in the use of various weapons - an odd mixture of talents that valued him as an employee of the CIA. Teaching the Arabic language at the university put an extra twenty thousand dollars into his money market fund, but he enjoyed it less and less. It was too much extra work along with his full-time job at the CIA. All day long he interpreted intelligence data collected by other CIA operatives in the Middle East. He would then leave his office and go to the university to teach Arabic to a lot of stupid people who would not learn. It wore him out.

The extra money was good but his social life suffered. A lot less time for his friends and he hadn't played golf in over two months. He loved golf.

He couldn't sleep and he usually slept like a baby as soon as his head hit the pillow...*a sleep disorder - great. That's all I need.* Behind a computer in a nine-to-five job staring into the face of that dumb machine made him restless and one of the reasons for the insomnia.

His increased restlessness and insomnia had multiplied since he had been assigned to a team to capture a person of interest on the streets of Chicago. He had been chosen because of his knowledge in the use of net guns. The capture team was led by an agent they called 'Clive'.

There was something very strange about that operation that stuck in his mind. It bothered him, especially the last minute instructions...*or rant*...from Clive just before the team disembarked the hummer to engage.

"Okay, you guys, just remember this guy is evil...he is dangerous so don't let your guard down. And he is powerful like no man you've encountered before. So, remember what I told you...don't let him touch you. It's imperative...and I repeat...no contact with him whatsoever."

The encounter with that person of interest on the snowy day in Chicago had left Ray with so many unanswered questions. He had been told so little and only on a need-to-know basis. There was something special about that man just from the protective rubberized clothing and the silly-looking metal toques that all the agents were instructed to wear during the capture.

He had helped to gun down that person and it left a bad taste in his mouth. The defense that the target had put up, who had so valiantly and with amazing speed and agility attempted to defend his companions from the aggressiveness of the CIA's capture procedure, impressed him. He couldn't stand by and ignore the plight of this one person. Ray was not a malevolent person and so he had reached out to assist this man in his moment of need after he had covered him with nets.

It was a simple gesture on his part, just to feel for a pulse after the heavy dosage of taser shots and tranquilizer darts that the targeted individual had absorbed. Then the net-covered man grabbed him by the arm. It gave him a slight electric shock and left him with an impression.

He had planted a simple message in Ray Jessome's mind: *My name is Baxter McPherson. Seek out Wendy Hunt of Homeland Security. Help me!*

Ray was then thrown but was uninjured.

That simple implanted message troubled Ray. He thought about it constantly and it added to his recent sleep problems.

Who was this 'Baxter McPherson' person who put that message in my mind? How could he do that?

Why had he thrown me away so vigorously just after he implanted that help message?

Maybe it was an instantaneous clever ruse on his part to disguise the mind-to-mind contact.

It had worked, since Clive and the other agents had not followed up on the interaction he had with this person.

Ray had to find out as much as possible about the so-called civilian terrorist named Baxter McPherson. He would go crazy if he couldn't remove the strong message that played over and over in his mind...*and who was Wendy Hunt?*

Ray had access to the grapevine that is so prevalent in any large organization. The capture of a high profile target was on the grapevine. A close friend of Ray's worked in the building where Clive had taken Baxter and his companions. Stories resounded that at times in the past screams filled the air from that specialized area of the building where the high profile target was to be housed.

Ray heard from his fellow CIA friend... *Baxter McPherson may be in there.*

The mystery of Baxter McPherson played over and over in his mind. He had to track down Wendy Hunt.

Wendy wore a bright red top with a front zipper that travelled from her neck to her slim waist, the day she met Ray

Jessome. It accentuated her sexuality and it was her favourite article of clothing. It gave her the option to uncover as much of her ample bosom as she wanted. Any prospective man would almost certainly be attracted to the best of her physical charms.

It was strange to her that a CIA agent had directly contacted her instead of higher up operatives at Homeland Security.

Why was agent Ray Jessome curious about the capture of some U.S. citizens on the streets of Chicago? She had her suspicions that the captured citizens were Doug Bannister and Baxter McPherson of Bannister Commodities Inc. along with a handful of trainees that had all disappeared in the middle of a training session in Chicago. It happened in her jurisdiction and it caused concern for her organization in their ongoing difficulties and conflicts with the CIA.

Wendy was attracted to Ray Jessome when they sat across from each other in the coffee shop where they had agreed to meet...*he sure is a handsome fellow*. His generous smile put her at ease. He was a man of considerable confidence with a gentle manner and quiet direct demeanour. She liked what she saw in this CIA agent. His slim athletic build had not been lost on her, She had to refocus for a second after she allowed herself the vision of a passionate sexual embrace. It had been a long time since she had a man in her life and she missed the pleasure of a man's touch. She was glad she'd worn her favourite top to this strange meeting with this agent.

She toyed with the zipper in her top - she raised it, she lowered it and exposed the deep cleavage of well-formed breasts. It was a provocative sexual message. Ray's head followed the motion of her hand on her zipper, but his eyes tried to stare straight ahead. His eyes strayed and darted lower. He took note of her inadvertent overture and had become distracted. She knew he was attracted to her obvious display of attributes.

"What do you know about a group of men taken by the CIA on the streets of Chicago - particularly a man named Baxter McPherson?" Ray asked, even as he couldn't help notice Wendy's forward movement, shifting closer to him with her top almost half-way unzipped. It revealed just enough of her breasts to attract attention. His.

"I don't know what happened in Chicago. You'll have to fill me in," said Wendy.

Ray was hesitant to reveal his full involvement with Baxter McPherson to a total stranger and especially to someone from Homeland Security. He would put his career in jeopardy if the information he was about to reveal found its way back to the CIA. But he had come this far in his quest to understand the implanted message in his mind...*what did Wendy Hunt know about Baxter McPherson?*

"Baxter McPherson was in a group of people captured in Chicago by the CIA," he said. He tried to conceal as much as possible about his role in the capture. "Unfortunately, I wasn't privy to any further information about these people, other than the CIA had determined them to belong to a potential home-grown civilian terrorists. But, I do know that this person of interest is a special person with amazing abilities that the CIA wants to acquire. I also know that the CIA will use extreme measures, including torture, to obtain the information they are looking for."

"The CIA is torturing US citizens?" she blurted out and sprayed a half-mouthful of coffee across the top of the table. "I know these people. Baxter McPherson and Douglas Bannister are business partners. They co-own Bannister Commodities Inc.

and they were involved in a commodities training session in Chicago when they, and some of the trainees, disappeared. She stopped for a brief instant and in a half-hearted attempt, wiped coffee stains off the table top. "The CIA took them and is now torturing them?"

"I think they might be," he said a little embarrassed. "But I must ask, what is your personal involvement with this case?" He didn't want to reveal how Baxter had implanted her name in his head. It would discredit him.

"I wrote a report for Homeland Security about Bannister Commodities Inc. as part of my job functions for Homeland Security, covering the Chicago area."

She looked him in the eye. "My report outlined that Baxter McPherson and Doug Bannister are involved in a marvellous venture through their company. They support and grow good morals and values in the human spirit that will only benefit America. Homeland Security appreciates their contribution to our country and they are considered to be valuable assets.

She hesitated.

"You have to stop the CIA."

***

Baxter resisted the first attempt to extract information by the waterboard technique. He was determined to resist as long as he could hold out. He held out longer than anyone had done before and his resilience impressed Clive.

"Congratulations, Baxter. You are truly an amazing individual," reported Clive. He clapped lightly in a sarcastic manner.

"But unfortunately for you, it gets harder to resist the next step."

Clive smiled while he tightened the leg straps that secured Baxter to the waterboarding table.

"That episode was only for five minutes and no human being can hold out losing the sweet breath of life for ten minutes and that is what is coming next. It is humanly impossible. So before we begin, I ask you again, can you read minds?"

Baxter could not resist for ten minutes. He gasped for breath while he still had it. He was determined to give up his life before he would do anything to assist the CIA from using his powers. He had resigned himself to his fate.

He responded to Clive's question. "I would rather die than give in to you."

Clive became incensed and kicked over the trash bucket next to the waterboarding table.

"Then you will die." He punched wildly at invisible air.

Clive motioned to the helper agent responsible for dropping water on Baxter's face.

"Give him ten minutes. Now!"

Water dropped on Baxter's blind-folded head in a light enough manner for him to gasp for breath. But with each breath he swallowed water which caused coughing spasms that induced a deeper consumption of the evil liquid. The water sapped away the air he needed to survive. Try as he might, he could not turn his head. The restraints were too strong. He tried to hold his breath, but with water in his lungs there was not much breath to hold. He commanded his body's blood supply to gorge his large muscles and exert every ounce of strength that he possessed to tear away the steel reinforced leather straps that held him down.

He had little time. Life supporting air was being sucked away. His lungs burned as he gasped for elusive air. But there was no air to be had, only water. One of the arm restraints started to give way under the immense pressure of his great strength. Two agents grabbed his arm, held it down as another re-secured the restraint and bolted it to the table.

Baxter tried to implant a message to the agent holding down his arm. "Please help me!" But the agent wore the rubberized clown suit and the silly metal cup on his head.

Baxter thought he was finished.

He had no air in his deprived, burning lungs. He could feel his life's breath slip away. His thought patterns became jumbled and cloudy. He thought of Linda. He loved her. Regrets was the last emotion he felt as he was dying. He heard yells and screams at the door to the torture room...the last sounds of his life. He let out one last scream of pain in anguish over the hopelessness of the situation... then lost consciousness.

Darkness.

I was swimming at my favourite swimming hole outside of Portland Maine. I was a strong swimmer and at ten years of age I would swim for miles and miles without tiring. I was halfway across the lake when something tugged at my leg from beneath. It dragged me down deeper and deeper into the murky depths. The further down it dragged me, the colder the water. I was losing my breath...water filled my lungs.

I looked at what grabbed my leg. It was a great fish with the face of the devil. It spoke, "Can you read minds?"

I struggled and freed myself from its grasp. My lungs burned, deprived of air and full of water. I broke the surface of the water and Linda was there in a boat looking for me. Beautiful monarch butterflies were everywhere fluttering above her.

Linda spoke. "You have so much more work to do. You cannot drown."

Wendy Hunt and Ray Jessome had very little time to intervene in the torture that they suspected was being undertaken on Baxter and companions. Wendy's report, written on the activities of Bannister Commodities Inc., was well received by Homeland Security and had been accepted and read at the top management levels of the organization. Once informed about Baxter's and Bannister's situation, Homeland Security contacted the CIA.

A quick series of events occurred which prompted immediate action.

The torture of U.S citizens would not be tolerated. Baxter and party were to be immediately released. Wally Campbell, Clive's immediate supervisor was to oversee the release operation. He was dispatched to Chicago to meet up with Wendy and Ray.

The door to the torture room was guarded by CIA agents when Wally, Wendy, Ray, other agents and a team of medical doctors approached. The CIA agents were under the direct supervision of Clive and initially resisted entry to the locked room to anyone without Clive's permission. Wally flashed his authoritative CIA identity badge and yelled out orders to step aside and open the locked door.

A sharp scream suddenly came from within the secured walls of the torture room. Clive's agents lowered their guard for an instant.

"Open that door or your careers with the CIA are over," barked Wally Campbell.

One of the CIA guards pulled out a swipe card and unlocked the room.

"Draw your weapons and follow me." Wally Campbell's jaw was set as he pulled out his revolver. The party stormed toward the limp figure strapped to an ungodly-looking table apparatus used for waterboarding. Clive jumped with a startled look on his face. He recognized Wally Campbell and saw his guards approach with drawn weapons. The medical team raced toward Baxter who was limp on the torture table, even as a CIA agent continued to pour water on his face. The agent was shoved aside and the straps that secured Baxter were released. The medical team administered aid to the lifeless form on the table. They were successful.

Baxter coughed and spewed water from his mouth on his way back from the dead. He cleared his lungs from the air-depriving effects of the water. The medical team placed an oxygen mask over his face. The gush of pure oxygen revived him and he guided the breath of life to circulate from his lungs and restore oxygenated blood flow through his body.

He sat up.

The torture room was in turmoil. Guards lead Clive's CIA agents out of the room. Clive stood in the centre of the room with his arms bound behind his back. He had a blank, bewildered look on his face. He did not speak. He had failed in his attempted conquest of Baxter. He glanced over at the rejuvenated form of his former adversary at the same moment Baxter jumped off the waterboarding table with the agility of an energetic teenager, much to the surprise of the medical doctors who attended him.

Baxter approached Clive. He stood in front of him and just looked without words. The look of resignation covered Clive's face combined with contempt and hatred for the man who had beat him. The two antagonists stared at each other.

Baxter spoke. "I told you that you made me experience hatred for the first time in my life. At that time, it was true. But right now, I have no hatred in my heart toward you."

Baxter reached out and took off the metal cup that Clive still wore on his head. He read his thoughts. There remained nothing but evil and hatred in Clive's mind.

Baxter could never change nor reach this man, so he turned away.

He walked over to Ray and Wendy and hugged them.

Ray and Wendy looked at each other lustfully. Exciting days did that.

CHAPTER TWENTY

Dreams

Cora looked out the window of her pleasant single-dwelling residence on the outskirts of Des Moines, Iowa and paused for a moment. She thought back to the bad, old days in Las Vegas where she was solidly entrenched in the grimy life of the prostitution trade.

God, I'm lucky I met Baxter McPherson. Where would I be now if I hadn't met him? How can I ever repay him?

If not for the chance encounter with Baxter, her life would have continued down the road straight to hell. She wished she could see him again and just hug him.

Her young daughter's cry interrupted her day dream. She walked into the nursery and with a wide grin picked up her one-year old daughter from the play pen. In perfect baby talk parlance, she said, "What's da matter, my beautiful little angel? You just love your mommy and want her to pick you up, don't you?"

Her mind wandered again. She thought of Donald, her wonderful husband.

He is so great...and loves me in spite of my past life.

Cora walked about the nursery holding and patting her beloved daughter. Again, she let her mind wander to the day she first started her now successful and thriving non-profit organization called 'United for Hookers' which helped young girls get off the streets, girls who were trapped in the sex trade. It had proven to be very successful and outreach centres had expanded across the country. It started with her move back to Iowa with over $100,000 in casino winnings.

Sometimes she just sat and thought about the irony of it.

The big, bad casinos paying for such a good cause.

She was due to leave her home the next day to attend an important meeting in Miami. She was in serious negotiations with prospective partners interested to set up one of her halfway houses. She was living her dream and happily packed for the trip. That night Cora woke up in the middle of the night. She jabbed her husband in the ribs and woke him up as well.

"Donald," she exclaimed to her half-asleep husband. "I just had a dream. It was about Baxter. He planted a time-delayed message in my head. I know he did. I know where Baxter is and he wants me to go to Halifax, Nova Scotia to meet him on the last week of September."

Donald had no idea what she was talking about. He knew who Baxter McPherson was because his wife often told him stories about her hero, but he was still groggy and could only think about rolling over to regain the joy of restful sleep.

Cora jabbed him again and exclaimed, "I have to go, but where is Nova Scotia? It's in Eastern Canada somewhere, isn't it?"

***

Ron Cooper had the same dream every night and it bugged him. It was like an unfinished, jigsaw puzzle that he could not piece together and he was a man who always finished what he started. The dream left him with no objective in his mind to put together. He couldn't figure it out.

It placed him in the coach car during a simple train ride to Chicago - a trip he had taken countless times over the years in pursuit of his many philanthropic projects. The dream was always the same.

> *People with blank faces, sat close to him and stared at him as they jiggled up and down to the rhythmic motion of the train bumping along steel tracks to its destination. None of them spoke. They just stared straight at him. Only one man had facial features. That man had a bright light shining on him when he turned around and smiled at Ron. The stranger always rose from his seat and walked toward Ron just as a flash of lightning burst in the air over Chicago. Ron saw the lightning from the train window.*

Ron did remember a stranger who spoke a few words to him on one of his long ago trips to Chicago. He couldn't remember the exact words the man spoke. Ron had written off the short encounter as just another chance meeting with a crazy person who had accidentally bumped into him. But he did recall that when they had contact, he felt an electrical charge throughout his body. Ron wondered if that strange feeling he'd felt on the train had anything to do with the lightning discharge he saw over Chicago in his dream. It was all a mystery to him since he couldn't decipher nor understand any hidden meaning that the dream might reveal.

Every time he rode the Amtrak train to Chicago he thought about the dream. The more he thought about it the more he became convinced that, indeed, it was connected to the chance encounter with the stranger some time ago. He wondered if he would ever see that man again. He decided that if he saw the stranger on one of his scheduled trips he would stop and query him.

Chances of seeing him again are remote.

Ron opened up a letter that he just received from the local car dealership. He first thought it was just another piece of junk mail. It wasn't. The message inside just about floored him. It was a congratulatory letter on the purchase of a new BMW for his son. He couldn't believe his eyes. He had a hard time holding back his anger. He read it one more time... it couldn't be true.

But it was.

"Janice, where is that son of yours?" Ron bellowed to his wife. "Get him. We got a big problem."

He read the letter to his wife. He stood in front of her and waited for a response. She stood there and didn't utter a word. He read the letter again but just the part that said 'Congratulations to Jason on the purchase of his new BMW.'

"How the hell does Jason have the audacity to go out and buy a BMW on my dime without informing me?" he said.

"Jason isn't around," she answered. "And what is so bad about buying something nice for our son... and he's your son too. You got lots of money and if you didn't give most of your money away to all those stupid organizations, there would be a lot more for our family. And besides, he needs a new car since he cracked up his Jag."

Ron didn't want to have this conversation about his philanthropic donations again. They'd argued about it so many times before and he couldn't understand her miserly way of thinking. But he had to respond.

"Stupid organizations! The Hospital for Sick Children, the Home for Unwed Mothers, the homeless... you think they are stupid organizations?"

He seethed inside. The difficulties about Jason and the BMW swirled inside him. Janice's total disregard or empathy for his worthwhile donations - the disposition of his large amount of wealth to do some good in society. He couldn't believe how unsupportive she was. No matter how often he explained, it didn't sit well with his ready-made family.

Every time he thought about his family it just reinforced his desire to give away more of his money and as fast as possible.

Ron groaned to himself.

The biggest mistake in my life was getting married again - to a woman with two worthless kids.

Everything was handed to them on a silver platter and they didn't have to work for anything. So they didn't.

At least I'm giving something back to those who aren't as lucky as me.

And my worthless kids, if I die tomorrow, I'm damn well sure not gonna leave anything to them.

Giving away his fortune to worthwhile causes and organizations satisfied him. He did it under the cloak of anonymity. It was his way. He had a problem, though. His financial resources were getting low and he worried about how he was going to inform his research associates of his lowered financial situation. It was difficult for him. The growth of worthwhile applications overwhelmed his dwindling financial resources and his philanthropic organization only had enough funds to continue to year's end before finances ran out... *Maybe sooner if I can't control the spending of those worthless kids.*

He had to tell his research team. Another trip to Chicago was in order. *Maybe this time I will see that stranger on the train...and get him to explain the dream.*

It was a sad day for Ron after the day's meeting in Chicago and he retired that evening with a heavy heart. Later that night, in the hotel, Ron had the dream. It started as it always started.

Blank empty faces of the many passengers in the same coach car, rhythmically bouncing up and down to the gentle rolling motion of the train as it moved along the tracks on route to Chicago. The difference was that the light on the single passenger with facial features, appeared brighter than in previous dreams. The stranger's gentle-looking countenance and pleasant smile reassured him that the unidentified and complete stranger did not have evil intentions.

He felt comfortable in the dream when the stranger rose from his seat and approached. But then the dream was different. All the formerly blank-faced passengers now had full facial features. They all smiled and faced Ron as the pleasant stranger in front of him extended his arm for a handshake. All the passengers simultaneously rose from their seats and approached to form a circle around the two. Ron raised his arm for the handshake. When their hands touched a bolt of blue-white lightning cracked above the train, in the Chicago sky.

The stranger spoke.

"Hello Ron Cooper. My name is Baxter McPherson and I know you are a good man with a good heart. This train is not headed to Chicago but instead, is going to Halifax, Nova Scotia with all my friends."

Baxter turned and extended his arms in a circling motion to include the other passengers.

"I want you to come to Halifax with us for the last week of September this year and I hope you'll consider joining our group."

All the passengers raised their hands and simultaneously said. "Join us."

Ron awoke from his sleep state. He felt refreshed and relaxed. His mind was at peace and unencumbered because the secret of his dream puzzle had been partially revealed. But he still didn't understand its full meaning. Many questions remained unanswered about the stranger and the purpose for going to Halifax and why he had been selected. Ron thought about the dream and concluded that the stranger, Baxter, must have a special purpose if he could implant a dream in Ron's subconscious. He had to resolve these unanswered questions if his dream puzzle was to be solved.

He had travelled throughout the Atlantic Provinces of Canada once before and had only pleasant memories of the beautiful rolling countryside, quant fishing villages, pleasant friendly people and the city of Halifax. He made up his mind that morning when he sat down for his freshly brewed morning cup of coffee in the Chicago hotel, that this coming September, he would travel to Halifax. What harm could it do?

***

I am cured.

Gerald Turner couldn't believe it. He felt his slightly pudgy body all over. It felt good.

And I lost fifteen pounds.

The cancer had been completely eradicated from his body. His death sentence was lifted.

So many people to thank. Dr. Shultz from Harvard University who had recommended him on advice from Baxter; the top-notch specialized stem cell medical team at St. Mary's University that had treated him with its revolutionary medical treatment that, while it was being developed, had been closely held under wraps - and of course Baxter. He owed so much to him.

He recalled Baxter's words.

"I want you to put your name and resources behind this research and champion its cause."

That message was not lost on Turner.

These procedures have to be brought into the mainstream of medical treatment as quickly as possible...and the treatment would have to be affordable for everyone. I owe it to every cancer patient out there.

It was a hard task he set for himself - to move the powerful anti-stem-cell pressure groups in Washington. He was determined.

The business community must get behind me. There will be profits to be made...and society will benefit.

He welcomed the challenge.

And he had to do something for St. Mary's University.

St. Mary's must become the focal point for a new world-wide medical research centre. I will make it happen.

Gerald Turner seldom dreamed. If he did dream, most of the time they were scary ones, more like nightmares. But in the early part of September he had a good dream.

> *Baxter rode up to him on a horse. The same horse, 'Susan's Gift,' that they had both bet on and won money at Los Alamitos. Baxter dismounted, walked over to him and said, "Meet me and friends in Halifax."*

He knew that Baxter planted this dream message in his head.

He is an amazing man. Halifax will be a great opportunity to meet him again - the man who changed my life.

He looked forward to the meeting and to discuss with Baxter the new directions that he set for himself.

***

Jefferson walked into Marie's office in Charity Cottage early in the morning, holding two cups of freshly brewed medium dark roast coffee. He sat down in front of Marie. He looked bewildered and remained strangely silent.

"Well are you going to speak to me and give me one of those coffees or do I have to wrestle you for it?" questioned Marie with a smile on her face.

Jefferson still didn't respond. He sat silent, deep in thought.

"The cat got your tongue?" Still no response from Jefferson.

There obviously is something going on in that thick head of yours," continued Marie in a more worried tone.

Jefferson stirred from his trance-like state.

"I had the strangest dream last night dat seemed more like reality than a dream. It was like a personal message - and it was from Baxter."

Marie knew about the meeting in Halifax. She had received email updates from Baxter since he had left Charity Cottage. But she couldn't share this information with anyone. Baxter had pressed this issue for cautionary purposes.

Until Jefferson had mentioned that he had a dream about Baxter, she was unsure that he had been invited. But she still had to make sure about Jefferson's dream.

"Tell me about the dream," she said.

"It's difficult for me to understand it, Miss Marie," said Jefferson, quickly reverting to his old talkative self.

"Baxter was walking slowly toward me from a long way back - out of da slums in da hood. As he gets closer and passes by each run-down house, da house and da hood change, become fixed up, clean, friendly and a welcome place with children smilin' and playing free in the street.

"Can you understand anything about dat, Miss Marie?"

"I think you know the message in the dream," said Marie. "Surely you do. Just look at the changes you see in our neighbourhood in the last year. People have been hired, family homes have been fixed up, local businesses have grown and people have moved back into the area. It has been like a touch of magic - people again taking pride in our community. Just like in your dream."

"You'se right, Miss Marie. I'd have to be plain blind and downright stupid not to notice the changes. Baxter had something to do with it. Am I right, Miss Marie?"

"First, finish telling me about your dream and I will try to answer your questions."

"Baxter comes closer and closer and with every step da hood gets brighter and brighter and more beautiful. Children are playin' everywhere and people are smilin' at one another again. The schools are full and da little ones are running around chasin' one another and playin' games."

Marie interrupted.

"It sounds like the way things are now. Remember the emptiness we faced a year ago."

"You'se right, Miss Marie. But I'm not sure how Baxter fits into it, 'cause the dream ends strange. He walks right up to me with a big smile on his face. He shakes my hand and hugs me at da same time and then he says something strange which I don't understand. He says, 'I want you to go to Halifax.' Dat's what he says, Miss Marie. I have never been to Halifax. Where is it? What does he mean by dat? It's a puzzle, Miss Marie, and then I wake up."

Jefferson still looked perplexed. "Miss Marie, I hope you can 'splain da dream to me 'cause it seems so real and I think Baxter is givin' me a message."

"I'm so glad to hear you mention Halifax. I needed to hear that from you. Baxter is a special person. We both know that and we were so blessed to have crossed paths with him. He has been in contact with me over the past while, and I give him all the credit for the tremendous changes that have occurred all around us. Without his support and advice all this would never have happened."

Marie became teary-eyed and wiped a tear from her cheek. "He has invited special and good people to join him in Halifax, Nova Scotia, in Canada. I don't know why he chose that place but he must have his reasons. You've been invited to go. Your invitation is that message he placed in your dream. That's the way he has been inviting special people that have come in contact with him."

Marie rose from her chair walked over to the window and stared at the children playing in the street.

"It's so good to hear the laughter of children again, don't you think?"

"Sure is, Miss Marie."

"You may not know it, but Leroy was also contacted by Baxter. Leroy told me and you know he has gone through a complete change and is no longer just another thug on the streets. He worked with the street gangs and the violence stopped. The drug trade has almost been completely wiped out, thanks to Leroy. Baxter totally changed him into a good man."

"And Jefferson, we are all going to Halifax. It's Baxter's plan."

***

Iron Tank pinned his opponent to the mat with his favourite finishing move - the 'boa constrictor' named after the snake. It took all his strength to hold 'Undertaker' down with his shoulders flat on the canvas for the required three count. The referee slapped 'One,' slapped 'Two,' held his count for four seconds - it seemed like a full minute to Iron Tank - before the final three count was slapped on the canvas mat.

Iron Tank let Undertaker up. The ref raised his hand in victory. The crowd roared. Tank reached across and shook Undertaker's hand. "Great match, Frank."

"You're still the best, Gary," said Undertaker. He held his shoulder. The boa constrictor move may have separated it.

Gary Brewer, a.k.a Iron Tank, never would've shaken his vanquished opponent's hand after a match - before the change. It felt natural now and it was the right thing to do... *we are all brethren - wrestlers*. Before the change in Oklahoma City, he would rather spit on a defeated opponent. But not now. He had respect for other wrestlers in his sport. Wrestling was the love of his life.

He ached when he woke up the next morning... head, arms, legs, torso...they all pained. They had been beaten on, twisted, pulled and contorted out of natural alignment. He liked the pain. He was alive, doing his thing. He looked at himself in the mirror. His forty-five-year-old body still retained a muscular appearance. It looked good.

How much longer can I keep doing this? I'm getting old.

The day after a match he would rest and let his body recover. A hot sauna, a steam and a massage helped the healing process.

His cell phone rang. It was his manager.

"Gary, great match last night. I arranged a three o'clock with Carlos. He wants to talk about a championship match with 'Grim Reaper'. The meeting is at the gym. Be there at three."

Gary loved the gym. He went early, around two o'clock. The smell of sweat was as aromatic to him as a red rose to a heart-stricken young girl making up with her boyfriend after a quarrel. His body still throbbed, even after the steam and massage, but his body's discomfort, faded when he walked up to the ring. It was home to him. Pain and life's troubles were left behind.

Congratulatory waves greeted him. Kids were allowed into the gym to watch the wrestler's workout. It had been his idea to increase the marketability of the sport to youth. They swarmed around him. He was their hero - the good guy. Their eager eyes and big smiles showed his popularity. They fired questions at him.

"The Undertaker is so much bigger than you. How'd you beat him so easily?"

"Can you show us the boa move?"

"Can you teach us?"

"Ho..aaah, ho...aaah, kids. I'll show you at next week's demonstration...and I will bring in the 'Terminator' to help show ya. You'll love him and he'll talk to you about wrestling."

The kids screeched.

Sailor Boy, an older, retired wrestler came up to Gary and pulled him aside.

"Gary, you're great with those kids. It was the best idea in years opening up the gym and giving them demonstrations. Gate receipts are way up...but you musta'heard... the dollars are not getting through to us wrestlers...especially the old retired ones like me. I'm one of the lucky ones. At least I got a job in the gym, as a janitor... But some of the other guys..."

Hurt showed in Sailor Boy's face. He had pride as a wrestler who helped build the sport. And now, all he did was push a broom around the gym floor.

"Don't worry, Jim...errr...Sailor Boy," said Gary. "I've got a meeting with the Federation today and I'm gonna' bring up the topic of the older, retired wrestlers."

Sailor Boy nodded. He didn't like being called by his real name. Everybody who knew him, called him Sailor Boy.

"We're gonna start at fifteen percent of gate receipts and work up from there," said Paul Conrad, his manager, as they walked into the gymnasium office.

Since the change, Gary took on a manager, although he didn't need one because he made all his own decisions. But it gave his old wrestling adversary a purpose after his career had ended. It had saved the old guy from the ravages of drugs and alcohol.

Gary nodded to him, but he had other priorities on his mind.

"The match with Grim Reaper will be the biggest championship match in years," said Carlos, the President of the Wrestlers Federation. "And we are heavily marketing it - at great expense. So let's come to terms."

"We want fifteen percent of gate..." started Conrad.

Gary cut him off. "You know what we talked about," he spoke directly to Carlos.

"How many times have I brought this up before? Pensions for the old, retired wrestlers, career counselling, job training, drug and alcohol rehabilitation and medical benefits. It's time - and it has to get done."

Carlos slammed his fist on the table in anger. He ruled the roost and was not going to be forced. "Those worthless old wrestlers are finished. They had their day in the sun and they're not gonna leech off this Federation as long as I'm running it."

Gary heard this many times before from Carlos, the fat, uncompromising dictator - rich from the spoils of the Federation.

"I'm finished with you and your Federation." Gary got up from his seat, grabbed his manager by the arm and said, "Let's go. The air in here stinks."

"You're obligated, contractually to the match with the Reaper," shouted Carlos as Gary slammed the door behind. "And after that I'll make sure you never wrestle again."

Paul Conrad had a wide-eyed look of disbelief on his face at what had just happened. He didn't know what to say. He didn't have to say anything. Gary knew.

"Paul." Gary said, "This was inevitable and I hope you're with me."

"I owe everything to you. Where you go, I go," said Paul.

Gary hugged him. "Good."

"I'm going to set up my own Federation," said Gary.

"I'm going to help the old retired wrestlers with job training, rehabilitation, medical benefits and a pension."

"The other wrestlers are on my side and will back me."

"I'm going to have a big fight on my hands. Carlos has a crime syndicate behind him. And he got loads of money."

"You know I never backed down from a fight in my life. But I think I just stepped into the biggest one I will ever face."

It was a week before the title match with Grim Reaper when Gary Brewer had the dream. It became imprinted deep in his mind as it unfolded.

It was Madison Square Gardens on a hot, steamy night in front of a large crowd of enthusiastic wrestling fans who had gathered for the championship match.

The ring announcer stepped up to the microphone at the ring's center. He was not your typical announcer dressed in a flashy tuxedo as was the norm for a championship match for a televised audience. He wore a full-length white robe and had the comparable facial features to Moses with the radiant white hair and beard.

"Attention world," the Moses-look-alike announcer shouted in a deep voice to the crowd of faceless fans. "Tonight's match determines the life direction of Gary Brewer. In the red corner we have the champion, Iron Tank and in the blue corner we have 'Hope for his future'

Gary looked over and saw no opponent in the opposite corner of the ring. He stood there bewildered, not understanding what was happening. Suddenly from out of the many in the faceless crowd sprang a familiar figure who entered the ring and stood in the center. It was the young stranger called 'Hope' who had defeated him in Oklahoma City in the Tough Guy Competition. Almost as quickly as Hope appeared in the ring, many previously faceless fans in the crowd also entered the ring and stood behind Hope. They were ordinary people of all ages and races. They extended their arms in a gesture of a warm embrace.

"Hello Gary," said Hope. "My real name is Baxter McPherson and I am welcoming you to join our group."

He turned around and gestured to the friendly group of people behind him.

"We all have a shared purpose, that of kindness to others and we want you to join us. Come to St. Mary's University in Halifax, Nova Scotia in Canada in the last week of September and set your life's course in the direction to benefit others. We'll give you the means to accomplish your goals."

Baxter walked over and shook Gary Brewer's hand.

Gary woke up. The dream was as realistic as any live activity he had experienced.

He lay in bed longer than normal that morning and thought about the dream's message. Since his match with Hope in Oklahoma, he'd been left with the impression that Hope was a special person. No normal man could have defeated him that easily in the ring and at the same time change his life. He wanted to meet him again and he recognized the dream revealed a message he couldn't turn down.

He would travel to Halifax.

***

Calvin McInnis knocked on John Shultz's campus office door a month after the disastrous amphitheatre meeting where Baxter had met Harvard's most distinguished professors.

"John," he started out. "You have no idea how badly I feel for the way I reacted to your special friend, Baxter. He was right all along about my research. I can't believe how much of an idiot I was, with my big bloated ego and all."

Shultz knew his friend was a proud man and had been wrong, but he was right to admit it.

He laughed. "Ya...you were a bit of an a-hole that day... but now I understand you believed Baxter shouldn't have told everybody about Meredith's cancer. You're my friend Calvin - overly arrogant at times I admit, but brilliant and with a heart of gold. That's what I love about ya."

"Our friendship is too strong to be busted by my arrogance," said Calvin. "I didn't give that young man a chance. And I tested his theory about my research. God Damn it, he was right... I owe him a lot. It would've cost me months of work and wasted research money if I continued down that wrong path. He must be brilliant to have picked up on my research so quickly."

"You don't know the half of it. He is amazing and I am fortunate to call him a close friend," said Shultz. "He is gone now, but he promised to get in touch with me...and he will."

"If there is any way I can make amends to him, I would welcome the chance...and just to talk to him again. Maybe, with another opportunity, I could listen and shut my big mouth. John you have to promise me that I'll meet Baxter again."

Dr. John Shultz felt the buzz of the cell phone going off in the inside pocket of his sports jacket. He carried Baxter's cell with him constantly. He rather enjoyed the tactile tingling sensation of the vibrating cell phone against his burly chest. It beat the noisy and somewhat intrusive distraction of a cell phone ring when others were close by.

Shultz hadn't heard from Baxter in a while. Baxter's calls to him had been more than welcome. They had become life-long friends and Baxter kept him abreast of his travels around the country and the calls reassured Shultz that he was safe and still thinking of him. But it did irritate him that Baxter didn't tell him about his upcoming plans, and that caused the good doctor much chagrin.

Shultz pulled the cell out of his pocket and tried not to attract the attention of the students in his freshman biology class. It was a strict policy not to allow cell phones in his class during a lecture. And to prove he meant business, Shultz deducted two percent of final class marks if a student violated the policy. But he was the professor and as distasteful as it was for him to violate his own policy, he had to take this call.

He excused himself from the lecture hall and stepped into an adjacent room He answered the cell and exclaimed, "Baxter is that you?"

A muffled voice replied.

"Yes John, it's me and it's so nice to hear your pleasant voice again. How are you, my old friend?"

"Are you okay? Why didn't you call? Where have you been?" Shultz couldn't control himself and threw out the flurry of questions in rapid succession. "It's been a long time since I last heard from you - since you called about Gerald Turner. Are you in trouble?"

"Slow down, John," responded Baxter. "Everything's fine with me. I had a harrowing experience recently that prevented me from calling you. But everything's fine now. I will tell you about it when we get together - soon."

Shultz calmed down.

"There is something more that you want to say to me," Shultz blurted out. "Thus the phone call. Am I right?"

"Yes you're right. I want you to come to St. Mary's University in Halifax, the last week of September. I'm starting something very big and I want you on my team."

Shultz felt proud. He could not restrain his inquisitive nature.

"Tell me more about it and how I can help. Of course you can count on me and I will come to Halifax, for sure. But what is it, Baxter?"

"I can't tell you now, but you will be pleased. I'm sure. You will find out shortly. And one more thing, before we hang up, please invite any of your esteemed colleagues I met that day in the amphitheatre. They're welcome to come along with you. I trust your judgement and there are good men in that group, despite that disastrous meeting with them."

"I will, Bax."

"I have to go now," finished Baxter. "I look forward to seeing you shortly in Halifax."

Professor John Shultz placed the cell phone back in his coat pocket. He had a pleasant smile on his face when he walked back to finish his lecture. He thought about Professor Calvin McInnis. He would invite him to come to Halifax.

***

The phone rang, just as John Shultz stepped out of the shower, dripping wet. *Goddam...it's a fact of life that the phone always rings when you're in the shower.*

He looked at the call display. It was Linda. He answered it in his birthday suit while he dried himself with a towel.

"Professor, it's Linda. How are you?"

"Good. And you?"

"A little heartsick about Baxter. I'm sorry, but I have to talk to you about him...again... You have common sense. I can't talk to my girlfriends about Baxter...they don't have any common sense."

She attempted a laugh between stifled sobs.

"Linda, I understand that you're upset. How can I help?"

"I'm troubled." Her voice cracked with emotion.

"You and Baxter had such a close relationship. Maybe you can help me understand. I love him and he left me so abruptly...with so little explanation...and it has been so long without so much as a phone call or a letter. I'm doubting my understanding of what we had." Her voice cracked even more. "I'm so sorry to burden you now. But there is an added complication in my life."

"Go on, I'm listening. Does it have anything to do with Baxter?"

"Sort of...in a way. You see my old boyfriend, John, has come back into my life. And I need someone to be close to, to be with, and Baxter's not here anymore."

"I think I understand your situation, Linda. John or Baxter - and Baxter's not here. I wish I could give you good advice but I don't think I can. It's not my place. You know how much I think of Baxter. I don't know your old boyfriend...but he's here for you now. All I can tell you is that Baxter had his reasons and I don't know what they are, for leaving. I'm sorry."

"John asked me to marry him. I don't know what to do."

For the second time...and he left me at the altar the first time... I don't know whether I can trust him. I have such strong feelings for Baxter. If he were here, we could talk and I could see if I've been living a fantasy, hoping he'd return...

"I'm sorry I put you in this position, Professor. I guess I wanted someone else to make up my mind for me, but now I know what I have to do. I guess I just needed someone to talk to."

"I can't give you an answer, my Dear…but you can always talk to me."

"Thanks, Professor. I'll talk to you soon."

She thought about John and what he said the day he proposed…for the second time.

"Linda, I am in love with you. After all, it's you I thought of every time I had sex with other women. That's what love is, isn't it?"

How can this man be so smart and say something so stupid to me. That has to be the worst romantic line I've ever heard. She laughed to herself.

I can't marry a man who thinks like that. Sometimes I don't know what to do. Sometimes I know exactly what I have to do…but I just can't decide what to do with my life. I'm a basket case…and I told John I would let him know by graduation. He graduates tomorrow.

It was a restless night for her. Just before daybreak she fell into a deep sleep.

She had a dream.

It was a surreal dream unlike any she had before - as if it were a living, active experience - in real time. She tossed and turned in her bed in the dream state as her emotions aligned with the movement of her body in the dream.

> *She was walking down a lonely, tree-lined country road. It was a cool autumn evening in Massachusetts and the light of the autumn moon shone brightly on the pebbled roadway and reflected a glimmering, silvery pathway along the full length of the road. It had the look of a magic carpet that reflected twinkling stars.*
>
> *Linda stopped and looked at the star-lined twinkling roadway in amazement. It was truly beautiful. Far off in*

the distance she noticed a solitary figure on the roadway's horizon. It moved slowly toward her. It stopped when it saw her standing in the middle of the road so far off in the distance. It was a man dressed in shining silver armour riding a magnificent white steed.

Linda couldn't believe her eyes. She stood motionless. To her the figure far off in the distance resembled the proverbial white knight on a white horse from the medieval fairy tales of her youth. The white knight recognized her and galloped toward her.

Hooves struck silvery pebbles with each gallop and created an explosion of sparkling fire with each contact on stone. It was magical and Linda froze on the spot, absorbed with the spectacle.

The magnificent white knight slowed his steed as he approached her. The steed trotted slowly toward Linda and stopped within snorting distance from her.

No one moved.

The white knight, steed and lonely lady faced each other in a stare frozen in the moment. The silhouetted figures of the three shimmered through the continuous sparkling of the silvery-lined roadway pebbles.

"Who are you?" she asked.

The white knight reached back and raised his face shield. It was Baxter. He spoke. "I'm the man who loves you."

He dismounted from his rock-steady steed, took off his helmet and walked forward until he was close enough to take her hand in his.

Linda stared into the eyes of her true love. She couldn't move. Tears swelled in her eyes and rolled down her cheeks.

"Where have you been and why did you not contact me?" She stammered as she wiped tears from her eyes.

Baxter responded with humility.

"You are the love of my life, Linda, and as much as I constantly thought of you, it was not possible for me to contact you till now. It would've put you and others I care about in grave danger. You have to believe me and believe in the message of this dream. I want you to contact Professor Shultz and accompany him in a trip to Nova Scotia where all will be revealed and where we can begin to pursue the rest of our lives together."

He leaned over, constrained by his heavy bodyarmour, and kissed her.

Linda woke up.

The next day she called John and then Professor Shultz.

CHAPTER TWENTY-ONE

Butterflies

The leaves in Halifax had turned to their majestic autumn colours. It was late September in the Halifax Public Gardens and Baxter strolled through the flowered grounds, unnoticed. He marveled at Mother Nature who rolled one season into another, bringing different palates of colourful bounty, year after year as if it set the seasonal changes to a template. His thoughts turned to current matters at hand. Within the next few days the Saint Mary's University campus would make history and turn into the launch pad for his start-up organization.

Dream messages had been implanted into the minds of many people he wanted to join his organization. The main body would be the Board of Directors; those men and women would be the first to arrive in Halifax and confirm the meeting agenda for a larger group.

Various thoughts raced through Baxter's mind when he poured over the items he wanted to address in the meetings. But foremost on his mind, as he continued to stroll throughout the winding pathways of the Gardens, was how he could make up for the hurt he had inflicted on the woman he loved and whom he had forsaken for so long.

It was noon in Halifax and Baxter sat down in the front row of the garden bleacher seats adjacent to the bandstand. He laughed to himself as he watched children race around in front of the bandstand chasing after the almost-tame pigeons. The youngsters squealed with delight while their mothers frantically ran after their energetic offspring to settle them down. *It looked like so much fun that maybe I should join in with the little ones.*

He saw Linda and Professor Shultz approach the bandstand from a distance. His heart jumped.

Linda... Good ol' Shultzy... I knew I could rely on him to bring her here unannounced.

He felt his mouth go dry and a wave of nervousness crept into his heart. Doubt overcame him.

God...I still have common human frailties... I know she loves me...but I'm nervous.

Linda and Shultz stopped in front of the bandstand, close to the statue of Diana, the Roman Goddess of the Hunt. Linda didn't notice the solitary man who sat behind her in the front bleacher seat. Shultz tapped her on the shoulder and whispered in her ear. "Turn around."

She turned and saw a dear and very familiar figure rise from the seat and step toward her. Linda's jaw dropped, revealing her surprise. She squealed and ran into Baxter's outstretched arms. They kissed in a long embrace and at his touch Linda became aware of the mystery and many reasons behind his long disappearance. She knew that he loved her and her love was returned tenfold.

"Let the inaugural meeting come to order." Doug Bannister slammed a gavel on the top of the desk with a heavy thud.

"You have all been chosen by Baxter to constitute the Board of Directors of our, at this point, unnamed organization. Many of you don't know each other. So the first order of business will be introductions. All of you have had a once-in-a-lifetime real experience with Baxter who has determined that your values represent the core values of our new organization. It's our hope and our goal to spread these values throughout our communities and throughout our lands. Starting with Marie here sitting next to me, please introduce yourself to our group and tell the others your story, how you met Baxter and your past and present activities."

Marie stood up.

"Hello everyone. My name is Marie Underwood and I take great pride that myself, and Leroy and Jefferson here, have been asked by Baxter to join this group. I'll try to keep it short because there are a lot of people here. We were lucky because Baxter randomly stumbled into our area and befriended Jefferson. We come from a formerly run-down area of Chicago where I ran a hostel. I say formerly, because since we met Baxter, the location has been transformed into a safe, thriving and prosperous neighbourhood from an area of poverty, drug addiction and gang-related activities...and I hope to use the experiences with my hostel - which by the way we call Charity Cottage - as a model for other locations with similar problems. And in a nutshell, that's our story."

Marie sat down and a loud round of applause followed.

One by one each of the people around the table introduced themselves and expounded on how meeting Baxter had changed their life and the lives of others for the better.

Something was happening in the room; a feeling developed - a commonality among like-minded people. Cora picked up on it and she leaned over to Gerald Turner.

"I think I know what's going on here," she said.

"There's a movement evolving here among us all... and it's growing. It's about goodness and helping people."

"I feel it too," said Turner.

"Me too," interjected Jefferson.

"It's in us all and it's powerful," said Gary Brewer.

"I think that's what this meeting is all about," said Leroy. "To set up an organization to promote our values."

They had become aware.

Baxter sat next to Doug Bannister and had not uttered a word. He acknowledged with a wide smile and a nod the praise that each person in turn bestowed upon him. His unassuming nature was obvious, visible in the pinkish shade of humility that began to colour his face. He accepted the kind words from the many friends he had encountered and influenced in his brief life.

They rose together at the end of the introductions and looked toward Baxter. They clapped in loud applause. He acknowledged the honour and the love that his friends had bestowed upon him.

"I thank you all, my friends," said Baxter as the group applause died down.

"I don't think I have to tell you why I brought you all together today. I believe you all feel it. I know I do and it must grow through each and every one of us and spread throughout our neighbourhoods, communities and lands. We have as our group goal to search out and support good, moral, righteous people and projects. You will be my advisory panel to spread our message of goodwill to all. But it won't be an easy task because, as sure as night follows day, darkness, hatred, evil, greed, corruption and jealousy do exist in our world and will be strong opponents to our movement. The challenges will appear in many forms. We must always be vigilant to the approach of evil. Each and every one of us must become a gate keeper to recognize and prevent these counter-energies from growing in our midst."

They rose again and applauded. Baxter motioned them back into their seats.

"Now the next order of business is to choose an appropriate name for our organization. Doug and I have gone over the many names submitted at the Chicago conference just before the CIA interrupted me. It was amazing that a large percentage of like-minded people chose 'Butterflies' as a symbol for our organization. This wondrous creature of nature represents the transformation from a relatively ugly caterpillar to a beautiful, graceful, elegant creature. Our organization will represent the change to a better society...just like the butterfly transforms itself. The butterfly flutters when it flies. It was suggested by one of the Chicago attendants that we use a fluttering hand movement symbol in an acknowledgement gesture when meeting others and fellow butterflies. As funny as it may seem, I like the idea."

Baxter mimicked a fluttering hand movement signal to the Board. They laughed and fluttered back in return.

"It will be the goal of our organization to give group support to as many good people as possible everywhere around us for the greater good of society. It is with the application of that common objective in mind that the beautiful butterfly will come to symbolize that transformation.

"All in favour of naming our group, the Butterfly Organization raise hands."

All hands went up.

"Approved."

The noise of the crowd sounded like a low roar that resonated throughout the auditorium. Two hundred people talked over one another, banged on desks and opened fold-out chairs while they waited for direction from the group assembled on the stage. Baxter stepped to the podium with the Board of Directors sitting behind him. He glanced down and smiled at his mother who sat in the front row directly in front of the stage. He remembered his mother's words of wisdom in his twelfth year when he'd asked her why he couldn't bring out the powers of suspension when he wanted.

"Baxter, you weren't put on earth to score ten goals in a hockey game."

He thought about those profound words. His family was there, including his father, brothers and sisters. His sister Joanne wasn't with them and her absence bothered him.

He had to talk to his mother about her after the meeting.

Baxter snapped back to the present when he heard Doug Bannister cough in the background. It was a signal that he lingered too long at the podium. Baxter looked out over the crowd. He recognized faces from the Chicago conference so many months back, before the terrible day on the streets of the Windy City. He opened up his great mind and intuitively scanned thoughts in the audience to sense their general mood. There were no malevolent or malicious thoughts present in the group's mind set. That pleased him.

My team has done a great job of assembling good people. But many of them are confused.

He tapped on the podium to quiet the restless crowd.

"Welcome to St. Mary's. You have so many questions for me. I will answer them in turn, but for now you have to realize that you are all good people who have been chosen by my team to spread the core values of our newly formed organization, the Butterfly Organization."

Baxter raised his arms in front of him in a gathering gesture. "You are all Butterflies."

He fluttered his hand.

In a collective moment of harmony the congregation saluted those close by with the new Butterfly salute.

He concluded with a short set of announcements.

"I have to make a few administrative points. You will now break into smaller sets of groups as outlined in the package kits you received. We have arranged that each group will represent a region, a similar location. In each group will be a collection of individuals from different backgrounds, ethnicities, educations, religions, age and sex. You will develop your own network and methods to identify and bring other like-minded people into our fold. You will name and elect a president to represent your group, who will in turn report to the Butterfly Board of Directors. Board members are on stage behind me."

He pointed to them.

"Get to know each other over the next two days. Have some fun. And a final thing. Financial training courses that were started in Chicago will continue and the full support of the Butterfly Organization will stand behind you. May goodness fill your hearts."

The Board of Directors, led by Doug Bannister, rose and applauded. The congregation also rose and joined in the loud applause.

Butterfly Org. was born.

"**Mom, you are troubled,**" said Baxter. He released her from a hug.

"I don't have to read your mind to know that. It shows on your face. It's about Joanne isn't it? She's not here."

"It's so good to see you, Bax. It's been too long. And you're doing so much good. We're so proud of you."

Tears welled in her eyes. "Yes, it's Joanne. She just ran away...left home. We don't know where she is."

"Mom, don't worry, I will find her."

"I know you will and I want you to protect her. She's special too. You know that."

He bookmarked a note in his mind to search out his missing sister.

***

Kathy Livingston stormed out of her principal's office for the last time. *My career is finished.*

Twenty-five years of teaching swirled down the drain when she slammed the door behind her. She glanced behind her as she walked away.

Maybe he'll change his mind and run after me and apologize... Not bloody likely...asshole!... At least I gave him a piece of my mind.

She glared down at the contract release notice she still held crumpled in her hand. She read the first two sentences again.

'It is with great regret that the Kansas City Board of Education releases you from Contract XS345 for conduct unbecoming a member of our Teachers Association.'

She couldn't read any further. She tore the letter up and tossed it in a nearby trash can.

God, I can't believe I'm fired... Conduct unbecoming!.. What a bunch of horseshit. They're the most inept and inflexible of associations in the world.

Her good friend and teaching associate was close by, in the office just down the hall. Kathy was steamed and had to tell herself to calm down.

"Oh, oh," said Sylvia her friend, when Kathy burst into her office without so much as a knock. "I can see by the look on your face that things didn't go so well with Robertson. Is that smoke coming out of your ears?"

Sylvia had a wicked sense of humour, but this wasn't the time for it.

"Not funny," said Kathy bitterly.

"You know what I said countless times. That stupid Board of Education keeps putting stumbling block after stumbling block in my way. How the hell can I ever reach those poor kids and prepare them for what's out there? Those Goddam rules, guidelines and policies the Board inflicts on us don't give the kids a chance to learn about the real world. It's hopeless... and they just won't listen. Most of the kids don't even know what a cheque is...and they want me to teach them history...stupid! You have to learn to walk before you can run."

"Kat, I've heard this from you so many times before. You're so stubborn and strong-willed," said Sylvia. "I know you're right. But you can't fight City Hall. They have all the power and you have none."

"Well I have a voice and I'm taking it to the press or to anyone who'll listen. Those poor kids are falling through the cracks...broken homes...parents who don't give a damn, except where their next drink or next fix is coming from....and the stupid Board wants me to teach them stuff they'll have no use for. They'll just drop out or get in gangs and get shot to death like poor little Johnny Stewart."

"Settle down or you'll get fired," said Sylvia.

"Too late. Robertson just canned me. Me and my big mouth. But you know I couldn't stay quiet and just accept my paycheque every month. It's not right and it's not me."

"Well, when there's no cheque in the mail next month, you might have second thoughts," said Sylvia.

"I've got a good mind to set up my own educational institution... just for those down and out kids and do things right. Give them a chance out there. Go to their homes if need be if they can't or won't come to school. Teach them to survive with life skills, not algebra or history...not yet."

Kathy gazed at her still-attractive features in the mirror. Her slim, curvaceous figure was still with her...*but for how long?* She had begun to feel the pressures brought on by her untimely dismissal, the loss of her teaching career and not receiving a regular paycheque.

I can still turn a few heads, but I'm losing weight...maybe too much... Most women are worried about getting too fat...and I'm worried about getting too skinny.

She laughed to herself. She also worried about the mild eating disorder she had developed - but that wasn't her main worry.

For one of the few times in her life, she didn't know what to do. She had to inform her son and daughter of her changed circumstances and she dreaded it.

They'll worry about me and I don't want them to do that. Good young kids on their own worrying about their mother... What the hell did I get myself into?

She smiled thinking about her kids - young adults now. They were used to her constant battles and had warned her about fighting the system. *God...maybe they were right...*and she worried about her diminishing bank account. Money was never the reason behind her career or life decisions. It had always been about teaching.

Now I have neither...money or a career.

Waves of doubt overcame her one morning as she sat on her balcony sipping a steaming cup of tea. Thoughts swirled in her head about how she was going to support herself and what she was going to do. The phone rang and for a moment it startled her out of her thoughts of self-pity. As she reached for the phone, hot tea spilled on her lap.

"Oh hell," she exclaimed as she picked up the phone.

"Good morning, Ms. Livingston," proclaimed a pleasant voice on the other end.

"My name is Ted Doherty and I represent the Butterfly Organization. One of our members heard about your release from the Kansas City Board of Education and we want to help you re-establish yourself. We will gladly support you in any way we can to help young, underprivileged children. We should meet and have a talk.

She paused for a moment and never being one lost for words, shot back with a question.

"What the hell is the Butterfly Organization and what are you trying to sell me? Are you a telemarketer? Is this a crank call?"

***

Greg Thorton would hear the roar of the shotgun blast over and over in his mind every time he lay down to sleep at night. It bounced from one side of his brain to the other and it did not relent. He couldn't escape this awful dream. He'd long since decided it was not a dream. It was his personal nightmare...a curse that he had to live with for the rest of his life.

It had been ten years since that dreadful night in Baltimore when, at eighteen years of age, young Greg Thorton couldn't take it anymore. His alcoholic, brutally vicious father had just come home from the tavern, drunk as usual. In the nightmare, Greg could still hear him stumble over the kitchen chairs in his drunken stupor and curse.

"Woman, make me supper."

His beloved, sweet mother, who had never harmed a person in her life, was in a hopeless situation. She had been beaten within an inch of her life, many times. She could not escape. She would take the beatings to protect her children as much as she could.

The nightmare was always the same.

A ten-year-old little boy yelling at his drunken father to stop beating his Mom and getting slapped in return. The nightmare scene repeated. A twelve-year-old boy screamed for his drunken dad to stop and then hit viciously again. A sixteen year-old boy tackled his father and was punched to the ground. The boy screamed, 'I'll kill you! I'll kill you if you don't stop.'

At eighteen he walked to the gun rack as the yells, screams and cries from the kitchen echoed throughout the household. Without so much as a second thought, he loaded the shotgun and walked into the kitchen and aimed it at his father. He heard his bloodied and beaten mother weakly scream when she saw him enter the kitchen with the shotgun.

"Greg no! No!"

Bright, red blood splattered throughout the kitchen and Greg woke up in a deep sweat.

Prison was rough. He fought for every inch of space and independence that could be mustered in the captive environment. There were evil, malicious men in prison who deserved to be there. The stories they told only confirmed the darkness that lurked in their hearts and souls.

Greg also met good men in prison. They made mistakes in life and paid for it. They deserved their imprisonment and only wanted to be given a second chance - to give something positive back to society. Greg saw himself as one of the good ones and he had paid dearly for taking his father's life.

After ten years of incarceration he was released from prison. The transition from prisoner to a free man was difficult for him. He had no job prospects or skills to enable him to function normally in free society. Government programs were available for recently released prisoners. He found out how useless they were when he walked into one of their offices.

"We can put you into the halfway house program," said the portly civil servant who flipped through his file. He didn't even lift his head to talk directly to Greg.

"I've talked to people who have been in that program," said Greg. "It doesn't work. The people running the program don't give a damn about former prisoners. It's all rules and procedures to them. And most of the former prisoners end up alcoholics, addicts, suicidal or return to crime."

"Well what do you expect from criminals," said the civil servant. "If they can't cut it on the outside and won't follow our rules, then they'll fail."

God...this simple silly servant has absolutely no empathy... Nothing but disdain and suspicion...probably for all of us.

He walked out of the office that day with little hope for his future.

He stopped at a Starbucks coffee shop nearby. He didn't feel good. No friends or family on the outside. His mother had died and he had no prospects for the future.

An elderly man sat down beside him. He wore a funny tee shirt with a brightly coloured butterfly on it. They talked... that is Greg talked... poured out his heart about helping other good men and former inmates get second chances. That's all they wanted and he told the old man how discouraged he was. Second chances, he'd learned, weren't available to them. The butterfly man listened.

Greg laughed when the stranger left and fluttered his hand to him instead of giving a normal handshake.

There sure are weird people on the outside.

Three days later two gentlemen, who wore the same odd butterfly tee shirts, knocked on his door.

***

Frankie MacDonald was in trouble when he saw his worst nightmare approach him in the school courtyard. He quickened his pace to avoid the inevitable confrontation with the school bullies.

"I am in deep shit now," he said out loud while he ran as fast as his skinny, little legs would carry him. But it was a futile attempt to outdistance the three older, bigger and stronger boys.

The three bullies recognized their prey in flight mode and shouted. "There goes that skinny, little prick. Get him."

They took off running. It was a footrace for Frankie to get safely to the school main entrance where most of the staff entered for their workday. The bullies would not confront him in front of the teachers. They'd try to grab him and pull him out of the teacher's line of sight before he made it to the door.

It was a race that Frankie could not win. He was weaker and slower than the other boys and was further restricted by the weight of his books and laptop computer that he carried in his backpack. The bullies were footloose without backpacks or laptops. It was a gallant effort by Frankie. He had never run so fast.

The outcome of the footrace came to its inevitable conclusion when the fastest of the three bullies grabbed him from behind by his loosely flying backpack buckle strap. They both went flying to the hard concrete and rolled into a row of thorn bushes.

The other two were on him in a flash.

"You gave us a little trouble catching you today, Frankie. You're getting faster. Have you been working out?" asked the lead bully.

He delivered a hard, sharp punch to Frankie's midriff. It buckled Frankie over and left him gasping for breath.

"You owe us ten more dollars this week because you made us sweat running after you. Now where is our money and what are we having for lunch today?"

Two of the bullies walloped him with fists and feet. The other one rifled through his backpack and threw his books and laptop to the ground. He found Frankie's wallet and took the twenty dollar bill that his mother had given him for his daily school allowance.

They left Frankie beaten, bloodied, bruised and humiliated in the thorn bushes. They shouted back.

"Next time don't run and we may take it easy on you."

They laughed and sauntered down the street looking for more targets.

"**We have to stand up** for ourselves," said Frankie, the next day at the computer club meeting. "Enough is enough. Just look at me with two black eyes, swollen lips and a broken laptop. This will happen to all of us every day unless we stand up together against them. We have to fight back."

"All the school does is post warm and fuzzy messages against bullying on bulletin boards, and they don't work because the bullies just keep bullying," said Jimmy. He was Frankie's best friend and was also a target for the bullies, maybe because he was a nerdy-looking geek.

"And a bully gets a three-day suspension and three days later he's back in class. And there aren't enough teachers to monitor the playgrounds and all the hallways. So what can we do to help ourselves?" said Karen O'Driscoll from the back of the room.

"All our parents do is have meetings with school teachers…and nothing happens. The school's hands are tied… they say. They got no control over off-school activities," said Frankie.

Karen spoke up. "It's not only the boys who are bullied. Girls are mean and vicious and their bullying is more subtle than the boys. They use Facebook and ruin the lives of girls they're jealous of. They hurt other girls in different ways and maybe more than what just happened to you, Frankie."

They turned and faced Karen. She seldom spoke at any of the meetings and had joined the club because of her newly formed crush on Frankie.

"Karen is right. We have to do something together to stop bullying in all its forms in our school," returned Frankie.

"Something that stands out," said Karen. "Why don't we all wear bright pink tee shirts with a slogan saying 'Stop Bullying Now!' and pass them out to everyone who supports us. We could do some marches. It should catch on with kids with another slogan on the back, like 'Kids Helping Kids.'"

"Fantastic. I like it," said Frankie. "We might even be able to get some television coverage of pink-shirted kids doing a march against bullying. My neighbour is a TV reporter and I'll talk to him about giving us a spot on the evening news."

"I love the idea and then maybe we can get kids wearing pink t-shirts to monitor the playgrounds and hallways…with a whistle…they could blow if they see someone being bullied. We can even monitor Facebook for bully attacks. I think this will really grow," said Karen.

"Now all we need is some money for the shirts. Maybe a thousand dollars," said Jimmy. "But that's a lot of money. How can we raise it?"

"I think I know where we may be able to get the money and maybe as much as we need," said Karen. "My dad keeps talking about a group of people he heard about that help others in need. They call themselves the Butterflies."

"The Butterflies!" said Jimmy.

They all laughed.

Frankie still giggled and with half a smile out of his swollen lips, said, "That's a pretty silly name for a bunch of adults."

***

"**Barbara, how can** you say that about your country?" queried Lou Leblanc to his sister. "You were born in America and it gave you so much."

"I'm not denying that," she replied. "I have so many friends and family I love in Iowa. But I love Canada and Toronto. It's my home now…and I hate the American health care system. You know I do."

"We are not having this argument again, are we?" asked Lou.

"Damn rights we are. It's so unfair to so many people, especially the low income people compared to the rich."

She had that look in her eye. She wasn't finished with her brother yet.

"Let me tell you a story about the rich girl, the poor girl and the American health care system. The rich girl talked about how great it was with the best doctors and care in the world. And the poor girl says 'Sure, if you got nine hundred dollars a month for the premiums. For my family, it comes down to a choice - food or health care - and just pray we don't get sick.'"

"And the HMOs are only interested in their bottom lines. If you have money, you get care," said Barbara.

She hammered home her arguments about the American health care system every time her brother came up from Iowa to visit. It was one of the never-ending topics of discussion. She was stubborn, a straight shooter and always spoke her mind. Lou loved that about his sister.

He also loved Canada - especially the anonymity - where he was not stopped on the street like in Des Moines, asked questions, berated, yelled at and even congratulated.

Ahhh...such is the life of a politician.

His visits to his sister gave him a lot to think about. Another perspective in a different country, but in so many ways a country similar to home. He needed that perspective...just to get away and think...away from the powerful pressure groups that tried to influence his decisions in Iowa in favour of their views. It gave him a break to sort out all the issues he faced and struggled with as an elected representative of the people.

But Barbara has a point. What is it she says all the time? Health care should be a basic human right for everyone.

He had valued his older sister's advice since childhood. She had become the head of the family since a car crash claimed their parent's lives. Her wise counsel kept the family together during those trying times. But her views ran opposite to his political party's health care policy and the debate that raged across America on the passage of the President's Health Care Reform Bill.

She wants some form of total socialized medical care for America...my party differs.

Steve Scanlon burst into Lou's office and clamoured. "You know I don't like your trips to Canada. It's not good for your political career and I know that your Canadianized sister tries to influence you."

"Well, she's my big sister and I still value her advice. But it doesn't mean I'll take it," replied Lou. "I just need to get away sometimes and clear my mind."

Steve threw a handful of papers on his desk.

"Well the numbers aren't pretty. We're down again in the polls and we're falling fast."

"That bad, eh?" said Lou. He laughed to himself about 'eh' in his speech.

Maybe I am spending too much time in Canada.

"I hate to see you lose. You're such a good man and Iowa needs you," said Steve. "But your opponents are bombarding the airways with their one-sided ad campaigns...and it's working. They got the money and the HMOs behind them. We don't."

He walked in front of Lou and stopped for a second...deep in thought.

"We need to get in touch with the Butterflies."

"What the hell are you jabbering about?" returned Lou.

"I've heard good reports about this start-up organization called the Butterflies. They're doing great things throughout the county and as far as I know further afield as well. They're becoming very popular and if we don't grab them and get them on our side, we'll lose them to our opponents."

Lou trusted his advice. Steve has been Lou's political advisor for years and had spearheaded his success in politics.

"Yes I've heard of them too. So I'll take your word on this. Get in touch with them then," replied Lou. "If you believe they will help, set up a meeting."

***

"**The values of goodness** and righteousness are roaring across North America like wildfire!" said Doug Bannister from the podium.

"You out there…all you Butterflies. You have a hand in it. I welcome you all to the third annual United States Conference of the Butterfly Organization."

He stood back from the podium and fluttered the butterfly salute to the large crowd directly in front of him. They responded with a wave of flutters in return and then broke into a thunderous applause that shook the building.

"Welcome to Boston, Butterflies."

The cheers rose higher.

"Street after street, neighbourhood after neighbourhood, community after community and state after state have embraced our goals and values. We have changed the moral fibre of America…and for the better."

The decibel level of applause and voices rose to new heights in crescendo fashion.

"I'm not saying this just to blow our own horn," said Doug. He raised his voice over the noise of the crowd. "Social statistics from every government agency across America have shown improvement since the inception of the Butterflies. Theft is down, murder is down, and crime is down everywhere. And household incomes are up, employment is up. Best of all happiness is up. I know you can't measure happiness...but I'm sure, it's way up too."

Thunderous applause again. Doug settled himself down.

"Butterfly income is in great shape...from profitable transactions in the financial markets and from generous gifts from people and organizations that believe in our cause. Just check out your copy of the financial statements."

"The Butterfly Organization is a resounding success. Everything is positively glowing."

Doug Bannister glowed too.

Baxter sat behind Doug. He didn't have the same glow that Doug exuded. He seemed disturbed, both at the level of exuberance in the crowd and from concerns that milled about in his head, even as regional representatives took turns on the stage and outlined the numerous projects, causes and people helped in their districts.

This is what the Butterflies are about, isn't it?

For Baxter, something was pushing them in a new direction, and he wasn't sure it was for the best.

That night he talked with his wife Linda and Shultz about his concerns.

"I see the slow but inevitable politicization of the Butterflies," he said to Shultz. "Political parties are lining up to jump on our band wagon. They notice our influence in their jurisdictions and are taking credit for these changes. They want our endorsement for their own political well-being."

"But is that a bad thing," asked Linda. "If they are supporting our values?"

"It remains to be seen," said Baxter. "You all saw how it troubled the Iowa Butterflies. It became a major debate for them. Should they support Lou Leblanc or not? A very good man...but he represented a major political party and a political view."

Linda saw that her husband was troubled. She didn't have to read his mind.

"So what are you going to do about it?" she asked.

"It's a dilemma for me. I have my own views and I don't want to overly influence the rest of the Butterflies. And they probably would if my views were known."

"You're right about that, Bax," said Shultz. "You can't let your views out, at least until you hear and are certain about what the majority think."

"Shultzy, you're right," said Baxter.

But I know what they are thinking.

It didn't ease his worry.

Shultz smiled and winked at Baxter.

"But you're way ahead of them, aren't you?"

Baxter winked back. "I still need to hear their views and that's why I placed 'Politics' as the last item on the agenda for tomorrow's meeting."

The political debate had begun at the meeting and it was heated. The Butterflies were like-minded on moral issues and values but they couldn't reach a consensus on taking a position of support for a political candidate or party. Many diverse and opposing positions were brought up. The health care issue was not the only debated item that many of the regional representatives had confronted. The abortion issue was raised by the Florida representative. The wars in Iraq and Afghanistan were also brought up. The environment and climate change versus economic growth was also a contentious issue. Topic after topic of mainstream issues that confronted pluralistic American society came to the fore and no one issue garnered unanimous agreement among the Butterflies.

Baxter sat back, silent as the debates continued. He did not offer his opinions. The delegates looked to Baxter for guidance. He gave none.

The representative from Massachusetts rose and raised his arms in a quieting motion to lower the chatter in the room.

"I have the floor," he said in an authoritative tone. The room fell silent. He looked directly at Baxter, giving him full respect.

"There is no consensus on many issues raised here today. Maybe we can't reach agreement on all these issues. But there is one item on the political agenda that we haven't broached and it must be raised." His statement piqued the attention of everyone in the room.

"Support for the Butterfly Organization is gaining rapid momentum throughout the United States, as Doug Bannister has cleverly shown in his statistical presentation. We're at the crossroads in our development. We're all aware of that."

The Massachusetts rep looked around the room. He noticed nodding agreement. Baxter also nodded.

"It's not surprising that both political parties are actively pursuing Butterfly support for their favour. They realize the growing power that is developing throughout America in our movement and they want our backing."

He raised his voice and in a powerful tone shouted.

"We are becoming a power in America to be reckoned with." Applause grew with some of the representatives rising to their feet. Baxter remained seated.

"America is changing for the better and the Butterflies are a large reason for this change. But this change is not enough. Not fast enough and not complete enough."

He hesitated for a second and scanned the faces in the room. The representatives hung on his every word. Many of them might have secretly held the same idea but had hesitated to bring it out.

He chose his next words with care.

"We need another major political party in the United States that represents our morals and values and those of the American family."

He pounded the table for greater emphasis.

"We need and want the Butterfly Party and we want Baxter McPherson to become President of the United States!"

A great cheer rose from the room. They rose to their feet, fluttered their hands in the Butterfly salute and chanted over and over in unison.

"Baxter for President! Baxter for President!"

They looked at Baxter for his response. He remained slumped in his seat and exhibited little emotion. But his great mind was at work. Strangely, it wandered back to the schoolyard fight many, many years ago when he was being beaten by the Hardiman gang. He had deliberately let the Hardimans beat him up, just so he could remain normal and not stand out. He flinched in his chair as if the fists and feet of the Hardiman gang still hit him.

The chant "Baxter for President" continued unabated. Baxter remained unresponsive to the chant and marveled at how the random wandering thought patterns of the human mind sent subconscious messages.

CHAPTER TWENTY-TWO

Joanne

The warm summer rain soaked Joanne McPherson through to the skin. She ran as fast as she could from the bus stop across the street to Billy Ray's Honky Tonk Bar in Fort Worth, Texas. She wore four-inch high heels which slowed her down and only prolonged her exposure to the driving rain. The sudden torrential downpour caught her by surprise and the twenty seconds running in the elements made her look like a drowned rat. Wet, stringy hair and mascara that ran down her face made her a sight to behold. When mascara ran, it was hideous and hers was running.

She didn't need the highlighting features of mascara like older women who applied it generously to hide the ravages of age on their face. Like most young women she just thought it was part of the female beauty arsenal, similar to lipstick.

She couldn't help notice her appearance in the mirror next to where she dripped water. She took a moment to look at herself. She shook loose moisture from her medium length mini skirt which highlighted her athletic shaped legs. Her tank top and flimsy, silky bra - wet from the rain - accentuated her well-formed breasts and protruding nipples.

I have to get to a washroom fast... If this was a wet tee shirt contest, I would immediately get the job.

At the best of times, she was not conventionally beautiful in the mode of a world-class female model, nor was she as sexy as an Angelina Jolie. She had a long, lithe figure with legs up to her waist. Any man who passed her on the street would turn to view her, coming or going. She had perfectly proportioned pear-shaped buttocks in a tight, young female body highlighted by a cheery, unblemished face with shocking, black hair cropped to her shoulders. She was looking for a job but right now, wet from head to toe, and despite being an attractive young female it was not her best job hunting look.

She approached the first person she saw just inside the front door of the bar.

"Sir," she said as she dripped. "Where is the ladies room and can you direct me to Mr. Jones's office?"

The fat, balding man lifted his eyes from her wet breasts and laughed as he spoke.

"Got caught in the rain, ehh? You certainly are a sight for sore eyes. The ladies' room is straight ahead and you're talking to Mr. Jones. If you're here for the cocktail waitress job, as far as I see given first impressions and all, you got the job, honey."

"That was the easiest job interview I ever had," returned Joanne. "Are you serious and when do I start?"

She wished her father could see her now. She remembered his constant rants.

'There's no way you will ever amount to anything in life and you'll never hold down a job... You're mediocre.'

Well...I got a job now and although he may not think much of me being a cocktail waitress...it means a lot to me.

She could never please her father. She was always compared to Baxter, and it was hard being compared to him. He was the apple of his father's eye and growing up she was reminded of his brilliance on a daily basis.

She both loved and hated Baxter at the same time.

He was good to her and as younger female siblings often do, she followed her older brother around whenever she could. She idolized him, imitated him and bragged about him to her girlfriends. Baxter never shunned her and had shown nothing but brotherly love toward her. He had helped her in every way he could. She loved him for that but she could never live up to his reputation: be as good as Baxter.

Baxter excelled in everything. She excelled in nothing and it only added to her frustrations and inferiority complex. It had been the story of her short life.

Her father picked on her even more when he lost control over Baxter's life. The tyrannical ten family rules that he inflicted on the household became unbearable for Joanne and it seemed that after Baxter left for university, her life became even more intolerable.

One night at eighteen years of age she just packed and was gone the next day.

***

Clive Dunlop wore a lead-lined cap 24/7. He wore it at work, at home without exception and would only take it off when he showered. He was paranoid about Baxter McPherson getting into his mind to control his thoughts...that Baxter would make him do things against his will. He was a laughing stock in the CIA and was somewhat of a recluse who remained tucked away from mainstream operations in a secluded small office in the back part of the building. But he was still the best at extracting information, which was a skill set coveted by the CIA.

After the Chicago debacle the CIA gave him a one-year leave for sensitivity training and then restored him to full time status. The training didn't take.

He was under direct orders not to go near Baxter again and to leave the McPherson family alone. The CIA had lost face after the revelation about the torture of a U.S. citizen captured on the streets of Chicago. But Clive was not finished with Baxter. He had one over-riding mindset and that was to uncover the secret about Baxter McPherson. It was the main focus of his life.

There had to be something that I overlooked just before I almost broke him. If I only had a little more time, I would've discovered his secret.

In his little nook-of-an-office he poured over the Baxter McPherson files, reading and re-reading them, again and again. He knew everything that was to be known about Baxter and his family from information that the CIA had gathered. But the secret was not to be found there.

His mother, father surely know the secret about Baxter's abilities. But...damn I'm under orders not to go near them.

However, there was something curious after he read Bud Brown's report on Baxter. He looked like a sympathizer. A light went off in his warped mind one morning while he took a shower without wearing his cap. It was as if his clown hat, once removed, had improved his thinking.

"Bud Brown," he screeched at the top of his lungs. "He knows the McPherson secret."

***

Bud Brown retired from the CIA after thirty-five years of service with a healthy pension. He was content now and close to his beloved family. He loved fishing with his ten-year-old grandson at his cabin deep in the middle of lake country. It afforded him time to be alone with his thoughts and to teach his grandson the pleasures of an outdoors life away from the hustle, stress and strain of the big city.

It was a splendid June day of fishing on the lake and the pleasure that Bud took when he saw his grandson land a three-pound trout with the first cast of his fishing rod made life's small joys become large.

"You're a great fisherman, Billie," said Bud and slapped him on the back with a congratulatory whack. They walked up the tree-lined path back to the cabin in the fading light of dusk. He looked forward to a fine meal, a pleasant evening with his grandson and his daily whiskey nightcap before he retired for the evening.

"Tomorrow I bet you'll catch an even bigger trout. And just wait till you taste your catch pan fried in butter. It will melt in your mouth. But first you have to clean the fish yourself."

"Do I have to Grandpa? It's so yukky."

Bud felt a strong stinging sensation on the back of his neck. He thought it was a horsefly. They were out this time of year and took a piece of meat with every bite. He reached back and felt a small dart that protruded from his neck. He felt blood run down his hand. Just before he passed out, he saw a man who wore a funny cup hat come into view.

Clive looked around the interior of Bud's cabin. He felt a twinge of jealousy. He'd always wanted a retreat far away from the hectic, fast-paced life in the big city that a cabin in the woods afforded. But he didn't possess the patience and know-how to build a fine comfortable cabin as Bud had done. It was a log-style cabin big enough to house about four people comfortably. He half expected to see the taxidermied heads of moose or bears mounted over the fireplace mantle... *Isn't that what crazy, outdoorsy people with cabins in the woods had as trophies on their walls?*

Bud only had a large two-foot speckled trout, stuffed and mounted above the mantle.

What a waste of a good fish. It would've made fine eating.

He let his mind think about the trophy fish a while longer, perhaps as a delay tactic against the unpleasantness he knew would come next.

Maybe the best part of the fish, the succulent pink flesh, had been scooped out and preserved for a meal over a bed of rice, a medley of fresh vegetables and a fine, chilled white Chardonnay. Stuff its skin with something and mount it while eating the flesh.

He stepped up to the mounted trout, touched its skin. He wasn't sure if the great fish had its own flesh and innards or some other hardened stuffing. Maybe, at another time he would seek out an answer.

Ten-year-old Billie's muffled cries through the gag in his mouth took Clive's mind off the fish. Billie was bound and strapped in a chair directly in front of Bud who was likewise confined. Bud was still groggy from the drug in the dart. He started to revive and opened his eyes only to appear shocked. He stared at his beloved grandson strapped and gagged in a chair in front of him. He screeched, completely bewildered, "Billie, are you okay? What's going on here?"

Billie couldn't answer. He made only a muffled cry in response.

Clive walked over to Bud.

"This is a wonderful cabin, Mister Brown. You have my utmost respect and admiration for building such a fine retreat. I hope you have willed it to someone close in your family, other than to Billie here."

Bud was fully conscious now and understood Clive's words. He interpreted them to mean they were not going to leave the cabin alive. He struggled as hard as he could and tested the strength of his bindings. They did not budge.

"You can't break those bindings, Mister Brown. I assure you. Baxter McPherson may be able to break them, but not someone like you with just normal strength."

"I don't understand why you tied us up. Who are you? What do you want and please don't hurt my grandson. He's only ten years old."

"I think you know who I am. After all, we have a lot in common. We both work, or have worked, for the CIA. We both know and admire Baxter McPherson - and all I need from you is to tell me everything you know about him, his marvelous abilities, and how he got them. And please, don't play coy with me. I know you found out about Baxter and your grandson's welfare is at stake if you don't cooperate with me. I can be a very persuasive man."

Bud recognized the lead-lined toque. The stories he heard about Baxter's capture by the CIA in Chicago and the agents with the lead-lined toques on their heads were clear in his mind. He remembered Baxter's own personal warning to him about the one-track evil intentions of the head agent named Clive, who he feared would still pursue him. Now Bud faced Baxter's worst nightmare. He was worried.

"Then you must be Clive, if I am not mistaken," said Bud. "Your clown hat gives you away."

"At your service and now let's get started. If you value anything about your grandson, Billie here, you will not hold back. And to prove my point...a little example."

Billie still struggled in his seat. He had a wide-eyed expression of fear on his face as he whimpered and cried muffled sounds from his gagged mouth. Clive ungagged him and looked directly in his eyes.

"Don't cry out. Just answer this simple question. What's your favourite sport?"

"Baseball," he said.

"Do you play?" said Clive.

"Yes, I'm the all-star shortstop in my league," said Billie with a sense of childish pride.

Clive re-gagged him and pulled out a cigar cutting tool, a six-inch cigar and snipped off its end with a quick snap. He lit the cigar and blew an aromatic puff of smoke into the air. He then placed one of Billie's fingers in the cutting tool.

"If you want your grandson to play baseball again with all his fingers, start talking."

Bud had to protect his grandson. He could not protect Baxter's secret. He feared for his life, but especially Billie's...and fear showed on his face. He had no choice. It killed him to talk but he had to reveal the McPherson family secret.

"It's Joanne, Baxter's sister. Her first born son will possess and carry on and even surpass Baxter's abilities. Don't hurt Billie...I don't care what you do to me but not Billie."

Clive was elated.

To hell with Baxter... I have to find Joanne. Maybe I will even impregnate her...my child would be the greatest human being in the world.

Clive was meticulous in his planning. He was trained to think on his feet. He figured the CIA could locate Joanne in about two days and on the third day, he would have her.

He took out his cell phone. There was no service.

"Good thing for you there is no cell service so deep in the woods. No one can get in touch with you. And there are no other cabins on this side of the lake. Chances of other cabin people finding you are remote."

"What are you going to do with us?" said Bud.

"Mister Brown I have good news and bad news for you. What do you want first... Okay the good news. I don't have to kill ya to keep you silent...thank your lucky stars."

He laughed.

"Now the bad news. I need your silence for at least three days...maximum, maybe four. Because I know you will contact Baxter after your release. So, here's what I'm gonna do."

He paused for a moment and patted Billie on the head.

"It will take three or four days for me to find Joanne McPherson, then I will call your family to come up here and release you. And don't worry; you won't be able to free yourself from those bindings."

"It was nice meeting you and little Billie here."

What a nice gesture on my part...I didn't kill them.

***

"This place is redneck heaven," said Joanne to a fellow cocktail waitress and close friend at Billy Ray's Honky Tonk Bar.

A wannabe cowboy had just fallen off the mechanical bucking bull and fortunately, in his drunken stupor, was unharmed. He yelled at Joanne to bring another round of 'buds for my buds.'

"I've never seen so many simple-minded rednecks in one place in my life. But they sure do tip well, especially if you show a little cleavage." She unbuttoned her blouse another notch and carried a full tray of Budweiser to the table of semi-drunk wannabes.

She had been at Billy Ray's for just over two years and made good money despite the bar's rowdy reputation. She was now the senior cocktail waitress in charge of a staff of eight waitresses. But she missed her family, even her dad...but especially her mom.

How could I not have called her for so long? I have to call her.

A solitary man who sat in the back of the bar beckoned to her for a drink. He looked out of place. She approached and her first impression of him was correct. He wore a dark suit and his short-cropped hair and clean-shaven appearance definitely placed him apart from the usual patrons.

"I see by your name tag that you are Joanne," spoke the clean-cut stranger.

"And since you can read, I can only assume that you're not a regular customer. How can I help you?"

"Bring me a Bud, Joanne. Where are you from?"

He seemed like a pleasant man and without giving it a second thought, she replied, "I'm a long way from home - originally Portland, Maine."

The man thanked her for the beer and took out his cell phone. He made a call directly to Clive's cell answering service about Joanne McPherson being located in Fort Worth, Texas. Clive's heart jumped in his mouth when he played back the message. Two days later, he and five hand-picked agents boarded a plane to Fort Worth.

CHAPTER TWENTY-THREE

Billy Ray's

It was a cool November morning in Portland, Maine, a morning that foretold the type of days to come with the fall season progressing into the dreaded cold winter that fast approached. Helen McPherson enjoyed the four seasons in Maine and the fall season was her favourite with the delightful changed colours of autumn leaves.

She had just finished preparing a breakfast of oatmeal, toast and jam with freshly squeezed orange juice for the youngest of her four kids at home and the usual Saturday morning plate of cholesterol for her husband. She tried to get Gordon to embrace a healthier diet but it was an exercise in futility. His habitual Saturday morning breakfast consisted of a feed of sausage, bacon and eggs, sunny-side up, with white toast and coffee. At least she had weaned him off his plate-sized steak that he ate every Friday night for the past twenty years. *It was a start...* She attempted to eliminate red meat entirely from the family diet. The children accepted the healthy food choices she planned in their lives, especially since it was all the rage in school these days, but Gordon was stubborn and set in his ways.

She looked out the kitchen window at the downed leaves that swirled in the wind, separated from mother trees. It wasn't time yet to get the kids out in the yard with the rakes until all the leaves were down - right now about half were still on the trees. She could never understand the stupidity of her neighbours who raked every day before the leaves had completely fallen. It just made extra work for them when the wind blew the rest of the leaves down and flew them from yard to yard regardless of how much raking had been done.

My neighbours are really stupid.

Just as she observed her next-door neighbour rake leaves in another futile effort, the phone rang. She picked it up. It had to be her best friend about the afternoon curling match. After all, it was Betty's turn to drive to the rink. Helen didn't wait for the 'hello' and hurriedly blurted out," It's about time you called. I'm packed and ready to go. What time will you pick me up?"

"Hello, Mom. It's Joanne. It's so good to hear your voice again."

Helen froze, speechless. She regained her composure and fired off questions in a choked voice. "Joanne, are you all right? Where have you been? Where are you? I've missed you terribly. We all have. I have so much to ask you, to tell you." She completely broke down and sobbed. She waited for her daughter's response.

"It's alright Mom, I've missed you too. I'm okay. Tell Dad I missed him too. But you know why I had to leave. And Barbara, David, Gerry and Susan... are they okay? And Baxter, what's he doing? I love them all and miss everyone."

Helen held back tears and replied, "Joanne, where are you?"

"I'm in Fort Worth, Texas. You can reach me at the number on your call display."

"Joanne, you stay put. I'm in touch with Baxter. Just got back from seeing him in Nova Scotia. He wants to get in touch with you. Remember me telling you how special you are. It's true, but I have to tell you how and to tell you in person. I can't tell you over the phone. We're coming to Fort Worth to see you.

It's very important. Email me your contact information and address. I have to call Baxter. Kisses all around. We love you."

Baxter was worried about Joanne. His mother had informed him she had gone missing. It troubled him because of the potential danger she could be in. He had set an alert in motion through the Butterfly Organization and its wide reaching tentacles to search for her. He didn't trust local authorities.

He received two messages on the same day in early November.

Only a few trusted people were given direct access to Baxter's cell phone. When his cell rang, he knew it was an important call from one of those people. The first call snapped him to full attention.

"Baxter, it's your mother." She sounded distraught but excited. She didn't mince words. She got right to the point.

"Joanne called. She's in Fort Worth, Texas. She's okay but we have to go there immediately to see her."

"That's great news, Mom. I was worried like we all were. I'll fly down immediately."

The singularity of Baxter's response made her motherly instinct kick in and she interjected before Baxter could continue. "If you think you're going down without me, you're sadly mistaken, my son. I'll drive to Boston right away to meet you and we'll fly to Texas together."

He didn't argue with her. But an overwhelming feeling of danger and foreboding permeated Baxter's thoughts. It was his extraordinary power of intuition that heightened his danger reflex. He thought of Clive Dunlop.

Clive had not been in Baxter's thoughts for some time, but Ray Jessome kept him updated about CIA developments.

Through Ray, Baxter had come to find out that Clive had returned to active duty. It disturbed him because Clive would find a way to come after him.

The second call that fateful day in November only reaffirmed the danger that his intuition had predicted. It was from Ray Jessome who reported that Bud Brown and his grandson had been found bound and close to death in their back woods cabin.

Red flagged danger signals raced through Baxter's mind as he put the pieces to a perilous puzzle together. They prompted him into instant action.

First, he phoned Joanne from the phone number his mother gave him. He reached her answering machine. He messaged her of pending danger and instructed his sister not to show up at work. He told her to tell no one, leave her apartment immediately, put on a wig, check into the Omni Hotel under a false name and not to use a cell phone or credit cards under any circumstances. He'd be down in two days.

***

Jonesy was in one of his foul moods at Billy Ray's. It was a busy time of the year and the bar rocked with noisy, obnoxious redneck cowboys who took advantage of advertised food and drink specials. It was Saturday night and it was crowded. Jonesy was a patient manager when things ran smoothly, but things did not run smoothly that night with his senior cocktail waitress absent from her shift without notice. He screeched at his short-shifted staff to fill the void. The other waitresses knew from past experiences to put up with him in one of these moods, since he would always apologize when things cooled down. But now he was in one of his yelling, ordering moods.

Clive Dunlop was evil and paranoid, but he wasn't stupid.

I have to get Joanne before Baxter finds out about Bud Brown.... He'll know I'm after her.

It was all about timing for him. Meeting up with Baxter again seemed more likely than ever.

One of his CIA agents was sent into Billy Ray's Honky Tonk Bar on that busy Saturday night to talk to the waitresses about Joanne. They didn't know where she was, but she was scheduled for this shift. The agent relayed a message to Clive about Joanne missing her shift.

Clive leapt into action and drove to the bar. He needed as much information as possible about her whereabouts.

Baxter reached her first.... Damn it!

Clive approached Jonesy and flashed his CIA credentials. Jonesy had a criminal record and was not one to rile the authorities because of his less-than-honourable past. He fully cooperated and gave out her address and phone numbers.

"That goddam bastard will not beat me again," shouted Clive to his agents in a tirade of anger and exasperation. "When we follow up on her address and phone numbers she won't be there."

I'm not finished yet! Joanne McPherson will be mine.

He stormed out of the bar in an ugly, cursing mood. There would be no bread crumbs, no leads that would provide clues to her whereabouts. No phone calls, no credit cards, receipts. Nothing. Baxter would make sure of that. But there was something that Jonesy had said to him that gave Clive some hope.

"Joanne made a lot of friends at Billy Ray's. Been here for almost two years. She won't leave Fort Worth without seeing them. It's just not her."

***

Joanne saw her mother, brother and a young, good looking stranger come through the entrance doorway of the hotel. She raced across the red-carpeted lobby with her arms outstretched like a long-necked pelican about to flap its wings ready to take flight. She wrapped her arms around her mother. Tears and warm hugs followed which captured the love between mother and daughter after a long absence.

Doug Bannister had accompanied Baxter and his mother on the quick flight down from Boston. They had become closer as trusted friends since their initial meeting in Los Angeles, their partnership with Bannister Commodities Inc. and the start-up of the Butterfly Organization.

Joanne had been at the hotel for two days after Baxter's warning of danger. She had followed his advice. But she had misgivings about why she was in danger.

How can I possibly be in danger? I've never had so much as a parking ticket in my whole life.

That evening they all sat down over a meal and had a long overdue talk. Baxter's trust in Doug made him privy to the McPherson family secret. Joanne's disbelief in the story and importance of her own biological nature was only overshadowed by her sideways quick glances at Baxter's best friend.

He's truly a good-looking man and he must be of good moral fibre if he gained Baxter's friendship.... and he's not a redneck cowboy wannabe...and he doesn't wear a cowboy hat.

She took her amorous glance off Doug and said in an excited voice, "Mom, you mean to say that my future son will be smarter and greater than Baxter?"

She reveled in the moment, wiggled her ears with her hands and stuck out her tongue at Baxter and in a songsy voice taunted, "My son will be smarter than you-hew!"

Laughter all around.

Baxter wiped a laugh induced tear from his cheek. "In all seriousness, Josie Babes," he hadn't called her by this nickname since he was about twelve years old. "You're still in danger until we leave Fort Worth. We're leaving Monday morning by car since airports will be watched."

Joanne interrupted Baxter. "I have to see my best friends at Billy Ray's before I leave."

"It's too dangerous. You can call them later," said Baxter.

Baxter doesn't approve.... I can tell by the look on his face...He always thinks he's right and only his opinion matters. Well this time it matters to me.

"Don't worry Bax, I always listen to you. I won't see them," she said tongue in cheek.

Baxter couldn't read her mind. It had something to do with her special DNA structure.

The next morning she left a note at the front desk, jumped in a cab and went to the bar.

The noon hour lunch venue was a busy time at Billy Ray's. It attracted the surrounding business community; men in suits and ties, business lunches and a more subdued, sophisticated and intelligent clientele. The bar's evening activities catered to the redneck wannabe cowboys who sloshed back beer, danced to live country music and rode the mechanical bucking bull.

Joanne actually preferred the redneck shift at the bar than the noon hour one. The cowboy wannabe's tipped more generously and more often than the noon hour suits. Maybe it was because of their alcohol induced generosity and the number of drinks they poured down their throats versus the tight-wad cheapness of the business people. She figured that's why the suits made more money than the rednecks...because they're so damned cheap.

Joanne headed to the employee quarters at Billy Ray's. But something felt different when she jumped up the stairway taking three steps at a time. At this time of the morning her friends would have arrived to start the noon hour shift. She looked forward to greeting her close friends and only planned to stay about ten minutes before she returned to the hotel for the trip out of town. She would miss her friends and wanted to tell them in person that she would Facebook them as soon as she was able. But none of the staff was around and it was strangely quiet.

She looked into the dining area and expected to see some late breakfast diners and early arrivals for noon hour meals. The diner was empty and silent without the clatter of dinner plates clanging against each other that was music to Jonesy's ear. Jonesy often said he knew how much money the bar made according to the loudness of the clattering plates.

But there was no clatter. No money being made.

The small hairs on the back of her neck stood straight up. She sensed danger. Baxter's words resonated in her head... *Some people and organizations will want access to your future son for their own purposes and they will do whatever they can to capture you.*

"God, Baxter is right again. Why didn't I listen to him?"

She heard someone behind her. She turned and saw three tall, well-built men in suits who wore strange-looking head gear. Her first impression was how funny they looked, but she also immediately understood who they were. The clown hats, as described by Baxter, gave them away as CIA agents and they meant her harm. She backed away, stumbled momentarily over the edge of the carpet before she regained her balance.

One of the agents reached in his jacket pocket and pulled out a fancy looking ID card, then flashed it at her as if to justify their presence and what they were about to do.

"Miss McPherson, I am agent Jackson of the CIA and you'll have to come with us," he said.

Joanne wasted no time, turned in an instant, and bolted across the room as fast as she could toward the exit on the far side, but without success. Two more clown-hatted agents appeared and blocked the exit. They grabbed her, forced her to the ground and handcuffed her. They hoisted her to her feet to face another agent who appeared smaller than the rest but who was obviously in charge. She struggled and screeched at the top of her lungs. "Let me go! Let me go!"

"Joanne, it's so nice to finally have the pleasure of meeting you. I've heard so much about you and your family - and of course, Baxter is my close personal friend," said Clive.

"I know who you are." She struggled against the large, muscular agents who held her still. Her arms were restrained but not her legs and one of the agents made a tactical mistake. He got too close in front of her. A well placed boot to the crotch, with all the force she could muster from her one-hundred-and-fifteen-pound frame, dropped him like a sack of potatoes. He moaned and clutched his privates.

"Your clown hat didn't protect you from that, did it you bastard!" The others grabbed her tighter and helped the fallen agent back to his feet.

"Come closer Clive and I'll give you one too." She kicked wildly in Clive's direction.

Clive laughed at the futility of her attack.

"You certainly are a feisty young lady with a lot of fight in you, just like your older brother. But for now you'll have to come with us."

They taped her mouth shut and with an agent on each handcuffed arm, they escorted her toward a back exit and a waiting van. She kicked and screamed muffled cries.

***

Baxter just missed Joanne. He saw her jump in a cab and drive away. He had sensed that she would try something and knew from her ironic tone the night before that she wouldn't be true to her word about goodbyes to her friends. He read the note she left at the front desk. She was going to Billy Ray's and would be back at the hotel around noon.

She's unprotected and Clive Dunlop is in town. Why didn't I padlock her to a door or chain her to a desk? I knew she would try something stupid. It's her way of showing me that I don't control her.

He grabbed Doug, hailed a cab and headed to Billy Ray's.

There was nothing out of the ordinary when Doug and Baxter arrived at the front entrance of Billy Ray's, probably about fifteen minutes after Joanne. But Baxter's senses became heightened. The smells, the sights, the sounds, the taste in his mouth, even the gentle touch of air on his skin all screamed at him that something was not ordinary. He could feel the full power of suspension kick in as if warning him of the danger he was about to face. He could feel the blood flow vigorously to his big body muscles and the rush of it engorged his brain to maximize his five senses. He picked up every detail of his environment. Everything about the surroundings seemed right, but his senses said it was all wrong.

He had hoped they would just meet up with Joanne, let her say goodbye to her friends and leave before the CIA arrived on the scene...that his sister's independent indiscretion would not be a costly one. That was not the case.

His worst fears were realized. Halfway up the steps to the dining area he heard Joanne's shrill cry. They raced to the dining room entrance, devoid of any bar patrons, only to catch a glimpse of Joanne, handcuffed and being escorted toward a back exit. One of the CIA agents trailed, walked backwards and checked for any rear end assault. He noticed Baxter and Doug. "We have company!" he screeched.

For Baxter, suspension made it seem as if time stood still like in one of those crazy science fiction movies where the hero could stop and hold everyone frozen in place while he walked normally around them. He made a quick assessment of the surroundings, the layout of the battlefield where a war was about to begin. He made his plan in a fraction of a moment.

There was a distance of about one hundred feet between the CIA group and Doug and Baxter. Between them were empty dining room tables and chairs set up with carefully arranged plates and cutlery on coarse linen tablecloths for the noon hour luncheon crowd. But there was no crowd and no staff present. The CIA had magically cleared away the noon-hour crowd and staff in some mysterious secret, organized way. The area was empty and quiet as a church.

Baxter had a strange thought enter his mind when he looked over the empty dining area. He thought of the Plains of Abraham and the Battle of Dunkirk where great historic battles had been fought. The dining room in Billy Ray's Honky Tonk Bar was to become his Dunkirk.

He looked across the expanse of white linen table cloths that separated him from his adversaries. He could use these table cloths to his advantage. His enemies would use the same weaponry against him as in Chicago. He noted they also wore lead-lined caps as shields against his mind-reading and message-implanting abilities. But he noticed that one of the agents did not wear his cap. It was the agent who was kicked in the groin by Joanne about a minute before. His cap had fallen off and he hadn't replaced it in his dazed state. Baxter finished his appraisal of the battlefield and the position of his enemies.

Clive recognized Baxter...his mortal enemy. He shouted out orders to take up defensive positions and to ready the net guns for instant deployment. They were the most effective weapon to use against Baxter. He had learned this from the Chicago incident. Five agents firing net guns would cover almost fifty feet of space from close range and would entirely negate the speed that Baxter would try to use to evade dart guns and tasers.

Clive screeched out an order. "Get that bitch down the steps to the van!"

Baxter projected the most powerful message he could send to the agent without the clown hat. He had never before implanted a message without touching a person. He didn't know whether he could do it or have the power over the distance that his electrical impulse messages could travel. He had never tested it before. It was something that had yet to be determined. But it was not the time or place for such a test. He just sent the message using the full extent of the impulses in his brain through the earth's magnetic field and along the airways.

"Hold on to Joanne. Do not move her. Protect her."

The message seared into the brain of the agent. He didn't move for a second as his brain interpreted conflicting messages. Then the large man moved toward Joanne. He grabbed her tightly from the agents who held her. They let her go. Was he going to obey Clive's order to take her down to the van or obey Baxter's order to hold and protect her?

He held her on the spot and shielded her from the other agents with his massive body.

Then everything happened at once.

Clive saw the agent who held Joanne hadn't obeyed his direct order. He also did not wear his lead-lined hat. Clive pulled out his taser gun and shot the man where he dropped to the floor writhing in pain.

Tables, chairs, cutlery, clattering plates and empty coffee cups and water glasses flew high in the air in an organized manner like the Red Sea parting at God's hand. White linen table cloths rose and floated in the direction of the four CIA agents. That distracted them from Baxter who rushed toward them from behind the white wall of linen. Soft explosions and sleek whishing sounds indicated that the net guns were discharged in the direction where the agents thought Baxter rushed.

Three of the nets were nullified. They encased fresh white sheets of linen as effectively as herring nets in the capture of a fast swimming school of fish. But Baxter was not in them. The fourth net hit Baxter and tripped him up from his headlong dash behind the white-out cover of the floating linen table cloths.

Clive had not yet fired his net gun. He had been distracted when he tasered one of his own agents. But now, he saw the opportunity that Lady Luck had placed in his hands. He had a clear view and fired at the fallen Baxter and completely covered him in more net. Drug darts and taser guns were discharged into the thrashing form sprawled on the floor. Baxter struggled against the confounding nets and the drugs.

Clive shrieked an ear-shattering victory cry. Once again he had captured the almighty Baxter, who had come so unprepared and weaponless to do battle.

"For a man so smart, you're a real fool," he yelled triumphantly.

The darts and taser shots had no effect on Baxter in his heightened state of suspension. He had blocked most of the shots and immediately pulled those that hit him. As for the few that did hit him and stuck - he commanded his body to fight off the debilitating effect they would have on a normal person. He had not come totally unprepared to do battle with his CIA enemies. He carried a small tool to counter the covering, immobilizing effect of their net guns.

A sharp knife.

"He's got a knife. He's cutting his way out," one of the agents screeched.

Too late.

Baxter was at full strength. He was free from the nets and he was angry. Angrier than he had ever been in his life...angrier than when he was being tortured in Chicago at the hand of the same individual.

Baxter's enemies were frozen targets when he jumped with amazing agility from the useless nets and chopped down the agents as easily as snapping a twig, with quick, forceful blows which knocked them unconscious, one by one.

Clive watched. He couldn't believe his eyes. Even as he trembled with the fear of being beaten by Baxter once again, he marvelled at this amazing human being.

While Baxter dispatched the agents one at a time, Clive made a beeline to Joanne who stood handcuffed and motionless by the agent downed by his taser shot. Clive's malicious mind snapped. He pulled out a pistol, holstered just above his ankle.

If I can't have her, no one will.

Doug Bannister had been hit by a glancing taser shot and was ignored as 'collateral damage' inconsequential in this battle. He jumped toward Clive when he saw the gun being levelled at Joanne. The weapon discharged only once before Baxter threw Clive ten feet in the air. When he landed it was with a thud - hard against the back wall that knocked both the gun out of his hand and the clown hat off his head.

Doug's headlong, frantic lunge at Clive and the discharge of the weapon in the desperation of the moment had made him unaware of his wound. He touched his shoulder and found it surprisingly sticky. Then he looked at his hand and found it surprisingly red. He felt no pain. He looked at Joanne and saw she was unharmed. Then he passed out.

Baxter retrieved the handcuff keys from one of the incapacitated agents and uncuffed Joanne. She rushed to the side of the man who had just saved her life at his own peril. Doug now bled profusely from his wound. She applied pressure to the wound... *I could love this man. Don't die!*

Baxter's rage subsided and he came down from his suspension high. He felt himself descend from Mount Everest to the serenity of the green field of normality. It was his preferred state. But before he reached that lower level green field where he could rest, he needed to perform one more important task under the influence of his heightened abilities.

Clive lifted himself to a sitting position from being prone and dazed on the floor. Baxter placed both his hands on Clive's head and downloaded every thought that was in his mind. Baxter stared directly into his frightened, bewildered eyes.

"I know you almost murdered both Bud Brown and his grandson. You shot my friend and I will do everything in my power to bring you to justice. And you know I have considerable power."

CHAPTER TWENTY-FOUR

Baxter and Linda

Baxter and Linda strolled hand-in-hand, through the flowered pathways of the small public garden in front of their hotel in Boston. It was a welcome retreat for Baxter to be alone with his beloved wife at this particular time. He loved the Butterflies but he needed to be away from them before he gave his thoughts about the future direction for the organization. A special meeting had been scheduled with the Board to discuss the issue.

Baxter was silent as they walked. Linda left him alone with his thoughts at these moments. It was his way of delving deep into his mind for personal reflection. She didn't have the ability to read minds, like her husband, but her female intuition was almost as accurate. She had a good idea what he thought. He was troubled and he would eventually open up to her. She would not force him.

Baxter's silence gave Linda a chance to practice her newly formed passion for photography combined with her love of nature. They walked over a small arching bridge which covered a babbling brook leading to a perfectly laid out bed of flowers.

"Stop here Bax," said Linda. He halted in his tracks. "I want to snap some pictures of these begonias."

They continued on their way in silence and stopped occasionally for Linda to capture more pictures of the beautiful flowers in the garden. Baxter would not read her mind. She was adamant about that and he respected her wishes.

They sat down on a park bench in front of another flower bed …nature's bounty at its best. Linda was tempted to take some pictures but she thought about Baxter's long silence. They sat for about five minutes without talk.

Seated beside them was an elderly couple, probably in their seventies. Baxter looked over at them. He didn't need to read their minds. Just the serene and loving look on their faces spoke volumes.

The elderly gentleman broke the silence. "Beautiful day. My name is Bill and this is my wife Mona."

Baxter returned the friendly gesture which started up a pleasant exchange between the two parties. The elderly couple had no idea who Baxter was and were not aware of The Butterfly Organization and this chance encounter of complete anonymity intrigued Baxter. He wanted the serenity, love and happiness that the elderly couple possessed to be his and Linda's future lot in life.

Linda immediately fell in love with the enchanting couple. She saw an opportunity to impress her opinion upon Baxter.

Baxter's thinking about his role with The Butterflies and its future direction.

"I have to ask you a personal question," she said to the couple.

"I hope you don't mind but you seem so content and happy together. If you could share just a little bit of wisdom about your life experiences that brought you to this happy place in your lives, we'd appreciate that."

Mona laughed. She smiled and completely opened up.

"Well my dear, it certainly isn't just one thing. We have had our share of ups and downs in life, like any couple. But we always abided by Christian values and maintained and cultivated our love for one another, our family and our friends."

Linda interrupted. "Yes I guess it's as simple as love for one another. But I have one final question about something that is affecting decisions in our personal lives. How did you mix your personal goals and beliefs, that I and Baxter admire so much, with your overall political beliefs that face the country at large?"

Baxter hadn't yet communicated his decision about The Butterflies to her. He didn't have to. She knew.

Bill answered Linda's question.

"That certainly is a loaded question and I don't think we are smart enough to answer for everyone and we certainly can't answer for you. There are so many complexities and issues in life that face our nation that are beyond our limited scope and knowledge. Even Mona and I may have opposing views on an issue, but all I can say is that as individuals we have to give our support to the candidate or party that holds our strongest beliefs. And collectively I believe that as a nation of mostly good and moral people, our values will prevail."

The older man concluded his political treatise by saying, "I apologize if I sounded stupid, but that really is the best answer I can give with my limited political background."

Baxter looked Bill straight in the eye. "You have no idea how close to my own view your answer is, Bill. Thank you for your great insight."

Baxter and Linda shook hands with Bill and Mona and continued on their walk through the park. They strolled for another few minutes, but Linda looked like she had just swallowed the canary. She wore a big smile on her face that made Baxter stop, laugh and wrap his arms around her.

"You knew I needed reassurance at this moment, didn't you?"

Linda kissed him deeply.

"Yes my dear husband, I did. I know how you will talk to the Board this afternoon. There will be no Butterfly political party and no President McPherson in America's immediate future."

They continued their walk.

"Bax, I know that you are the most amazing human being in the world. Even as much as you try to hide it, I know it's true. But soon after Joanne and Doug's wedding, I suspect that a little boy will be born who will even surpass your tremendous abilities."

She stopped and looked at her husband.

"What do you think he will be like?"

Baxter walked a few steps ahead, turned and laughingly replied.

"I don't know. Maybe he'll be able to fly!"

Linda punched him in the arm.

"In all seriousness, he will be a national treasure or better still a world treasure," said Baxter.

They approached the gate at the exit to the gardens.

"Well then what are your plans after the meeting?"

They crossed the street back to the hotel. Baxter answered.

"After the wedding, how'd you like to go to Europe?"

www.ingramcontent.com/pod-product-compliance
Lightning Source LLC
LaVergne TN
LVHW040136080526
838202LV00042B/2930